Praise for Isabel Cooper's
No Proper Lady

Publishers Weekly Best Book of the Year

Library Journal Best Book of the Year

RT Book Reviews Seal of Excellence

RT Book Reviews Reviewers' Choice Finalist,
Best Book of the Year

RT Book Reviews Reviewers' Choice Finalist, Best
First Historical Novel

"A genre-bending, fast-paced whirl with fantastic characters, a deftly drawn plot, and sizzling attraction…"
—*RT Book Reviews*, 4 ½ stars,
Top Pick of the Month

"Sexy, edgy, and stunningly inventive...will have readers begging for more."
—*Library Journal* starred review

"A compelling debut that smartly mixes history, action, romance, and magic."
—*Publishers Weekly*

LESSONS AFTER Dark

ISABEL COOPER

sourcebooks
casablanca

Published by Sourcebooks Casablanca, an imprint of Sourcebooks, Inc.
P.O. Box 4410, Naperville, Illinois 60567-4410
(630) 961-3900
Fax: (630) 961-2168
www.sourcebooks.com

Printed and bound in Canada.
WC 10 9 8 7 6 5 4 3 2 1

*To Abby Laughlin, who was there at the beginning.
I can only hope that future generations of teenage girls
will stay up late to giggle over this book—and that
they'll have as much fun as we did.*

Chapter 1

WHEN OLIVIA BRIGHTMORE ARRIVED AT ENGLEFIELD, THERE was nobody to meet her.

That wasn't absolutely true, she told herself as she stood staring at the house, bag weighing down one arm. There had been the carriage when she got off the train, and the elderly and taciturn coachman who was even now driving it back out of sight. Someone had sent him. Someone was expecting her, and it wasn't as though she could expect Mr. or Mrs. Grenville to come out and greet her. She was a new teacher, not a weekend guest. She'd just have to go inside, find someone appropriate, and give him the letter Mr. Grenville had sent when he'd hired her.

Very simple, really.

Olivia swallowed hard, smoothed her free hand down the side of her best skirt, and still couldn't make herself move for a minute or two.

Englefield was a pleasant country house, square and red brick and Georgian. She'd lived eighteen years in one much like it, before marriage and widowhood and London. There was nothing Gothic about it, but just for a minute it seemed to loom against the cloudy evening sky, full of unpleasant possibilities. If they hadn't sent for her at all and it had been some kind of horrible mistake—if she was too young or too soft looking now that she was here—if they'd changed their minds and that letter had reached her rooms too late—

She started forward with all the dignity of a rabbit bursting from cover. It took until the foot of the curved set of steps to bring her feet under some sort of control, and none of the meditation she'd learned managed to slow her heartbeat a jot. When she knocked, her hand looked very small, the gray leather of her good pair of gloves startlingly pale against the varnished wood of the doors.

You absolutely must get hold of yourself, my dear.

The voice was a memory: Lyddie, the woman who had taught Olivia most of what she knew, speaking before Olivia's first night performing on her own. Olivia's hands had been shaking so badly she'd spilled one glass of water already. Lyddie had gripped them in hers, her black eyes as calm and pitiless as a raven's. *You're not asking them for anything they don't want to give you. Remember that.*

Olivia sent silent thanks to Lyddie, wherever she was in the Silent Land or beyond, and managed to put a proper and distant smile on her face just as the door opened.

It helped that the maid on the other side looked rather flustered herself. She was young too, perhaps eighteen at the most, and she started talking as soon as she saw Olivia. "You're the new teacher, aren't you? The one from London?" Before Olivia could reply, the girl put a hand to her mouth. "Oh—I'm dreadfully sorry, ma'am!"

That phrase was certainly on the list of things Olivia hadn't wanted to hear. If she'd actually faced the icily composed butler or suspicious housekeeper she'd been expecting, she might have frozen again, but the maid's youth and confusion let her get the words past the sudden tightness in her throat. "Sorry?"

"Well, there's nobody at home, just about. Mr. Grenville's gone to see his sister off today, and he won't be back until nightfall at least. And that would've been fine, only Mrs. Grenville's just gone out to have a word with the builders, and Mrs. Edgar's...talking...with Cook."

"And the butler?" Olivia asked, surprising herself with the laughter in her voice.

"Quit a week ago, ma'am. Said no decent man would put up with—well, never mind." The girl seemed to abruptly become conscious of her place, or that Olivia was still on the doorstep. She stepped back. "Why don't you come in, then? We can take your bags—oh—well, we can put them somewhere until Mrs. Grenville and Mrs. Edgar can say which room you're to have."

She looked at Olivia's bag dubiously and didn't ask where the others were. Olivia knew she was blushing and smiled quickly to cover it up. "I try to travel lightly," she said.

Very lightly: two shirtwaists, a skirt, underthings, her other pair of gloves, two books, and a few magical tools. The rest of her clothes hadn't been worth seeing. In any case, the books lent some weight to the bag. Olivia thought the maid might have been truly shocked, otherwise, when she handed it over.

"What's your name?" Olivia asked once the girl had closed the door.

"Violet, ma'am."

"I'm Mrs. Brightmore."

Violet bobbed a curtsy, Olivia's bag tucked under one arm. "I—" She bit her lip and stopped. Olivia saw the question in her face and knew what it was. Even such a raw servant as Violet would know her place better than to ask, even of someone who'd been as informal with her as Olivia had. It was far too personal.

Besides, there really was no polite euphemism for *witch*, even for a woman who was coming to teach at a school of the occult.

It was to her and Violet's mutual relief when a door on one side of the room opened and a head of neatly cut auburn hair poked out of the doorway, a little less than six feet up. The gentleman behind the door glanced around the hall, frowning, and then frowned more when he saw Violet and Olivia.

Violet, on the other hand, broke out in a smile. "Oh, I'd forgotten the doctor! Dr. St. John, sir," she said with another curtsy in his direction, "this is Mrs. Brightmore, the new teacher. She's just come from London, and—"

"Simon isn't back yet, I suppose? Or Mrs. Grenville, from wherever she's gone?"

"Just down to the new building, sir, and I'll send someone for her directly." Violet looked from the new arrival back to Olivia. "I was just going to show you to the drawing room, ma'am."

With, to some credit, only a very faint sigh, Dr. St. John stepped fully out of the room. "I'll escort the lady."

"Thank you, sir," said Olivia as Violet nodded and sped off. "You're very kind."

Now that she could see him entirely, Dr. St. John proved to be on the thin side, perhaps more so than he should have been by nature. His features were strong but a touch drawn, and a fading tan didn't quite mask the faint shadows under his eyes. His eyes were a rather striking green, and while he was dressed for practicality rather than fashion, his clothing was neat and well cut.

Handsome, in his way. Not that it particularly mattered, since this was a school and not a ballroom, but it was no bad thing to have an attractive man about the place.

"A pleasure to make your acquaintance, Mrs. Brightmore," he said, looking down at her as they headed through another of the doorways. "I'd apologize for the improper introduction, but I wouldn't wish to raise your expectations for the school."

"I had no impression this was a precisely regular establishment," Olivia said, trying a hint of a smile on him and getting no response. She glanced around the drawing room. "Although it's certainly *looked* unexceptionable so far."

It was a nice enough room: blue paper, dark wooden furniture with blue cushions, plenty of windows, and a small piano in one corner. It could have been a dozen others she'd seen. Olivia realized she was surprised, and inwardly shook her head.

"Doesn't look precisely like a school for magic, does it?" asked Dr. St. John, who *probably* couldn't read her thoughts.

Like *witch*, *magic* sounded more than faintly ridiculous. Olivia had never used the word in her previous profession. It put the customers in the wrong frame of mind. And Mr. Grenville's letter had thrown around lots of camouflage. "Talents of a certain nature" here, "a singular variety of human service" there: enough for any reasonable person to get the hint, but still never coming right out.

Still, there it was, and one could only dance around the subject for so long.

"No," she said and glanced over to find Dr. St. John

studying her face almost as intently, if somewhat less subtly, she hoped, than she'd been regarding him earlier. Curiosity about a colleague was natural. Nevertheless, Olivia could have wished he'd been less curious, or she'd had time beforehand to freshen up from the journey. "But then," she said, "I suppose it wouldn't. Not the public rooms. One so rarely sees busts of Pallas in the best houses these days."

She hadn't known Dr. St. John nearly long enough to expect anything from him. Even now, it was something of a surprise when he grinned. He looked surprised too, and Olivia wasn't sure that was any compliment to her. "Quite right," he said, "and I suspect keeping eye of newt in the pantry would lead to a number of catastrophes."

"You might encounter—" Olivia was going to go on and talk about problems keeping servants but stopped as Dr. St. John suddenly turned back toward the door. It was a second or two before she heard footsteps running toward them, and only a little longer until a boy burst into the doorway.

He was perhaps fifteen or sixteen, dark haired and well dressed. He was also quite alarmed. At first, "Sir—" And then the words nearly burst out of his mouth. "Sir, Dr. St. John, you've got to come upstairs. It's Elizabeth. She's…" Only then did he seem to notice Olivia, and his face turned red even as he went on. "She's on the ceiling, sir, and she can't get down."

Chapter 2

"You may as well come," Gareth St. John said. "You might do more good than I will."

He hadn't thought to say it. He hadn't, really, thought at all, other than to wonder if Fitzpatrick thought Gareth could do anything about the situation or had just come to the first authority figure he could find. Not that it mattered. He *was* the one at hand. Fitzpatrick was fifteen and terrified, and Gareth's body was headed for the door long before his mind snapped itself out of the shock.

Simon had hired the Brightmore woman for *some* skill with the occult, presumably. It wouldn't hurt to have her along. Gareth glanced over his shoulder to see how she'd taken the order.

She was nearly neck and neck with him. Either she moved with inhuman speed—not wholly impossible, given the circumstances—or she hadn't been waiting on his invitation. Not one to sit on her hands in a crisis. Gareth had to give her that, just as he'd had to concede a few moments ago she had some measure of wit.

Naturally, he told himself as they followed Fitzpatrick into the hall, Mrs. Brightmore hadn't seen the case yet. Neither, in all fairness, had he.

"Has someone gone to get Mrs. Grenville?" he asked.

Fitzpatrick nodded. "Charlotte."

Better she than me was all through his voice. Modern

youth wasn't much for chivalry, it appeared. Not that
Gareth could entirely blame the boy.

By the time they'd gotten halfway up the stairs, his
leg had already begun to ache. He could slow down,
but not in front of the Brightmore woman, and it probably wouldn't be a good idea even if she wasn't there. If
Elizabeth's powers shut off suddenly, as they sometimes
did—then there *would* be something he could do. If he
and Elizabeth were lucky.

One bit of fortune was on Gareth's side. Until the
builders could finish the new dormitory that occupied
so much of Mrs. Grenville's attention, the female students stayed on the second floor in a hastily refitted
guest room. If climbing the stairs in a hurry was painful,
dashing across the grounds would have been a study in
agony. It was lucky too, they had been inside: here there
was a ceiling.

A year or two ago, Gareth had never had time to think
during a crisis. They'd always been right at hand. Half
the time, he'd no sooner stumbled out of his bed than
there'd been some broken and bleeding young man in
front of him, and his mind had turned itself swiftly and
wholly to the task. He'd never thought, then, he might
actually miss those days.

When he reached the landing, Mrs. Brightmore by his
side, he could hear Elizabeth sobbing. It was honestly
something of a relief. The girl clearly hadn't damaged
herself too badly. It took a certain amount of strength to
cry, particularly at any volume, and it required that the
person crying have lungs in relatively good condition.
Death, in Gareth's experience, was quiet, more often
than not.

Nonetheless, he covered the length of the hallway quickly, despite the pain in his leg. It didn't take long before he drew in sight of the open doorway and glimpsed the figures inside. Fitzpatrick had dashed ahead of him and now stood a little to the side. Waite and Fairley were nearby. All three had their heads tipped backward, the better to stare the six or so feet to the ceiling.

Elizabeth Donnell floated there. "Floating" gave the impression of serenity, though the girl was anything but serene. She twisted and shrieked, kicking her legs and clawing at the air as if she could find some purchase on emptiness. Her red hair had come loose from its plaits sometime in the struggle and tangled about her as if in an unseen wind. As Gareth came in, she looked down at him with red-rimmed eyes and, with some effort, made her crying coherent.

"Oh, Dr. St. John," she said and gulped, "can you get me down from here? *Please?*"

Poor little thing. Gareth's own talent had been quite bad enough at thirteen, but it had been far more subtle, and controllable, than this. He'd have been screaming too, in her circumstances.

Pity wouldn't get her down, though. Admitting he didn't know what would get her down would probably only make matters worse. The last thing the students needed was further panic. None of that meant he had the slightest idea how to begin. At a minimum, he could talk calmly to her until Mrs. Grenville returned, and be on hand in case the situation got…out of hand.

Gareth drew a breath to speak.

"I can." It was Mrs. Brightmore. Her brown eyes

were a little wide, but her face, although pale, showed no signs of panic.

It was a familiar face too. Gareth had thought so since a few moments after he'd met her and was more convinced now. He couldn't place the connection, and it didn't matter. If the woman thought she had the situation in hand—it was more than he did. "This is Mrs. Brightmore," he said by way of an introduction. "She's come to be your teacher."

The boys turned briefly, but only briefly. A new teacher, even a young and pretty one, held no fascination beside the scene playing out above them. Gareth shot them a reproving look—*this is not a sideshow, gentlemen*—and was glad to see a general embarrassed shuffling.

More to the point, Elizabeth turned a gaze to Mrs. Brightmore that was both surprised and hopeful. "You are? So you know about—?" She gestured vaguely around her.

"Yes, of course." A quick smile. "It won't be any problem at all, so long as you do what I say."

"Yes, ma'am!"

Mrs. Brightmore took a few steps into the room until she was standing almost directly below Elizabeth—just enough off to look easily up at the girl. "First of all, I'd like you to shut your eyes. Good. Now take a very deep breath. Fill your lungs and hold it for a second."

Elizabeth fell almost silent, but Gareth saw her lips moving and heard a very low mutter. Some of the words sounded a bit like Latin. None of them seemed quite to correspond with the short, neat woman in the brown checked wool. However, the lamplight casting a shadow across her face and darkening her chestnut hair made her look more suited to her role.

"When I say 'go,'" she went on, "open your eyes, look at me, and let your breath out. Slowly. Count to ten."

The whole room was silent now, silent enough to hear the first puff of Elizabeth's breath, and attentive enough to notice when her body started to descend. It was only a few inches, but her nose no longer brushed the ceiling.

"Good God!" Waite whispered.

Gareth knew he should reprove him, but he'd only barely controlled the urge to swear himself. "I suggest," he said, "that the three of you go and explain the situation to Mrs. Grenville."

"But Charlotte—" Fairley said.

"Miss Woodwell won't know about this latest development, will she?" Gareth used the voice that had always worked on orderlies and assumed the sound of footsteps meant it had worked. For his part, he didn't take his eyes off the center of the room, where Elizabeth was slowly but surely drifting downward.

Now, as he hadn't had time to do earlier, he took a closer look at Mrs. Brightmore. Pretty, yes. Even now he wasn't blind to a pleasantly rounded figure or a cheerful, heart-shaped face. She hadn't dressed to play up either asset though, or to show off her wealth. Her clothing was plain and her hair pulled back in a simple knot. Necessary, perhaps, since she didn't travel with a maid. She was no schoolgirl, but she was no more than his age, if that, young to be so certain of herself under these circumstances.

Nothing in her appearance explained how she'd

learned whatever she was doing. Nor did it account for the feeling Gareth had met her before. That was highly improbable. He hadn't been more than half a year in England, he'd been recovering for most of that, and she was no nurse.

Elizabeth continued her descent. Mrs. Brightmore didn't give her much time to realize it, from the way things looked. She kept talking, lengthening her words slowly, and her hands moved in slow patterns in the air. Her fingers were long and slim, nimble looking.

"Now in for another count of ten. Imagine letting out everything that makes you float, as if you're a great big balloon. Someone's untied the end, and the air's coming out. But it's not all at once. I am right here, and you are safe. Just breathe out now, slowly—and hold—and then in again."

There was a faint accent to her voice now, almost but not quite French. It was familiar, again, like the movements of her hands.

"In once again—hold—and out—and we're done!"

Gareth almost jumped when the heels of Elizabeth's boots touched the carpet. By the look on her face, though, he wasn't half as surprised as she was. "I-it worked!" the girl said.

"So it did. I'd go downstairs, if I were you, and see if I could get some bread and butter out of Cook. You'll be able to eat a horse soon." Mrs. Brightmore smiled.

It was the smile that pulled all the other hints together. A dimple in one cheek made it look slightly lopsided, and suddenly Gareth knew he'd seen that precise smile before. In person, yes, but also on a poster. Not a very good print, but the girl had been pretty, the night had been quiet, and they'd all been flush with pay. *I've never been*, James had said. *Don't you think we should, before we leave? Don't have these in Egypt, I'll wager.*

Gareth and Edward had been willing enough to go along. Wine had helped.

It should have been gin. Spirits to talk with spirits. Gareth remembered Edward's voice. A month or so later, Edward had lain on a filthy cot in a hot country, sweating and bleeding and dying for nothing particularly right or true. Edward had been whole that night, though. Merry going in, melancholy after. He hadn't been able to say why.

Madame Marguerite, the woman had been called then. Medium Most Magnificent. Part of something called Hawkins's Wonder Show. She'd sounded more French, or more like her audience had expected French to sound. Her hair had been down in ringlets and her wrists clinking with cheap bangles. Her dress had been white and cut much lower. But she'd moved her hands the same way, and her voice had been just as coaxing when she spoke to "The Realms Beyond."

Gareth had almost been able to see the wires.

He took a step back without thinking. He'd started to admire her—that was the worst of it. The way she kept her head in a crisis, her quiet humor, her ability to calm a scared child. Downstairs, perhaps he'd even started to like her.

Now—

Gareth reminded herself he didn't know. He *couldn't* know for sure. It had been six years. Plenty had happened, plenty of faces had passed through his vision on the way, and women did look and even sound similar.

And Mrs. Brightmore could do what she claimed. She just had.

Except...she'd simply talked, for the most part. Any half-shilling fortune-teller could talk a decent game, and most of them could manage a few tricks of mesmerism—certainly enough to work on a scared child. The invocation had been the only blatantly magical part of the process, and even that might have been for effect.

He didn't want to offend an innocent woman, nor did he want to offend a woman he would have to work with. Nevertheless, he had to know. More than that, he owed some information to the Grenvilles.

"I realize it's an unusual question," he said abruptly. "But I think we've met before. May I ask your Christian name?"

Was it his imagination, or was her smile a touch fixed now? "Olivia," she said. "But I don't—"

"Ah," he said and watched her face. "I was almost certain it was Marguerite."

She was very good. The recognition on her face—and the guilt—was there for only a minute. Just long enough to tell him what he needed to know.

Chapter 3

AT ANY OTHER TIME, SHE COULD HAVE HANDLED THE question.

Oh, it would have thrown her a bit. Olivia hadn't expected anyone to remember her from her past life. In her experience, a significantly different way of dressing or doing one's hair would fool most people, and she wasn't so distinctive looking as to be an exception to the rule.

At any rate, she'd been dimly aware the possibility existed, and the last ten years had made her good at thinking on her feet. She could have brushed off the speculation firmly, asked Dr. St. John what gave him license to presume he knew a lady's given name, or even acted puzzled and innocent. No. She thought she had a cousin named Margaret, the closest English equivalent, but she hadn't seen that branch of the family in a while. It wouldn't have even been quite a lie, though she and Margaret Drew had looked nothing alike in their youth, and Olivia doubted time had increased the resemblance.

"I—" she began now, watching Dr. St. John turn away from her.

He glanced back, impatient and distrustful and…hopeful, perhaps, that she had an explanation? Or was that wishful thinking on her part?

Olivia didn't know what she was going to say. Talking itself was an effort, after the strain of gradually pulling power from Elizabeth and grounding it, after trying to seem as if the process was completely familiar to her, when she'd done it only a few times before and only once with someone's natural power. Her mind felt colorless and sticky, almost half a moment behind where it should be.

It was part of the reason, she knew, she'd botched her response so badly, and it would do nothing to help her attempt to explain herself, if, that is, there was any explanation Dr. St. John would accept.

Nevertheless, she had to try. "I'm certain it—"

Through the open doorway, she heard the sound of rapid footsteps on marble and of another door firmly closing. Voices rose from downstairs: one male, two female, none of them particularly familiar.

"That will be Simon," Dr. St. John said. He drew himself up, and whatever hope Olivia had seen or imagined vanished from his gaze. "If you'll excuse me, madam, I believe I should speak with him."

She was still doing a very good imitation of a landed fish when he bowed, very slightly, and headed out. The door closed behind him, and the sound of the latch clicking felt like a blow. It wasn't a hard hit or one from which she couldn't recover, but a slap was a slap.

There was a chair by one of the narrow beds. Like the thick carpet and the patterned wallpaper, it was a rather ludicrously ornate clue that this room hadn't held students for very long. The chair was upholstered in brown plush and overstuffed. More importantly, it was at hand.

Olivia mostly fell into it.

She sat with her fingertips pressed against her closed eyes and told herself various reassuring things. The Grenvilles had known about her past before they hired her. She hadn't deceived them. Dr. Gillespie could assure them—and had, Olivia thought—that she actually could work magic. Dr. St. John could tell them nothing they didn't already know.

He could, very easily, force Mr. Grenville to choose between retaining Olivia and retaining him. Or his disgust could simply make the Grenvilles reconsider their decision, no ultimatum required. If one of the staff reacted so strongly, what might others think if the truth came out? What would the students' parents do if they got news of it? Olivia had never been particularly famous, or tried to be—Helena Blavatsky could have all the Theosophical Societies and published books she wanted—but she had always been content with rent for the month and an occasional roast dinner. But this afternoon had been proof enough that she wasn't anonymous either.

I should have dyed my hair. But she'd been trying to stop practicing that kind of deception.

She wondered if that had been part of the reason she'd fumbled.

Not that it mattered.

The room was more comfortable than the parlor she'd kept as a young wife in London. Nonetheless, she could have been back there, sitting on a tiny sofa and working out her accounts, trying to ignore the doctor's murmurs overhead and the sound of her husband's coughing. Waiting for the tread of footsteps on the stairs and the doctor's judgment of how much worse Tom was ailing this time. Preparing for bad news never seemed to get any easier.

Olivia took a breath, held it, and let it out slowly,

trying to calm herself the way she'd helped Elizabeth relax. The process had been easier in some ways for the child, who was as yet free from such distractions as tight corsets and too many hairpins. Then again, Olivia wasn't hanging in midair.

Not literally.

—◇◇◇—

Gareth had been hoping to talk with Simon alone. He didn't have anything against Mrs. Grenville, though the woman did remind him of several sergeants he'd encountered not always on the best of terms. However, the situation concerning Mrs. Brightmore was delicate. Even he knew that, and he hadn't been moving precisely in Polite Society in the last few years.

He found himself strangely reluctant to embarrass the woman publicly, much as she might deserve it. It was far better to have a quiet word with an old friend and put the matter in his hands. Discretion is the better part of valor, and all that.

So he'd hoped. On the other hand, Simon had not picked his wife for her overabundance of feminine delicacy. On most occasions, so far, Gareth had thought Simon's judgment sound. On this, however, he could have wished the new Mrs. Grenville had been altogether shrinking and dainty, although her presence in Simon's study was largely his own fault. Mrs. Grenville had said she'd heard the new teacher had dealt with Elizabeth. Gareth had cleared his throat and said he'd actually like to speak with Simon about the teacher in question…

…and here they were. The Grenvilles sat in chairs by

the fire, Gareth stood while trying not to put his hands in his pockets like a nervous schoolboy, and the Turkish carpet stretched between them like a small sea of good red wine.

Or fresh blood.

"Mrs. Brightmore is—" Bluntness, Gareth decided, would probably serve him well. If it wouldn't, he was still not capable of anything else at the moment. "She's a fraud."

Mrs. Grenville frowned. When she spoke, her accent—vaguely American, though Gareth didn't have the ear to place it—made a startling counterpoint to Gareth and Simon's voices. "She didn't get the Donnell girl down?"

"Yes, she did. Through some trick of the mind—useful, I don't doubt. But I recognized her. She wasn't using the same name then."

"I didn't know the two of you had met before. I would've said something." Simon was leaning back in his chair, almost lounging, in sharp contrast to his wife's straight back and intent look.

"We hadn't," Gareth said more sharply than he'd intended. "One doesn't *meet* fake mediums."

There it was. Except the statement hadn't provoked the shock or dismay Gareth had thought it would. Mrs. Grenville actually relaxed a bit.

"I wasn't suggesting you'd signed her dance card or taken her for a carriage ride," Simon said, half-smiling. "Though I must say I thought the Army made a man less alive to distinctions of class, not the reverse."

Gareth felt himself flush. "I hardly meant it like that. I wouldn't take issue with a colleague's birth or wealth, but she was a confidence trickster or the next thing to it. She hasn't admitted to it in words, but, Simon, I would swear I'm right about this."

"Yeah," said Mrs. Grenville, "you are." She shrugged. "We should've told you earlier, but we didn't think it'd come up."

"What?" It was hard to be proper with Mrs. Grenville under normal circumstances. Surprise made Gareth blunt. "You knew?"

Mrs. Grenville lifted her blonde eyebrows in her own rather sarcastic version of surprise. "You didn't think we'd check her background?"

"It was good of you to inform us," Simon interrupted, "but yes, we had some idea of her past."

"And you hired her?"

"I said *past*." Simon smiled in a way Gareth recognized from university, a smile that said he could be patient because he was right and you were wrong and he was just about to show you how. It had always made Gareth want to push him into a mud puddle, though there had never been any puddles convenient. "She was a charlatan for several years, and I'd wager you met her then. Now she isn't."

Gareth snorted. "What proof has she shown you?"

"The same sort I showed you that evening after the Boat Race. I can ask her to demonstrate, if you'd like."

"No, thank you." Gareth repressed a shudder. The window Simon had opened for him in their youth hadn't shown him anything *bad*, precisely, but what he'd seen had made his mind hurt. "Simon, are you absolutely certain? There must be someone else."

"Nobody willing to drop their own lives and teach

a pack of odd youths out in the countryside," Simon replied. He glanced over at his wife. "Besides, it's been…suggested…certain of the lady's other skills will be useful, given the end we're teaching toward."

Students, Simon had said when he and Gareth had first discussed the school, and then agents. People to stand against the dark forces of the world when they appeared. Gareth supposed a certain amount of deceit might, under such circumstances, be a necessary evil.

He wasn't at all certain about trusting a woman who'd turned to it in order to make an easy shilling.

"I'm willing," Simon added slowly, "to take quite a few chances in this endeavor. The school, the students, my ability to teach what little I know and find out more…one woman hardly seems like much of an obstacle."

"And I suppose she can't do a great deal of harm here," Gareth admitted slowly. The town was small, the housekeeper had relatively sharp eyes, and Simon knew what he was doing.

"You'll be able to work with her, then?" Simon smiled hopefully. "We do rather need you here."

There were lines at the corners of Simon's eyes Gareth hadn't seen before he'd left. No gray in his friend's hair, not yet, but he moved and spoke more slowly, with more purpose, as if he were climbing some mountain in his mind.

Gareth wondered if Simon knew how the years had changed him. He wondered what alterations he had yet to notice in himself.

Better a little bad company in a good cause than a little good company in a bad one.

"Certainly," he said. "I can be civil to the woman.

After all, you want me to mend cuts and inspect sore throats, and she's to be a teacher. It's not as though we'll have much to do with each other."

––––––

A clock downstairs chimed the quarter hour, jolting Olivia out of her thoughts and making her realize two things. The first was she had about reached her limit as far as waiting was concerned. The second was she was sitting in a bedroom, even though there was nobody else in it.

Making herself move briskly, she got to her feet and brushed her skirts into some semblance of order, then checked her reflection quickly in the small mirror on the wall. Acceptable, she decided, if tired. At least she'd kept herself from weeping. If she was to stay, after all, it wouldn't do for her students to see her so discomposed.

If she wasn't—well, with any luck the Grenvilles would pay her train fare, and she could still earn a living back in London. Regardless, she wouldn't break down when she heard the news. She wouldn't impose herself on the Grenvilles that way, and she certainly wouldn't give Dr. St. John the satisfaction.

Olivia lifted her chin, straightened her back, and stepped out of the room.

At the other end of the hall, an older woman in a dark dress started as she saw Olivia then hurried toward her. "Mrs. Brightmore? I've been looking for you."

"Oh?" Olivia struggled to keep her voice neutral and pleasant. "I'm sorry to be so hard to find. I'd just sat down to catch my breath for a moment."

"Of course," said the woman. Tall, noted the part of

Olivia that had spent the last few years reading people for a living, and neither thin nor stout. About forty but well preserved, and not badly off. The dress was plain, but the broadcloth was good material.

The rest of Olivia tried not to beg for information. She smiled politely. "I hope I haven't been any trouble."

"Not at all. I'm Mrs. Edgar, the housekeeper." The woman curtsied. Hers was practiced and stately, very far from Violet's uncertain bob. "Mr. Grenville sent me to tell you he and his wife are dining by themselves tonight, as he assumed you'd want to do as much after such a tiring day."

That sounded almost promising. "It *has* been a little long," Olivia ventured.

"I don't doubt it. Violet's been unpacking your belongings, and we'll have a tray sent up to your room."

"That's very kind of you," said Olivia but didn't let herself relax yet. A room could be temporary. "The students?"

"They'll eat on their own. God willing," said Mrs. Edgar with the first real emotion Olivia had heard from her, "there won't be any more incidents tonight. Mrs. Grenville said she'd introduce you tomorrow and take you 'round the place as well."

It was an utterly offhand comment, but it almost made Olivia slump against the wall with relief. "That would be very kind of her," she said, fumbling for words. "Please thank her for me. And thank you too."

"Of course, ma'am," said Mrs. Edgar, neither smiling nor frowning. "Just follow me, and I'll show you your room."

Olivia followed, half-blind with joy. She could stay. She could teach and learn in her spare time; more than that, there'd be a steady wage, ready meals, and a roof over her head she needn't worry about losing every month.

She hadn't let herself realize just how much the position meant to her or how terrified she'd been when she thought the Grenvilles might send her away. Now clarity had arrived all at once. Olivia was surprised to find anger came with it.

"How long has Dr. St. John been here?" she asked.

"Hmm? About two weeks, ma'am. Keeps to himself a fair bit—when the students allow it. Without any other teachers here, it's fallen to him to keep the children in line when the Grenvilles are occupied."

"I'll do my best to relieve his burden," Olivia said and tried to sound pleasant.

The vicar of her girlhood and Dr. Gillespie, her old mentor, would have reminded her that forgiveness was divine. Even Olivia's common sense told her Dr. St. John's concern was understandable. However much it embarrassed her to admit it, he thought his employers were being practiced upon. Loyalty was a virtue.

It was all very good in the abstract. It was harder to let go the time, short as it had been, where her hopes for the future had suddenly seemed to slide just out of reach. Harder, too, to overlook the look of disgust on the doctor's face or how bare his attempt at civility had been.

He hadn't even let her try to explain.

None of that mattered, Olivia told herself sternly. She was a grown woman. She could and would be reasonable and civil and too sensible to let resentment color her behavior toward a man who would be only a remote colleague. And she had plenty of other duties to occupy her mind.

Dr. St. John, she decided, would be a very minor factor in her life.

Chapter 4

"YOU MEAN SHE'S GOING TO BE OUR TEACHER TOO? NOT just for the girls?"

It was probably Fitzpatrick speaking, Gareth thought. Fairley's voice hadn't changed yet, and Waite was more inclined to drawl. He looked up from his papers and sighed. That wasn't the kind of question that began a short conversation. From the sound of it, the boys would need to learn several lessons in punctuality. "How to knock" would also be a decent subject to cover.

"You can't be serious!" That was Fairley. Gareth winced. He didn't mind that his office had been hastily converted—that it was, essentially, a drawing room divided in two and refurnished. The room was clean, warm, and indoors, and it featured a total absence of scorpions: all a nice contrast to his quarters in Egypt. If the new walls and swinging door occasionally let a voice drift through, he wasn't going to complain.

The problem was, Fairley's voice didn't drift. It stabbed.

"Oh, I most certainly can." Waite said. "Though I generally try to remain otherwise. If you can't laugh at life's little surprises—"

"A female teacher?" Fairley again, sounding even younger in contrast to Waite's typical attempt at playing worldly. "As if we were in the nursery?"

Gareth, getting to his feet, glanced quickly out the

window. It was a clear day so far, with perhaps a wisp or two of cloud floating in the blue. Nothing outside would be terribly susceptible to Fairley's moods. All the same, it was good to be certain.

Through the window, he glimpsed a figure in blue and recognized after a second it was Mrs. Grenville, walking toward the stables with her husband beside her. She'd finished showing the Brightmore woman about the place, then. Gareth had seen them going out earlier but thankfully had been too far away to speak. Since then, he'd been conducting preliminary examinations on the students and administering vaccinations to those who needed it, which had kept him quite nicely in his office.

Eventually, he would have to talk with Mrs. Brightmore. Eventually, he would have to die. Gareth saw no point thinking about either longer than was strictly necessary.

Outside, Waite chuckled knowingly, or what he thought was knowingly: a seventeen-year-old boy trying to act like a thirty-year-old model of dissipation. At any rate, their temperaments were normal, whatever their knowledge might end up being. Gareth smiled, even as his throat tightened. Memory was really the damnedest thing that way.

"Oh, cheer up, old man. There's quite a bit you can learn from a woman, you know. Especially a woman like that." Waite let out a low whistle.

The smile died on Gareth's face.

"Really?" Fitzpatrick speaking again, his voice dropping. "You think—?"

"Well, she's probably here for the conventional things, you know. Shakespeare and geometry and that.

Perhaps a little bit of contacting the spirit world. Women are good at that sort of thing, you know. Think how impressed she'll be when she hears what we already know, or when Fairley here shows what he can do."

"She did get Lizzie down," Fairley began.

"Any half-bright sort of a girl can talk a child like Lizzie into behaving sensibly. I don't think there's much in her but—"

The opening door cut off Waite's speech. It almost hit him in the side, as well. Gareth hadn't been intending the second effect, but he didn't think he'd lose a great deal of sleep over it. "Gentlemen," he said, slipping back into his orderly-commanding tone, "I believe we were supposed to begin ten minutes ago."

Fairley ducked his head and looked at his shoes, and Waite had the sense to stay quiet. The door had evidently made an impression. Fitzpatrick, though, spoke up. "We didn't know you were in, sir."

"You could see the door," said Gareth. "You have hands. Next time, I suggest you use them. Since you were suffering from so much suspense, however, we can begin with you."

Fitzpatrick winced but stepped forward.

"By the way," Gareth added, looking between all three boys. "I would suggest not underestimating the ability of any teacher at this establishment. Mrs. Brightmore is both intelligent and knowledgeable…and if the Grenvilles appointed her as your instructor, magical or otherwise, I would imagine it's because they think highly of her fitness for the task."

He paused.

"It is not one I envy her."

In his old life, he'd not had much cause to take such a tone, not even to issue many corrections. Most of the orderlies—most of the men—had known their job, tried their hardest, and not made much trouble, or not much that had been Gareth's responsibility. Now it had been twice in two days. Not a good sign. In any case, he hadn't lost the skill of it. Except for blushing, all three boys were studiously blank faced and still.

Too still, in fact, for a mere dressing down, emphatic though it may have been. Waite wasn't even looking at Gareth but past him—

Oh, no.

Now he was starting to smile a little. Not triumphant or smug, though. Embarrassed. Almost apologetic.

Oh, no.

It could have been Simon or Mrs. Grenville, and Waite might have been squirming because he'd been caught out by more than one authority at a time. If Fate had been kind, it would have been.

Fate was hardly ever kind.

Stomach sinking, Gareth turned away from the boys.

He had to concede that Mrs. Brightmore did a very good blank face herself. A little flushed, obvious above the plain white shirtwaist she wore, but that could have been from the wind. She had clearly been outdoors. Little wisps of hair had escaped their knot and were clinging to the sides of her neck. Other than that, she looked eminently respectable, she was certainly standing within speaking distance, and Gareth had made no effort to keep his voice down.

He was generally quite good at hearing footsteps. Egypt had taught him that much.

He had no idea how long she'd been there.

As Gareth hesitated, Mrs. Brightmore glanced over the small and flustered group of boys, and back at him. Then she smiled. It was very polite, no hint of gloating in it, but he couldn't read anything else in her face. "Good afternoon," she said, and she might have been meeting an acquaintance at a garden party. "I seem to have lost my way to the library."

"Oh," said Fitzpatrick, as apparently none of the others could speak. "Go back to the hall, only right instead of left. Ma'am."

"Thank you," said Mrs. Brightmore, ignoring the belated title. "I do hope you're all well."

"Quite," Gareth said and hoped it didn't sound as strangled as he felt. "Thank you. Behind schedule, though, so please excuse us. Fitzpatrick?"

Not waiting for the boy to respond, he turned on one heel and sought the refuge of his inner office.

The "Charlotte" Fitzpatrick had mentioned the previous night turned out to be Miss Charlotte Woodwell, a tall young lady with curly black hair and vivid green eyes, apparently fond of aesthetic clothing and wandering the gardens in her free time. She was by far the oldest of the students, by the look of her, no more than eight or nine years younger than Olivia.

"Hardly the model of a schoolgirl, I know," she said with a wide grin and an easy shrug in response to the question Olivia had carefully not been asking. "But I don't know nearly enough to teach, and I've been dying to *learn* for years. Packed my trunk and came down as soon as I heard about this place. I've got absolutely heaps of questions. So now you're warned!"

"I'll do my best to answer them," Olivia replied, smiling back. It would have been hard not to like the younger woman, and it was a relief to meet anyone remotely adult who was so straightforwardly glad to see her. Violet had been nervously cheerful, the Grenvilles had been kind, but it hadn't been the same.

She hadn't even actually seen Mr. Grenville yet. "Reinforcing wards," his wife had explained. "You'll help eventually. Simon says the land's got to get to know you first, though."

The tour she'd been given hadn't been much help there. If the land was getting to know Olivia, she wasn't reciprocating. Mrs. Grenville—a tall, thin woman with reddish-blonde hair and a sort of American accent—was friendly enough in a brisk way, and she certainly had been exact. Stables are there. Town is that way. Don't go in the forest unless one of us is with you or you mark your path with a ball of string. It wasn't her fault Olivia was used to streets with signs and a two-room flat. Nevertheless, the phrase "whirlwind tour" had never felt quite so accurate.

She'd eventually managed to find the library. She'd gotten to do no more than stare at the shelves, somewhere between gluttony and lust, before Mrs. Grenville had found her again and taken her outside to make introductions. All the same, she'd gotten there. The process had proved unexpectedly gratifying too, if also confusing. She'd expected the boys to be skeptical about a female teacher. She hadn't expected St. John, of all people, to set them right.

"Woodwell," Mrs. Grenville said, breaking into Olivia's thoughts while they walked up the path away from the gardens, "will probably be the easiest to deal with. She'll end up teaching in a year or two, or going into the field, depending on how things work out."

"Into the field?"

Mrs. Grenville nodded. "You know what they're here for, right?"

"Yes." If the letter hadn't made that clear, the interview would have. "But—" Olivia began and then stopped. Somehow, she didn't think *but she's a girl* would hold much water with Mrs. Grenville. "But she's very young. They all are."

"You send them to war and sea younger. Down the mines too, I hear, or into the factories, though that's not so glamorous."

Memories of London came back. Pinched, smudged young faces above tattered clothing. Girls selling flowers and ribbons in dirty streets. Boys with brooms. Those weren't the worst off, she knew, not by a good ways.

"Not as young as Elizabeth," said Olivia, though she wasn't sure how she dared say it. Mrs. Grenville had a stare like a gauntlet when she wanted to. She also wasn't sure what the woman had meant by *you*—America had both factories and armies, after all. "Or, um, Michael?" She recalled a tow-headed boy, all freckles and puppy fat, who hadn't looked more than thirteen.

"Fairley, yeah. We won't take them that young, generally. Simon thinks it *is* too young to volunteer for this kind of service…except when it's worse for them to go untrained."

"The levitation?"

Mrs. Grenville nodded. "The levitation. Donnell does that when she's upset. Fairley can make it rain."

"And the others?"

"Nothing uncontrolled. Woodwell talks with animals, she says. Fitzpatrick and Waite don't have any natural talents, but they want to learn. Like you and Simon."

Fitzpatrick's first name was William, Olivia had learned a little while earlier, and the third boy was Arthur Waite. They were fifteen and seventeen, respectively, both dark haired. Fitzpatrick was slightly taller and broader shouldered, despite his youth, which would allow Olivia to tell them apart for the moment.

"They'll be the easiest to teach, then, I'd imagine," Olivia said, hopeful despite what she'd heard from both young men earlier.

"Probably. The most trouble otherwise, though." Mrs. Grenville sounded perfectly casual when she spoke, even amused, and there was nothing in her expression to suggest she knew about the incident near St. John's office.

"Oh?" Olivia looked carefully off toward the house.

"Seems likely. Woodwell's old enough to have grown some brains, and Donnell's scared of her own shadow. That's its own issue, especially since she starts floating around when she gets scared. But she won't give you attitude. Fairley might, but the naturals mostly want to get their powers under control. Waite and Fitzpatrick…" Mrs. Grenville pulled a face. "Recruits, right? Signed up of their own free will, and you've got to give them credit for that, but the problem is they know it."

She sounded very familiar with the situation. Her

father had been military, Olivia thought, or maybe her first husband. Olivia wasn't inclined to ask.

Mrs. Grenville gave another shrug. "You might have to beat them back into place a few times. Don't worry about it when it happens. The rest of us have your back."

Olivia took a few seconds to figure out what the other woman meant. She'd never heard the phrase before. When the meaning did become clear, she had the impulse to ask if "the rest of us" included Dr. St. John. Nothing about Mrs. Grenville encouraged idle questions, though.

Besides, Olivia already knew the answer.

Naturally, St. John had dressed down the boys. He'd had to. Olivia had realized that almost as soon as she'd headed back toward the library. A slight against one of the teachers was a slight on Mr. Grenville's good judgment, and St. John was his friend, or so she'd heard from the servants. Letting the boys say whatever they were saying—Olivia had overheard only a little but could guess at the rest—would have undermined the whole order of the school.

There was no point mentioning the incident, really. Waite, Fitzpatrick, and Fairley had learned their lesson, and if having to defend a woman he so clearly despised had pained St. John at all, Olivia couldn't bring herself to be sorry for him. It repaid, a little, that half hour of terror she'd spent the night before.

Still, she couldn't help remembering the tone in St. John's voice or the way the door had hit the wall when he'd pushed it open. Upholding authority was all well and good, but Olivia was surprised he'd be so vehement about it.

Chapter 5

OLIVIA HELD HER FIRST CLASS IN ANOTHER ONE OF THE converted downstairs rooms, this one a small drawing room fairly near the library. The alterations here hadn't been extensive, since there weren't many students. Olivia's five pupils had arrayed themselves over an assortment of yellow-cushioned couches and upholstered blue chairs. Someone had taken up the carpet, though. Olivia wasn't sure whether they'd anticipated blood sacrifices or spilled tea or both.

Either seemed likely enough.

It had taken all she knew about disciplined breathing to get a good night's sleep, and she hadn't been able to eat much at breakfast. But now, as she faced the class, she felt no fear at all. Her nerves hadn't vanished; they'd been transmuted, as they always were, into a fierce, cheerful energy that lifted her chin and straightened her back.

Take the curtain up, Olivia thought as she smiled at the class.

"Good morning," she said. "We will begin with theory."

They were with her so far. Patient. Curious. Not enthusiastic yet.

"This world has certain rules," Olivia said. "Some are obvious and well known." She held up her pen for a moment then dropped it. It hit the floor with a *clack* and rolled toward one of the couches, where Waite picked it up.

The students' faces showed a little more interest, as any physical demonstration would command. Olivia took a breath.

Modulate the voice, a little louder than before, catch their eyes.

"Some are less so." She spoke the single word she'd been repeating in her head since she'd woken up.

A foot away from her, a hand-wide pillar of bright blue fire burst up from the floor.

Olivia kept her eyes on the students as they gasped and stared. She had to admit the reaction was satisfying. Well worth the effort, even though Enochian was even harder to master than Latin. But more to the point, she didn't want to watch the fire. That would make her look uncertain. It was only after half a minute that she let herself glance over, and she made sure it *was* just a glance.

The flame had coalesced into a small ball, leaving the floor unmarked, and was hovering around shoulder height. The fire had always behaved before, but she was never completely certain. Olivia let herself relax a little, inwardly, and turned her attention back to the room.

St. John was standing at the back.

How long had he been there? Why was he there at all? He showed no signs of retrieving any of the students. He was standing with his hand resting lightly on the back of a chair. He intended to watch the class, then. Olivia could think of no flattering reason for him to do so—certainly not without consulting her first—and half a dozen insulting ones. For a moment she froze, and her tightly held balance wavered.

Then she saw his fixed gaze and his slightly open mouth. St. John might have arrived in order to make sure Olivia didn't corrupt the students or steal the candlesticks, but he was staring at the fire like everyone else.

She could handle this. And she'd be damned if she let some officious prig of a doctor throw her off her game.

"Let us consider an analogy" she said. Her voice was clear and calm. Six pairs of eyes turned back toward her. Olivia met St. John's, smiled as politely—she hoped—as she'd done in his outer office, and went on.

"Let's say the world is a city. The way most people live, and even the way we live most of the time, is like a visitor with a carriage and a map. He can follow the main streets easily enough, and he'll nearly always get where he's going as long as he has the address. It's not the quickest way, and he might miss a few things, but he'll be all right."

She paused, ostensibly to let that sink in, really to take a breath and ready the next part of the lecture. Everyone in the class was looking at her, and it was a thrill again rather than a burden. She'd regained her footing in this particular dance. She did not feel St. John's gaze any more than the others, and if she did, it was only because his presence was so wretchedly unexpected.

"Now think about a man who's lived in this city all his life," Olivia went on. "He knows he can cut across *this* back street, make a turn just before *that* crossing, and use the other bridge if there's too much traffic on the main one. That's what magic—the kind I just did—is like. Mr. Fitzpatrick?"

The boy put his hand down just enough to point at the ball of fire. "You can't do that normally, ma'am, no matter how long you take."

Olivia smiled. "Precisely. A native won't just know routes. He'll know about *places* a visitor wouldn't. Perhaps this"—she gestured to the flame, still careful not to look—"is like, oh, that little tearoom that does the best sandwiches but won't stand a crowd, or the bookshop you have to get to through a back alley and two flights of stairs."

There might have been a surprised chuckle from the back of the room where St. John was still standing. Olivia didn't look. Charlotte had her hand up, after all. "Miss Woodwell?"

"What about the other kind of magic?" Charlotte was leaning forward, elbows on her knees. "You've generally got to prepare a spell or say something, like you did before. What about people who can just do things when they want…or even when they don't?"

Everyone very carefully did not look at Elizabeth, who turned red.

"Good question." Olivia spoke quickly, getting the class's attention again. She smiled apologetically at Miss Woodwell. "I hate to disappoint, but I have to admit I don't know for certain. I *think* it breaks a lot of the rules, and there are a couple of theories about why, but nobody's really very sure."

Also, it's not diplomatic to suggest that your students have a fairy or a demon somewhere in the family tree. That is, not on the first day.

Olivia looked around the room slowly and deliberately. "All of you here," she said, holding Charlotte's gaze for a moment, moving to Michael, who was frowning a little, then on to blushing Elizabeth, "are part of something very new. The whole sum of human knowledge, where magic is concerned, amounts to perhaps one book in a vast library. Perhaps not even that. Mr. Grenville knows a few things. I know a few. There are others who know still more." Fitzpatrick had his head tilted to one side, listening. He grinned when she met his eyes. Even Waite, lounging against one end of the couch, had an unexpected alertness in his face. "I expect to teach you. I also expect we'll all learn. We'll have to if we're to fulfill our purpose at this school."

On impulse, Olivia looked past the students, straight at St. John. She couldn't read his face. It didn't matter. She smiled at him.

Then she stepped back and let silence fall.

"You may each come up and look into the fire, if you want," Olivia said at the end of the class. They'd all behaved well, as far as she was any judge, and a reward would carry them forward nicely. "It won't burn you, and it can be a sort of fortune-telling. Most people see a face in the flame."

"What, their true love?" asked Michael, mouth twisting in thirteen-year-old male scorn.

Olivia laughed. "Someone who'll be important to you by and by. An employer, a political opponent, a friend, a child…or a sweetheart, in some cases."

"Or an enemy?" asked Waite, more serious and less eager than Olivia would've expected from him.

She nodded. "Or that." They were all, as she'd said, here for a purpose. There was no point concealing what that purpose might involve. "Line up neatly. Youngest first," she added and left the front of the room.

A few glances over her shoulder showed her that the students did as she'd instructed, either impressed by her trust or under the belief that she didn't have to be looking at them to catch them in misbehavior. Neither would be a bad thing—and they couldn't hurt themselves with the flame. It was only a little bit of shaped aether.

St. John had started toward the door, but Olivia met his eyes as she crossed the room, and he stopped. He was polite enough to remain, or simply too proud to flee. The latter seemed more likely.

He watched her warily as she approached, and obviously braced himself for anger: threats, tears, something of the sort.

"I hope you enjoyed the lesson," Olivia said in her most pleasant tone of voice.

For an instant, St. John's face showed both surprise and alarm. Then he inclined his head toward her—the movement slightly rough, as befitted a man a little out of practice with Polite Society, but not bad at all—and smiled. "It was highly educational and extremely surprising. I couldn't have asked for more."

He was quick. Part of Olivia wanted to kick him for it, but part felt the same thrill she'd gotten stepping out on stage for the first time.

"I'm glad to hear it," she said. She paused momentarily, tilted her head to look up at him, and added, "I hadn't expected to give a lecture to such an important guest. Some women might have found it extremely intimidating, you know."

Another hit. Olivia could see his eyes narrow at *some women*, the *some* slightly emphasized. A rather interesting shade of green, those eyes. Darker than

Charlotte's, not quite hazel. More…moss? She was no artist. Besides, she didn't care.

"I'd hate to cause any distress," St. John said, almost curt. He stopped there for a second. Olivia fought the urge to smile in triumph and wondered why that triumph should be faintly disappointing as well. Then St. John shrugged and went on. "But I'm sure a woman of your experience is more than capable of disregarding any opinion that fails to please her."

Experience carried just enough weight to make the meaning clear. Anger swept up Olivia's body, and she knew it showed on her face. Not for the first time, she wished she'd managed to acquire a suntan, no matter how unfashionable it was.

Never mind. Carry on.

Olivia smiled. She bared her teeth, at any rate. "I assure you, sir, I am quite capable of doing so. But the respect of a colleague is a very different thing, wouldn't you agree?"

"Certainly," said St. John. He took a step forward and looked down at her, raising his dark eyebrows. "In fact, given the mission of this place, I would say we have even more responsibility than usual for the character of its students…and so more responsibility toward each other."

In other words, yes, he had been watching to make sure she didn't somehow corrupt the students, and no, he wasn't going to stop.

If Olivia had been ten years younger, she might have slapped him. She didn't like to think it. She preferred to believe her self-control had been very good, even at seventeen. Still, the temptation was very strong, even at twenty-seven.

"Your dedication does you credit, sir," she said and managed not to grit her teeth. "It gives me great comfort to know you'll be as attentive to your role as I will be to mine."

St. John waved one hand, a gesture of concession. Olivia didn't believe it for a second. "I'll do what I can," he said. "Of course, my experience with…occult matters…"—there might have been distaste in his voice—"is slight. I'm no judge of such things."

"I'd imagine," Olivia replied, "a man such as you could consider himself qualified to judge any number of significant matters."

"Some situations are considerably easier to judge than others." St. John turned abruptly away from her and toward the front of the room, where Waite was looking into the blue flame. The boy's face had lost the amused look Olivia had already come to expect. He was biting his lip, and his brows were furrowed. "Could I see a face in that?"

Olivia blinked. "I…er…yes, if you looked."

"Even if I'm not trying to?"

"I would imagine so, yes," Olivia said crisply, recovering herself. "You're not trying to see the fire itself, after all, and yet it persists in being there."

St. John looked from her to the flame and back, then made a noncommittal noise in his throat. "I take it," he said, "you've seen everything you'd care to of your future?"

"Certainly as far as faces are concerned," said Olivia and turned away.

Chapter 6

ALL BUILDINGS STARTED OUT UGLY. THERE WAS PROBABLY some moral lesson in that. Gareth hadn't seen the plans for the dormitory, but he thought it would end up handsome enough. Simon's taste wasn't bad, and he could afford competent builders. At the moment, there were only jagged, unfinished brick walls rising out of a muddy scar in the earth.

The dingy sky overhead didn't help either, nor did the raw wind put Gareth in a more appreciative mood. Nonetheless, after three days of rain, and another when the ground was too wet for his leg to support him, he was just glad to be outdoors.

"Ten people are far too many for one house," he said half to himself.

Simon lifted his gaze anyway, turned from inspecting the brickwork, and shook his head. "More than ten, old man. You forgot the servants."

"So I did." Gareth shook his head, abashed in the face of his friend's good humor. "And it's not as though I've ever precisely lived alone. I'm sorry. You've been quite hospitable."

"Oh, the students count for two or three people apiece," Simon replied easily. "Particularly to those who aren't that young anymore. I confess I don't know how we stood our crowd, and we had only four in our rooms."

"Wine, as I remember. And the occasional brawl." Gareth touched his left eye as a particularly vivid memory crossed his mind.

"Mm, yes. Particularly where you and Edward were concerned."

"Yes, but I never started it. Hardly ever," Gareth admitted. "And Alex was—" He stopped as he realized what he'd said, but couldn't find any other way out of the sentence. Simon was inspecting the wall again, a bit more carefully than anyone needed to. "Was no stranger to temper either," he finished. "Sorry."

He wasn't exactly sure what had happened to Alex Reynell, only that it had involved Simon, the woman who was now Simon's wife…and blood. There'd been the official story: plucky widow menaced by deranged man of fortune, saved by equally wealthy but hopefully saner gentleman, pistol shots, and mysterious escapes. Gareth didn't believe it, particularly not once he'd met Mrs. Grenville.

Gareth also hadn't asked. He'd been sad when he'd heard, and surprised, but he'd never been close to Alex. Simon had, and so Gareth hadn't asked.

He didn't now. If Simon wanted to talk, he would, but Gareth doubted it. The man had another confidant these days.

Something silver-blue glimmered on the wall. Gareth took a few steps forward, peering at the bricks. He could just make out an outline, although he couldn't tell what it was. The shape was almost runic, yet curved: a long, graceful loop. "Very pretty," he said dryly. "Won't the builders ask questions or gossip?"

Simon shook his head. "At this rate, the physical sign

will be gone by morning. It's already fading fast. It was much brighter when I made it."

"Oh," said Gareth. No paint he knew of was that shade or would fade so quickly.

"Do you want me to tell you?" Simon asked, glancing sideways at Gareth.

"I doubt I'd understand it if you did. I'll leave those details to you and your…apprentice?"

"Kindly refrain," Simon said cheerfully, "from giving me a beard and a pointed cap in your imagination. And if you mean Mrs. Brightmore, she knows as much as I do—her expertise is simply in different areas. As I hear, you have reason to know. And no," he added, lifting a hand, "she didn't tell me you were there."

Of course not. She wouldn't have needed to. "Is it a problem?"

"It doesn't seem to be, yet."

Gareth lifted his eyebrows. "What do you think I intend to do, Simon? I promise I've no wish to put a mouse in Mrs. Brightmore's desk—not that she has one at the moment—or pour ink down anyone's back."

"That's a tremendous weight off my mind," said Simon dryly, "but it's possible your presence could distract the lady."

The *lady* was used to performing for twenty or thirty people at once. Gareth very carefully didn't point that out, just as he didn't mention his real reason for attending the class. He'd already gone around once with Simon over Mrs. Brightmore's past. He would rather not point out the need for someone to keep an eye on her.

Even if he wasn't precisely sure what he was keeping an eye out *for*.

"It doesn't," he replied instead. "She assured me of as much herself."

Simon smiled a little. "Likewise," he said, "when I asked her about it."

There was no reason why that should feel like a betrayal. Simon had a school to run, and it was best to be straightforward. Gareth had always thought so. All the same, the knowledge that Simon had consulted Mrs. Brightmore about his behavior stung. He took a few steps, rounding the corner of the half-built wall. "She teaches well," he said. "That's not a surprise, I suppose. Certainly wasn't as surprising as your wife teaching…boxing?"

"Fighting. There's *honor* in boxing." Simon made a wry face. "Marksmanship as well, eventually."

Gareth lifted his eyebrows and whistled. "One doesn't often meet an Amazon in Britain these days," he said. "I take it the parents don't know all that you're teaching their children."

"I'd assume not. Colonel Woodwell might, but he, from all reports, is eccentric enough not to care, and Miss Woodwell has attained her majority, in any case." Simon absently ticked off students on his fingers as he spoke. "Fitzpatrick's mother, pardon both the language and the slight, probably doesn't give a damn as long as he's out from underfoot and not disrupting her performances, and there's no father in the picture there. The Donnells and the Fairleys were at their wits' end, so I can't imagine we'll have much trouble from them."

"Waite?"

"Could be trouble, if he writes home too tellingly and too soon. His parents are both radicals, by Society's standards, but I'm not certain they're radical enough to accept some of what happens here."

"A pity you don't just accept orphans."

"I've thought so myself, at times," Simon said, "but we do need some fees coming in. I can't impose myself entirely on friends and family, you know. They start fleeing to the Continent before too long."

Gareth laughed. "Only those of us who can travel in style," he said. "Have you heard from Eleanor?"

"A letter came this morning. She should've reached Rome by now. She was in Paris when she wrote." Simon chuckled. "If Ellie ever tires of helping me with this madhouse, by the way, she'd have an excellent future writing for Baedeker or Murray. I'm surprised France has any stationary left."

That sounded like Simon's younger sister, whom Gareth remembered as an intense, bookish sort of schoolgirl. She'd been somehow connected with Alex too, which meant her trip abroad might not have been entirely for pleasure. Something else he didn't ask.

"Does she forget you've been there?"

"I think she rather assumes I didn't appreciate it properly." Simon glanced over at Gareth. "How about your family? Have you seen them since you've been back?"

It wasn't a tentative question, but Simon asked it with a diffident tone that was almost worse than boorishness. Still, he meant well.

"Went up to Kent a month before I came here. They're well." That was true. There'd been no tragic homecoming, no stormy scenes. His mother had embraced him, and his father had been proud of him. Gareth knew he really shouldn't ask for more.

Particularly because he didn't know what more he could have asked.

"They all send their best," he added and turned the conversation to lighter things, as he might have steered a balky horse. "Jenny, my niece, wasn't exactly heart-broken when she heard you were married. Sorry to hurt your pride."

"Been replaced, have I?"

Gareth nodded. "By the grocer's lad, if I hear cor-rectly. I think Helen had more peace of mind when it was you. Especially as this one might actually return Jenny's affection—she can actually speak complete sentences around him. Clearly he doesn't have your overwhelming charm."

"Yes," Simon said, "I'm sure it's that, and not the difference between twelve and sixteen."

Both of them fell silent. Gareth watched a flock of birds, starlings, he thought, cross the gray sky, heading south.

Four years had passed since Simon had come home with him, that week when they'd roamed the country-side, talked late over wine, and shared gentle laughter at Jenny's moon-eyed infatuation when they were sure she wasn't around. Simon had left for town shortly after that. Gareth had gone to Egypt. He'd climbed rocks eas-ily back then, and the buzz of a fly hadn't made him go rigid with anticipated horror.

Not even the light parts of his past quite worked any longer. Everything ran into what came after, just as the gentle slope on which they stood rolled inescapably downhill and into the dark fringes of the forest.

"They all seem quite healthy," he said. "The students, I mean."

"Ah," said Simon, briefly disoriented. Then he seemed to find his place in the conversation. "Good."

Gareth clasped his hands behind his back and forged onward. He'd gotten used to carrying conversation over gaps. That skill had been one of the things he'd learned on his visit home. "Do you expect many more?"

Simon laughed, and the constraint eased a little. "I dearly wish I could say. It's a tricky business, you know."

"I suppose one can't simply post advertisements in the *Times*," Gareth agreed.

"Hardly." Simon gave the brickwork one last moment of scrutiny and then turned back toward the house. "I've a few connections here and there," he went on as Gareth fell in beside him, "but I'd as soon not be too public. The servants are sworn to secrecy. That's one of the reasons we don't have as many as we should. Even the village thinks this is just an odd sort of bohemian establishment, like something Morris or Ruskin might have founded. Better that way, for a number of reasons."

Gareth thought of the symbols on the bricks. "Sensible," he said and tried to keep his voice neutral.

Something must have shown through, because Simon looked over and shook his head. "Poor St. John. From one war to another?"

"I'd imagine that's how most people feel," said Gareth. "This one's—" He stopped for a second. If the general subject of his past brought up too much darkness to speak of, his time in the army was worse: like the bottom of a well rather than the forest's shadows. "At least it lets me be more comfortable in the off hours."

He looked away from Simon's gaze. There were a

hundred unasked questions in it. He braced himself for one of them.

Instead, Simon looked back toward the house. "We do strive to please," he said lightly. "Speaking of which, it's just about time for dinner."

Thank you, thought Gareth, and said nothing.

Chapter 7

"GOING INTO THE VILLAGE?"

At Charlotte's voice, Olivia looked up from buttoning her walking jacket. "I thought I would. I've a few errands there, and honestly, I'd like to get a look at the place. Care to join me?"

"Wouldn't I?" Charlotte laughed, gesturing to her elegantly styled coat and hat. "As long as you don't mind my trailing along. I promise I can keep up. I'd rather have someone to talk with, and I couldn't go with Waite and Fitzpatrick this morning, you know. Scandal and all that rot."

"I'd be glad of the company," Olivia said, smiling. "Especially company that looks as good as you do."

Charlotte's dress was a rich green-and-brown wool, made along much more flowing lines than was common in popular fashions. Some of the ladies who'd come to see Olivia in London had worn similar styles, but few had worn them as well. As far as she could tell, "artistic dress" was reform clothing for those who didn't want to take the plunge into bloomers. Ribbons, some brown and some green, trimmed Charlotte's hat, and her brown coat looked considerably newer than Olivia's faded gray one.

At the compliment, Charlotte laughed again. "Thank you, and thank God you don't twit me about dressing like a normal female. I was scared to death of a lecture the first time I saw you."

"I find it hard to imagine you ever being really fright-ened," Olivia said as they went out the door. "Besides, you're not the first girl I've seen in such clothing."

"Oh, yes, you lived in London, didn't you?" Charlotte sighed a little theatrically. "I've never been. Well, not really. Passed through a bit on the way here, you know, but all I saw of it was the inside of the station, and that very briefly. My first train was late, and I had to move like anything to catch the second, and that's the very devil to do in skirts and a crowd. Er, sorry about the language."

"Quite all right."

Good humor was easy just then. Outside was one of those cold but brilliant days that came in late September, where the sky was almost a sharp shade of blue and the trees blazed golden and red beneath it. Autumn in the countryside. Olivia hadn't known until just then how much she'd missed it in London, where the only change of the seasons was the thickness of the fog and the fre-quency of the rain.

The money in her purse didn't hurt either. Money, in Olivia's experience, had come in the form of rather battered coins. What notes she'd handled had been crumpled and stained more often than not. Those she'd received that morning, in a discreetly wrapped paper bundle, had been crisp and new. Not a significant detail but one that made her happy nonetheless.

She'd put half her pay into a small wooden box in her room, as she'd always done, but that had still left her with enough to order some new clothes.

As she walked, Olivia looked down the road, smiled, and then looked back at Charlotte. "You might have to be immensely proper later on, you know," she said.

"I don't know what…well, what you'll be doing once you've had an education here."

"Oh, I can act the lady when I have to," Charlotte said easily. "Papa saw to that. Well, the governesses he hired, mostly, but he always said a man, or a woman, ought to be able to fit into any society necessary. He said we're adaptable creatures, and we should act like it."

"A follower of Mr. Darwin, then?" Olivia asked.

"A little. He's quite a naturalist when he has time for it. When we were in Egypt, he used to take me out to look at the crocodiles." Another laugh as Olivia's eyes widened. "From a distance, of course, and with a rifle. Is your papa much for nature?"

"Not crocodiles," Olivia said. "He fished a great deal, though, and he was very fond of gardening." Had Stephen and Mariah, her cousin and his wife, kept his design for the gardens at Redford, her childhood home? They must have. They were very kind, and there were Mother's feelings to think of. But then, Mariah was very fashionable, and Father had been rather the opposite. Olivia cleared her throat. "I think he proposed to my mother because she was the only woman he knew who preferred irises to roses."

"I'm sorry," said Charlotte, hearing the past tense. "I didn't know—"

"Not at all. It was several years ago, and he went peacefully. He'd had his threescore and ten."

Charlotte gave her a long look. "Did—may I ask an impertinent question? You can slap me or walk ahead if it's *too* impertinent. I'll understand."

"Yes, you may," said Olivia, and read the question in Charlotte's face. It could be nothing else, Miss

Woodwell's curiosity being what it was. "No, I never tried to talk with him afterwards."

"Oh." To her credit, she didn't ask why not.

Olivia wasn't sure *she* knew. At first, she'd known very well she couldn't actually speak with anyone's spirit. After she'd discovered a way to really do so, she just hadn't thought of it. In any event, he'd probably passed beyond by then. People did. "I suppose I didn't want to disturb him."

Charlotte thought for a moment, dark brows drawn together, and then nodded briskly. "Makes sense enough to me. You were dealing with the spirits of everyone else's relations. Naturally you'd want a rest when it came to your own. I asked about Mama once," she added, more slowly than usual. "A few years ago. We were back in England by that time, and there was a woman who said she could talk to the dead for a few shillings."

Her eyes were on the road ahead of her. Olivia tried to keep her gaze ahead too, and not to tense. "What happened?"

"She twitched a lot and spoke in a different voice. Said she was Mama and she was very happy where she was, but nothing specific." Charlotte shrugged. "Then again, I didn't go in with much. Mama died when I was very little, you understand."

"And your father doesn't talk about her often?" Olivia asked, relieved and sad at the same time. In the ten years since her father had died, every letter from her mother had mentioned him in some way.

On the other hand, she barely even thought about Tom anymore, and what did that mean?

If Olivia's emotions showed on her face, Charlotte

didn't notice. She merely shrugged again. "Not in any tiresome Gothic sort of way. He hasn't covered her portrait or forbidden me to mention her or anything. It's just…been a while. Life goes on. He married again," she added. "Two years ago. That's part of the reason I'm here. She's kind and all, but—"

"I'd imagine it's difficult having another woman in charge of your house after all this time."

"That's it exactly. I wish her and Papa well, I truly do, but if I'm not going to be mistress of the place I live, I might as well get an education out of it."

Olivia smiled. "No wicked stepmother either, then."

"Afraid not!" Charlotte said cheerfully. "The only fairy tale about me is the godmother. Unofficial godmother. I've two official ones, very respectable, but they didn't do anything interesting for me." At Olivia's blank look, she continued. "When I was born, Papa's regiment was up north, on the coast. He did a favor for one of the local families, took their side against one of his men in some kind of dispute. Papa wouldn't ever tell me what exactly, so I think it was a pretty nasty business."

Tom had alluded to similar nasty business when he'd been alive, skimming over the parts he'd thought a lady shouldn't hear. Olivia had guessed them later, when she'd started working in London. "Quite probably," she said.

"The day after, an old woman came to see Papa— the grandmother or great-grandmother or something of the family he'd helped. She said he'd made an effort to understand, and so his children would always be able to understand others."

"And what does that mean, practically speaking?"

Charlotte stopped, held up a hand, and looked around.

They stood alone in the road, with the village just around the bend. There were a few farmhouses in the distance, but mostly the road was lined with trees.

"Please come down," said Charlotte, and there was a strange not-quite echo about her voice. "We won't hurt you."

There was a brief flurry of wings from a nearby tree, then a shape winging down. Olivia stood staring for a moment before she recognized the shape as a blackbird.

"Hello," Charlotte said to the bird as it lit on her hand. "No nipping off anyone's noses, right? We're not nearly the right rank, and nobody's tried to put you in a pie." The strange quality remained in her voice.

"Does it understand you?" Olivia asked.

"More or less. Birds are harder than mammals or reptiles. I can't talk to insects at all, or the smaller sort of fish, and even the bigger ones are difficult." Charlotte stroked the bird briefly then lifted her hand again and watched it fly off. "I've a theory it's to do with the elements, but I really don't know."

They started walking again. "Do you command them?"

"Hardly! That's why I picked a blackbird. They're curious enough most times, as long as they know nobody's going to hurt them. The gift works on human languages too," Charlotte added, "only I didn't think you'd be as impressed if I understood you speaking Latin."

"I don't know about that," Olivia said, laughing. "My Latin still isn't very good. It's probably the worst part about studying magic. So many books are written in Latin or Greek, and the translations aren't very good even when they do exist."

"Maybe you should ask Dr. St. John for lessons,"

Charlotte said offhandedly. "Doctors have to know Latin, don't they? And I'm sure he'd be glad to help."

"I'm sure," Olivia said and tried not to sound sarcastic about it. She looked ahead to where a neat row of houses lined either side of a small, cobbled street. "And I think perhaps I should start trying to find my destination."

Navigating proved to be fairly easy. The dressmaker's shop was small, but her sign was in good condition. The cold weather kept most people indoors, so there weren't crowds to deal with, and Charlotte and Olivia didn't even get many curious looks as they headed down the street.

Inside the shop was a different story. When Olivia opened the door, three women were leaning over a table of fabric, studying various weights of black wool. At the sound of the bell, one of them, a slim brown-haired woman, looked up. When she didn't greet the new arrivals familiarly, or perhaps when her face didn't show any recognition, the other two turned to look.

Farmers' wives, Olivia thought, casting a quick glance over them. One middle-aged, one considerably older, probably mother and daughter or daughter-in-law. Not hostile, but definitely curious. She smiled politely at them and hung back with Charlotte, waiting until they'd finished talking with the seamstress.

Not that the women left. They simply concluded their conversation and then lingered to "think it over." Olivia approached the dressmaker—a Mrs. Simmons, as it turned out—introduced herself, and discussed the possibility of a dress for evenings. "Nothing too elaborate," she said and smiled. "I'm a teacher, after all, so I'd best look plain and stern." Part of Olivia still wasn't sure she'd have anywhere to wear even the plainest silk, but there might be village concerts or parties, and it would look well to have people from Englefield attend.

"We've got some wine-colored silk," Mrs. Simmons said, moving briskly to take down bolts of fabric. "It should make up nicely and wear well, and you're young yet to be too severe." She glanced over her shoulder at the other two women who were going through the dance of introductions with Charlotte. "Are you from Englefield, then? We'd heard there was a school starting there."

"Yes," said Olivia, "we both are."

"Strange notion," said the older of the two customers, "starting a school all the way out here. Or coming to one, though I'm sure the two of you had good reasons."

"It's good for young people to be out in the fresh air, Mama," said the middle-aged woman, "and away from, the sort of thing that happens in the cities. Especially now."

"Mm," said her mother and turned her gaze back to Olivia and Charlotte. "Do the two of you teach there?"

"Mrs. Brightmore does," Charlotte replied easily. "I'm a rather overgrown student, but they've been kind enough to take me nonetheless."

The younger of the two customers smiled. Her mother shook her head. "My father used to tell stories about that forest, you know."

"Oh?" Olivia looked up from examining the silk.

"Mm. Lightning on clear nights sometimes, he said. And a white bird with gold eyes, once, that acted…queerly." The woman gave Olivia a somewhat rusty smile, then glanced from Mrs. Simmons's blank face to her daughter's nervous frown. "Fireside tales,

I should say, and he had most of them secondhand. Probably no more than a barn owl and some lads setting off fireworks."

"I wouldn't be at all surprised if the fireworks started up again these days," Olivia said, "though I'll do my best to prevent it."

She tried to sound simply amused and thought she did a good job. After all, the woman's father probably had been in a condition to see things. Olivia refrained from asking what precisely he'd been doing in the forest at the time. Stories got exaggerated in the telling. She turned back to examining the silk, said a polite farewell to the women, and didn't ask any more questions.

Still, the fittings gave her time to wonder and to think that if the weather held and she could find a map, she might go for a walk in the forest sometime soon.

Chapter 8

WHEN IT STARTED RAINING, GARETH THOUGHT THERE WAS probably something wrong.

Granted, that was no sure thing. It was autumn in England, and the last few days had been sullen and drizzly, enough so he'd been keeping to the flagstone paths in the garden rather than risk his leg on the wet ground. He'd been expecting to feel a drop or two any moment and to go inside when they became steady.

Instead, the clouds overhead opened.

By the time Gareth reached the shelter of the house again, he was muttering under his breath, curses he'd picked up from his men and which, therefore, he cut off quickly as he glimpsed a female figure at the end of the hall. Wiping the water away from his face, he saw it was Mrs. Brightmore, gripping Fitzpatrick's shoulder firmly and glaring sideways at Fairley.

Outside, he heard the rain already beginning to slack off.

"Because other people aren't there for our convenience, that's why," Mrs. Brightmore was saying. "Even—especially if we can do things they can't."

"So I shouldn't bother—?" Fitzpatrick began, his voice muffled and nasal. Now Gareth saw he was holding a handkerchief to his face. Blood had already liberally spotted the white cotton.

"That's entirely different."

"Why?" asked Fitzpatrick.

"I'll explain later. When your nose isn't broken." She turned back toward the hall, saw Gareth, and gave him a look that mingled relief and apology. She didn't quite hide her resentment at feeling both. "Dr. St. John," she said, "I'm so sorry to disturb you, particularly now, but we seem to have a situation."

"So I see," he said and repressed a sigh.

"We can, however, wait for you to"—Mrs. Brightmore waved a hand—"to be more comfortable. Michael, go upstairs and have one of the servants bring some towels. And a pot of tea. Then go to your room and wait for me there."

"But—"

"I really don't think—" Gareth began even as Fairley opened his mouth to protest.

"*Now*, please," said Mrs. Brightmore.

The tone sent Fairley up the stairs without further ado and even made Gareth flinch. Inwardly, of course. He cleared his throat. "I'm much obliged, ma'am, but I'll see Fitzpatrick now. I have," he added in response to the dubious look on her face, "worked under far worse conditions."

The nose was indeed broken, Gareth saw once they'd gotten into his office, and bleeding copiously, as such things often did. Fitzpatrick was bearing the pain decently well for a boy his age, but he stifled a yelp when Gareth touched his face. There was some bruising as well, or would be. "Will I be seeing the other fellow after this?"

Fitzpatrick shook his head. "Not a fight," he mumbled. "Practicing." He glanced over at Mrs. Brightmore, straightened his shoulders, and added, "Broke a lamp too. One of the round ones with pendant things."

"Having trouble telling the difference between the library and a cricket ground, are we?" Gareth asked, recognizing the description. From where Mrs. Brightmore was sitting, hands folded very properly in her lap, he heard a sound that might have been suppressed laughter. He fought back a smile of his own, reminding himself he didn't actually like the woman and therefore didn't want to join her in anything so comradely as humor.

"We'll pay. Pocket money and that."

"Mm." Not really his concern. Gareth placed one hand under the boy's chin. "Hold still. This is going to hurt."

Straightening a broken nose was, by now, one of the tasks he could perform in his sleep. To Fitzpatrick's credit, he didn't cry out, just sucked in air and grimaced. Gareth had seen worse from men twice his age.

"That's the worst of it," he said and shifted his hands, putting one on each side of Fitzpatrick's face, fingertips pointing to the nose. He tried to be careful of the bruises. "This is just going to be a bit odd."

Had there been another sound from the side? A sound a woman might make perhaps if she were shifting her weight to get a better view? No matter. Mrs. Brightmore wasn't his concern either.

Gareth closed his eyes. Shifting his focus was easy—he'd done it since he was younger than Fitzpatrick or even Fairley—and correcting the injury would be almost as simple. Child's play, one might say, certainly compared to what he'd been doing a few years ago.

When he opened his eyes and looked at Fitzpatrick,

he saw a man-shaped web of gray-and-silver threads in all different sizes, thickest near the boy's heart and brain, thinner out near his hands and feet and on the surface of his face. Now a few of the latter were broken, the thickest running down the bridge of his nose. It hadn't snapped entirely, Gareth saw as he looked closer, but it was worn away in parts, and the rest was unraveling.

It didn't take much effort at this point, or even much thought, to reach out and weave part of his energy into the threads, shoring up the unraveling parts and bridging between the broken ends. He worked, carefully aware of how long he'd been out of practice, making sure all of the fastenings joined snugly to one another. He pulled his senses back a little and saw the threads were whole again. Not as good as new—he could still see the edges—but they'd heal the rest of the way soon enough. He closed his eyes again and refocused on the world as he usually saw it.

Fitzpatrick's face was still covered in blood, but his nose had stopped bleeding. The straightening had held too, and there was no incipient swelling or even bruising. The boy raised a hand to touch it. "It…doesn't hurt!"

"No," Gareth said, turning away to run a clean handkerchief under cold water. "It won't. Though I don't recommend hitting it with anything for a little while. Certainly not a cricket ball."

"I'll take it right out of my plans, sir, I promise," Fitzpatrick replied, clearly regaining his old self by the minute.

"Right," said Gareth and handed him the handkerchief. "Wash, and let's make sure there's no bruising."

Now that he had a moment, he reached for the buttons of his jacket. He'd already gotten rid of his hat. There was only so much he could do about the rest of his clothing until Mrs. Brightmore took herself and Fitzpatrick out of his office. Furthermore, she was a widow. She was, or had been, a fraud, and Gareth didn't feel particularly obligated to retain his soaked jacket for the sake of her theoretical modesty.

Healing always made Gareth hungry and a little cold. Under the circumstances, neither was doing much for his temper.

He glanced over at Mrs. Brightmore, not sure whether it was to warn her or gauge her likely reaction, and found himself meeting her eyes. She'd been looking at him, it seemed, and Gareth thought he saw surprise in her pretty face. Perhaps even astonishment.

A greater man wouldn't have found the realization gratifying. Gareth had no pretense to greatness.

Of course he was smug. Wretched man. His smile, polite enough to the casual observer, was only barely on the correct side of a smirk.

Olivia looked straight back at him, refusing to drop her gaze. She couldn't do anything about her blush, curse it, but she told herself she had nothing to be embarrassed about. "I had no idea you were so talented, Dr. St. John," she said, trying to sound casual and knowing she didn't quite manage it.

"As you said, it's an extraordinary school. I don't think the average doctor would have sufficed." A lock of his wet hair was hanging in his face. It should have made him seem less equal to the conversation. Instead, Olivia had the purely idiotic urge to brush it back.

She didn't look down at her hands, but she flexed her fingers, making sure they stayed laced together and her hands stayed in her lap. "A sound judgment. And certainly one that's been helpful today."

No, she still sounded breathless. Damn her stays, Olivia thought. She should have followed Charlotte's example and left them off long ago.

"Much obliged," St. John said again. He looked away, and Olivia felt a moment of satisfaction, but it was only to continue unbuttoning his jacket. "Towel, please," he added, and she wasn't sure if he was speaking to her or Fitzpatrick. She passed him a towel anyway.

The jacket came off slowly, not that Olivia was watching, and the white shirt underneath had been considerably dampened by the rain. She caught a glimpse of tan skin and dark hair, and observed that St. John's arms and chest weren't badly developed, for all that he was thin. Not badly developed at all.

Not that she was looking.

She swallowed, lifted her gaze to the shelf of books above St. John's head, and found an opening. "I hope my classes have been helpful, then," she said. "I didn't know you were seeking information for yourself."

St. John paused, towel midway to his head. "I hadn't been," he said mildly, as if it were a matter of no import, and resumed drying his hair.

A hit, Olivia thought, but a quick recovery. She pressed what advantage she had. "I beg your pardon," she replied, trying to echo his offhand tone. "I should've known you'd be well schooled in theory."

"I wouldn't say that. Practice does well enough for me." The towel came down, and St. John met her eyes again. "I've had a few years of it, after all."

"I've washed my face," Fitzpatrick announced. "May I go now, sir?"

St. John snapped his gaze back to the boy with a speed that made Olivia smile. To his credit, he did provide a quick but thorough inspection before he replied, "You can," but the words were too quick. There was a retreat there.

"Thank you, Dr. St. John," said Olivia, rising from her seat. "I'll try to avoid any further interruptions."

"Please do," he said. "Or wait until I've dried off."

Olivia took herself out, wondering who'd won that round. It was a waste of time to consider it, she told herself. Scoring points was childish. She didn't want to fight with the man, and she certainly didn't wish Fitzpatrick hadn't interrupted.

Not at all.

Chapter 9

Olivia finished the final line of a pentagram and then lifted her pen from her journal and tried to shake the cramps out of her aching wrist. Teaching was no joke, not even with as few pupils as she had, and teaching magic was proving to be harder work than she'd thought. Her practice in London and her time under Gillespie had given her a head start, but not a particularly large one, and there were some areas that greatly needed filling in.

Protection, for example. Olivia had learned how to guard a room or a person against accidents and even the occasional predator that lurked in the realms beyond, but she'd skimmed lightly over protections against anything someone had purposefully sent. Nobody who could command demons, she'd thought, would have bothered setting them on a medium of no great fame or fortune.

The young men and women who would come from Englefield would be a different story altogether. Mr. Grenville *did* know protective spells—she was doing research in his library, after all—and would certainly cover anything more advanced, but there would be times when he was away or otherwise unavailable.

Those last two words covered a great deal. Olivia tried not to think about certain possibilities.

Instead, she leaned back in her chair and looked out at the rainy landscape. Rainy *without* Michael Fairley's influence this time: either her lecture or an hour washing dishes in the scullery had driven home certain points. Olivia hoped so.

Where powers were concerned, Michael's control was better than Elizabeth's, who *still* tended to react to any alarm by rising half a foot off the floor. However, Michael tended to cut corners in practice, and the incident with Dr. St. John hadn't been the first time he'd used his talent unfairly. According to his parents, by way of Mr. Grenville, it had been common for the clouds to open whenever Michael's governess tried to take him on an unwanted walk. So far, there hadn't been much self-indulgence of that kind at Englefield, but there also hadn't been much opportunity for it.

Olivia closed her eyes, pentagrams and circles still dancing in front of her lids, and let herself slip into further assessment. Elizabeth's problem was mostly being afraid of her own shadow. She was getting better, but as soon as she felt herself losing control, she'd grab and clutch and try to shut off all her talent, which usually only made the situation worse. She had nightmares too, with all the loss of control *that* implied, and Olivia was usually in her room to ground the energy no less than once a week. Elizabeth had never gotten as far off the ground as she'd done that first day, though, and Olivia counted that as a victory.

The older students were coming along well, she thought. William tended to rush things. Michael and Charlotte were also hasty about ceremonial magic, the spells anyone could do, which didn't surprise Olivia. Growing up able to do one form of magic simply by thinking about it might naturally render one impatient with the sort that took time and intricate planning. Elizabeth was the exception to that rule. She was as careful in spell casting as she couldn't be at levitation. She had the makings of an excellent magician, as did Arthur, who had an eye for patterns.

Much she knew, Olivia told herself with a small smile. She had all she could do keeping up.

That was no complaint. There'd been a vigor and a challenge about the last month Olivia hadn't known she'd craved. Teaching and research had been like taking a brisk walk uphill after weeks indoors.

*Speaking of that...*With a sigh, she turned toward the windows.

The week since her visit to the dressmaker hadn't often provided her with weather suitable for walking much of anywhere, much less the forest. Olivia had also remembered Mrs. Grenville had told her not to go in without her or Mr. Grenville, and she wasn't inclined to flout that advice. She'd been a country girl once, but that had been ten years ago, and even then she'd been much more used to farms than forests. So she'd waited.

Neither of the Grenvilles had been available long enough. They generally weren't. Even now, Mr. Grenville was talking with his steward, and Mrs. Grenville was teaching the older students hand-to-hand combat in the ballroom. One could hear the shouts and thumps from fully three rooms away. The younger students, who would have their turn in an hour, were upstairs studying their normal lessons.

Absently, Olivia put aside the book from which she'd been taking notes and turned back to the shelves to retrieve another. *Spirits and Omens of Our Grandfathers' Time.*

She'd seen the title a few times before and had mostly looked over it on her way to something more substantial.

The book was no more than thirty years old and came complete with colored illustrations. It did not, Olivia quickly discovered, have an index, though the authors had been considerate enough to lump related incidents together. She idly flipped the pages past descriptions of black dogs and phantom music and paused at a section on ravens.

According to the authors, in a Greek myth, Apollo had turned the then-white raven's feathers black because it had informed him of his *inamorata's* faithlessness. Not much useful information there, except perhaps not to bring bad news to the ancient gods. She wondered what Apollo had thought the poor beast should have done, and flipped back a page.

Oh. Peck out the young man's eyes.

Lovely.

She looked up as the door opened. Dr. St. John stepped inside, then frowned as he saw her. Probably surprise, judging by his expression, though one never could tell with the man.

Oh well. She'd made good progress today, it was vile outside, and she wasn't going to let St. John put her in a bad mood.

"Your patron god," she said, thinking of the myth, "does not strike me as much of a gentleman."

It wasn't fair, Gareth thought. He'd spent a useful morning filling out records and arranging new equipment in his office, he'd come into the library to reward himself with a novel, and he'd found Mrs. Brightmore with the lamplight gold on her fair skin, looking like some Pre-Raphaelite's idea of the Spirit of Knowledge, and talking like a madwoman.

A man of his age should have been able to expect *some* order in his life.

"Pardon?" he asked. "Patron god?"

"Apollo," Mrs. Brightmore said and then paused. Gareth noticed she pursed her lips just a little when she thought. It drew a man's attention, made him consider the shape of her mouth and the slight fullness of her underlip. She was probably doing it on purpose. "I believe he's in the Hippocratic Oath," she continued.

"Oh. Probably. Greek gods aren't really the memorable part. Nor are they generally gentlemen, if memory serves." Gareth took a few steps closer to the desk. Now that he was here, it wouldn't do to retreat.

"No. That's why—" Mrs. Brightmore abruptly stopped herself. Gareth watched a blush spread itself up her neck and over her face. She cleared her throat. "I do hope I'm not in your way."

"Not at all. I came to borrow some reading material. Something a little more lighthearted than yours," he said, casting a quick glance over the books at Mrs. Brightmore's elbow. A small, leather-bound journal lay on top of a much larger, much-older-looking book. Gareth couldn't make out the title, and he didn't know that he wanted to. The book in front of her was about omens and spirits. "Not seeing any black dogs at crossroads, I hope?"

"No, I haven't seen anything. I'd heard a story or two in the village, but it's probably nothing." She talked quickly. Other than that, there was no sign of relief that he'd moved on.

"Mm," Gareth said. He put a hand on the desk, letting it support his weight without leaning too obviously. "'That's why' what?"

Mrs. Brightmore bit her lip and was silent for a moment. She didn't pretend ignorance, though. He had to grant her that. "It's only a theory," she said, "and it's not...some people could find it a bit insulting. I shouldn't have mentioned it."

"And yet you did," he said, "and now I'm curious."

It wasn't entirely embarrassment coloring her face now. Her eyes flashed. "I won't have you stalking off in offense if I tell you, sir," she said. "Not when I have to work with you. Or if you do, I won't have you blame me for it."

"I promise," he said, holding up a hand in a reassuring gesture, "I won't take it badly."

Mrs. Brightmore relaxed a little, though there was still a certain wariness about her when she spoke. "In that first class, Charlotte asked why certain people could do magic at will. I said there were a few theories on the subject."

"So I recall."

"One of them, and I have reason to think it's true, is those people are somehow connected to...other beings." She spread her hands in vague illustration and absently began to rub one of her wrists as she spoke. "Beings from places that follow different rules, or none."

"Fairies?" Gareth lifted an eyebrow.

"Or angels. Or gods. Beings who call themselves gods, at any rate. All of them have supposedly had the appropriate sorts of…association with humanity. The, um, blessings in fairy tales, for instance."

"Or the, ah, seductions in myth?" Gareth mimicked her hesitation and let a smile drift across his mouth. "I'm a grown man, you know. I'm not going to faint."

"Just challenge me to pistols at dawn, perhaps." Her fingers moved from her wrist to her hand, and she winced.

"Are you all right?"

"Hmm? Oh. Fine." Mrs. Brightmore blinked up at him. "Thank you," she added, sounding less grudging than surprised. Clearly she hadn't expected his concern, which Gareth found unexpectedly annoying.

"Let me see," he said.

"It's nothing, really. I've just been writing for a while."

Gareth stepped around the desk to her side. "They do pay me for something. Give me your hand. I promise you'll have it back afterward."

The implied challenge did the trick. She extended her hand quickly and held very still as Gareth took it. He might have said something about that, but the feeling of her small, smooth palm beneath his thumb was more distracting than he'd thought. Flesh and blood, he told himself. Nothing out of the ordinary here. No reason warmth should spread from their linked hands; no reason to relish each circle his thumb made on her palm.

"So," he said, "my connection to Apollo might not be just a symbol?"

"Ah." Mrs. Brightmore's voice was a little distracted, a touch breathless. "Perhaps. Or Airmed for the Celts, or beings, perhaps a being, using those names." Gareth pressed harder for a moment, and her eyelids drifted half-closed. "None of it's very clear yet. Probably, um, not Raphael, not if we're talking descent."

"Probably not," Gareth agreed. He'd stepped a little forward at some point, he noticed now, and he was looking down at the top of her head. There were strands of red and blonde in her chestnut hair, and a few that were almost black. His fingers moved down to her wrist, tracing lines and then circles over the tense muscles there. "Did you come up with this theory yourself?"

Mrs. Brightmore shook her head slowly. "No, I—had it explained to me. And then I studied considerably."

She had done that. There was a callus on her right forefinger where she would hold a pen. There were the ink stains. There were the books. "Ah."

Gareth thought if he reached out his free hand he could just touch the side of her face, tilt her chin up, perhaps, so she was looking at him with those rich brown eyes. Her skin would be like silk beneath his fingertips.

Mrs. Brightmore's breath might have been quicker now, or Gareth might simply have been noticing the way her breasts rose and fell. They were easy to notice. Even in her plain skirt and shirtwaist the woman had the sort of lush curves no man would find easy to ignore. Perhaps it was just his perception.

All the same, under his fingers, he thought he felt the pulse in her wrist speed up. Mrs. Brightmore did look up at him then, and her eyes were dark. Her lips parted a little.

"I think that should suffice for any further studying," Gareth said. He dropped her hand and stepped back quickly. "I assume you have quite a bit of it ahead."

"Ah," she said. In both distraction and acceptance,

her tone was a mirror of Gareth's from a moment before, only with slightly more surprise. Did she sound disappointed too? He couldn't tell. He didn't want to tell.

"I won't intrude on your time any longer," he said, his voice thicker than he would have liked. He turned away and heard her take a breath.

Fabric rustled.

Gareth didn't stay to hear any more.

Chapter 10

A PILLAR OF SHINING MIST ROSE FROM THE CENTER OF THE ballroom, thinner and prettier than the gray-brown fogs Olivia had become used to in London. Prettiness served no purpose, but because the mist was more transparent, she could easily see the two children who were standing within it. It was brighter around them too, as it siphoned off the energy that glowed like a second skin within them.

"Michael," Olivia asked, focusing on the boy's face now and letting her other awareness recede a little, "how do you usually begin to make it rain?"

"I go up to the clouds, in my head, of course, and—"

She held up a hand. "Let's start there. How do you do that?"

Michael fell silent for a moment. Olivia let him think and switched her focus back to the flow of energy in the room. As she'd hoped, the patterns she'd chalked on the floor held the mist in place, and the mist was steadily but not too quickly conducting energy away from Michael and Elizabeth. Olivia could see its lower edges glowing as it transferred power away and grounded it harmlessly.

Theoretically harmlessly, that is. She hadn't ever read that grounded power in floorboards would be a problem, any more than it was for electricity. Hopefully neither the floor in the ballroom nor that in Elizabeth's room would suddenly take a dislike to everything above it, turn to rubber, or start sprouting trees.

She turned her attention back to Michael as he started talking again. "I think about what the clouds look like right then," he was saying slowly, "and how they're made, and then…it's a little like talking to them, maybe? Not like a conversation. More like riding. You dig your heels in, and the horse knows it means 'go.'"

"All right," said Olivia. "Elizabeth, is there anything in what Michael said you think you could use?"

Elizabeth bit her lip and looked at the floor, tracing a pattern with the toe of one stockinged foot.

All three of them had removed their boots on entering, Elizabeth and Michael following the habit Mrs. Grenville's practice sessions had instilled, and Olivia because the thought of wearing boots across the smooth expanse of floor made her wince. The ballroom, with its gold-papered walls and its large windows framed by amber-colored drapes, was one of the rooms that still looked like it belonged in a well-appointed country house, and she found she wanted to keep it that way.

"Maybe," Elizabeth said, her forehead wrinkled, "if I think about how my power works? I know how *gravity* works, everyone does, so maybe if I think about that and then tell it to, um, stop working for me? A little?"

"A little," Olivia agreed firmly. "Michael, do you tell the clouds how much rain you want?"

"Not so you could measure it," Michael said, shrugging, "but a general sort of idea." He looked over at Elizabeth. "Try and make a picture of what you want."

"Now?"

Olivia nodded. "Now."

The girl closed her eyes. Her face was squinched up into a mask of nervous concentration, and Olivia could see the power inside her start dancing like boiling water. Teeth firmly set in her lower lip, she took in a deep breath—

—and rose a foot in the air.

"Well done," Olivia said, not allowing Elizabeth time to get distraught. "Much more controlled than last time." That was true. She'd risen, not shot up, and didn't show any signs of going higher.

"It's more than I meant to move," Elizabeth said, and she was doing a decent job of keeping her voice optimistic now too. "But it didn't feel as…as downhill as usual."

"Right. You won't, in here." Olivia gestured around the room. "And once you've practiced a little in here, you'll have more control outside. Do you think you could move? Fold your legs, for instance?"

"I…maybe?" Slowly and uncertainly, Elizabeth crossed her legs in front of her tailor-fashion. She folded her arms too, for either symmetry or self-protection, and floated like one of the djinn from the *Arabian Nights*, if djinni had worn bloomers and blouses and had twin braids of red hair.

Mr. Hawkins and Lyddie would've given their eye-teeth for someone like Elizabeth, Olivia thought. She would have done so herself. Her hardest evenings had been when she was up against a Child Prophet or Girl Medium. Back then, she hadn't thought those girls had any power. Back then, she hadn't thought anyone did.

Now she wondered how many Elizabeths and Michaels had been among those children, and how many were still earning their living a step or two above side-show exhibits. Had they looked down on women like Olivia, whose only abilities until three years ago had lain in swift talk and sleight of hand? Envied them for their control? Hated them, perhaps, as the reason people doubted them…or the reason people went to see them at all?

Past is past, Olivia reminded herself. It had been one of Mr. Hawkins's favorite sayings. *You can't live there, and it's best you don't visit too often.*

For a man without much education, he'd been remarkably wise.

"Good," she said quickly. "Now hold that as long as you can, and let me know if you feel yourself slipping. Michael, I want you to make it rain, but not too much. We've had enough in the past few days, I think." She made a face, and the children, as she'd intended, laughed. "Just a shower *and* just over this part of the house."

"How'll you be able to tell, ma'am?" Michael asked. "There's only the one window. Unless—is there a spell so you can see two places at once?"

"Probably, but I haven't cast it. I'll depend on your honor."

Also, it didn't really matter whether Michael succeeded or not. The important thing right now was how the power drain affected his control.

He clasped his hands behind his back, recitation-style, closed his eyes, and took a breath. Concentrating, he looked even younger than usual. Power began to move inside him, but much more gradually than it had in Elizabeth. A few bubbles surfacing rather than a full boil. Olivia watched his face through the mist and restrained a sigh when she saw a fading bruise on his left cheekbone.

Olivia had glimpsed only a few of Mrs. Grenville's practice sessions, but what she'd seen made her wince even in memory. Necessary, perhaps—probably, since neither of the Grenvilles seemed the sort who'd indulge in wanton cruelty—but certainly brutal. Part of her was even surprised Mrs. Grenville had forbidden boots during practice, given the resources at hand.

Then again, as far as the students and their parents were concerned, broken bones probably crossed a line even if they could be easily mended. Mrs. Grenville seemed smart enough to realize that. Perhaps, too, she hadn't wished to put an undue strain on Dr. St. John's strength…or his patience.

Olivia wanted to make a catty remark about his lack of either quality, in the privacy of her mind, but couldn't quite make herself agree that he *did* lack them. She was no real judge of strength, either physical or magical. The only other natural talents she'd encountered were Michael, Elizabeth, and Dr. Gillespie, and they were all so different in form as to make comparison almost impossible.

As for patience, she'd rarely seen Dr. St. John display anything but control. Even a few days before in the library, one couldn't say he'd been *impatient*. Quite the opposite. Remembering, Olivia blushed and felt heat spreading to places lower on her body. The strength of the feeling was as surprising now as it had been at the time.

She turned to face the closest window, looking out at the overcast sky and the half-built dormitories down the hill. No rain yet. Olivia watched for it, trying to compose herself as she did so.

Olivia was no sheltered girl. She'd enjoyed the physical aspect of her marriage a great deal. That had been long ago, though, and memory faded. In the time since, she'd not become precisely a fallen woman, but she'd touched men and taken a few hands. There'd been the occasional spark, since neither her heart nor other parts were in the grave, no matter what Society thought was proper. There'd been nothing like what she'd felt with St. John's fingers on her, as outwardly close to innocent as the contact had been.

And what, exactly, had the man been playing at?

Olivia didn't believe for an instant he'd taken her wrist purely out of either duty or altruism. If he'd been trying to seduce her, he wouldn't have stopped, certainly not so abruptly. A magician might have been using the contact to better target her in the future, but St. John had admitted he was no magician. Besides, irritating as he might be, she'd never thought he was a danger.

The first fine drops of rain appeared on the window. As Olivia had requested, it was very light, almost a mist outside to match the one indoors. She turned back to face the children, fairly certain her face was its normal color again, and smiled approvingly. "Very nice, Michael. Is it more difficult than usual?"

"A bit, ma'am," Michael said, sounding more cheerful and less petulant than Olivia had come to expect from him. Energy was flowing steadily inside him. Not particularly quickly, but more so than it had been when he'd worked under normal circumstances. "It's not too much trouble, though. I'm keeping it over this part of the house too."

"Well done, then," Olivia said. She looked from him

to Elizabeth, who was still sitting cross-legged in mid-air. The girl's face was rigid with concentration, and her power didn't flow as steadily as Michael's. It seemed to stutter and skip on occasion. Even so she'd stayed about where she was, and that was a beginning.

Olivia smiled at them. "Now," she said, "I want you both to stop what you're doing, as gradually as you can. Michael, let the rain stop, but don't send the clouds away. Elizabeth, float back down to the floor. Then we'll start the next exercise."

Chapter 11

DESPITE THE PRESENCE OF AN ANNOYINGLY BEAUTIFUL confidence trickster, Gareth was beginning to like Englefield. He'd managed to get his office set up and the necessary paperwork dealt with, Simon was as amusing over port and cards as he had been in university days, and there were far worse things than spending a crisp autumn evening in the countryside with a bit of time on his hands.

Balcony doors that suddenly opened were one of them. The sudden noise yanked Gareth away from contemplating the view. He didn't flinch—he'd stopped doing that after a few weeks back in England—but he turned to regard the newcomer with no great joy.

"I'm sorry to disturb you," said Mrs. Brightmore. She spoke politely enough, but her set chin and narrowed eyes conveyed a different message: she had as much right to be on the balcony as he did, and what was he doing glaring at innocent passersby anyhow?

Gareth considered adding her to his growing list of less fortunate things. Her past, her tone, and her presence on the balcony all argued for it. Her general competence argued against. Her figure, her eyes, and the intriguing curve of her lower lip could count for either side.

"Have you seen Arthur?" she asked, pulling Gareth out of his internal debate.

"Waite? No, not in the last hour or two."

Mrs. Brightmore frowned. "He didn't show up for practice, Mrs. Grenville said. You're the last person we've asked."

Gareth abruptly stopped thinking about the view—either one. "Who saw him last?"

"William. It was after my class, a few hours ago. They were in their rooms. William left to see if he could get some bread and butter from the kitchen, and Arthur was gone when he got back. He didn't think anything of it until practice."

Although Gareth hadn't been to any of Mrs. Grenville's practice sessions, he couldn't imagine any of the students casually deciding to miss one. Still, he spoke lightly as he got to his feet. "He's probably just gone down to the village and lost track of time."

"That's what we're hoping. All the same..." She glanced over toward the forest waiting beyond the gardens and buildings of Englefield. To Gareth, it looked damned uncomfortable. To a teenage boy, it might suggest adventure, or an afternoon of fishing. "We should take a look before dark. Accidents, you know."

"I know," said Gareth.

He followed Mrs. Brightmore back through the door and downstairs, noticing how stiffly she held herself. Worried, almost panicked, and trying not to show it. Doing a fairly good job too, Gareth thought, and dismissed the urge to reach out in some reassuring gesture or other. He was not in a position to offer comfort to this woman. He didn't want to be. That was important to remember.

Simon met them in the hall. "The servants are checking the house, and Joan's gone down to the village," he said, "since I know the forest best. St. John, sorry about the leg, but I think you'll have to come with me in case the young idiot's fallen down and hit his head. Mrs. Brightmore—"

"I'll keep an eye on the students," she said, very calm. "Unless you think another magician would be helpful out there."

"I wish I knew," said Simon. "I'm not as familiar with the forest as I'd like to be. But one of us should stay behind."

———∿∿∿———

"At times like this," Simon said as he and Gareth made their way down the path to the forest's edge, "I rather agree with those people who say the youth of England travel too much."

"I don't think you could say Waite's *travelling*," said Gareth.

"Not Waite. Me. Until a few months ago, I was at Englefield only for school holidays, and not always then. I don't know a great deal about the forest my-self. And"—an odd half smile crossed his face—"it's a strange place, really. There are a bunch of standing stones in it, somewhere, nothing big enough to excite much comment, but I suppose we did have druids here in the old days. It's..." He sought for a word, then spread his hands in a gesture of defeat.

"Strange?" Gareth suggested dryly.

Simon laughed shortly. "Rather. How are you hold-ing up?"

"I'll be fine," Gareth said. He'd found a walking stick, which helped a bit. His leg would probably pain him that night, particularly if he had to use his power on Waite, but that happened. He'd had worse. "Don't worry about me."

The forest didn't seem particularly unusual when they entered it. The trees were the usual mix, red and gold leaves standing out against the darker evergreens. The grass was the usual faded gray-brown of autumn. The dirt was, well, dirt. None of the shadows moved.

On the other hand, the place was large. A number of paths led away from theirs, and if Waite had come this way, he'd left no signs of his passing. "I'd rather not split up," Simon said and sighed.

"We need a bloodhound," said Gareth.

"Miss Woodwell could find something, but we don't have much time before dark." Simon frowned. "I hate to try divination without the right implements, but it looks as though I might have to. Do you—?"

A branch cracked on the right-hand path. It sounded too loud to be wildlife, or to be the sort of wildlife one encountered on an English estate. "Hello?" Gareth raised his voice. "Is someone there?"

A figure came around the bend. Tall and slim, with dark hair currently hosting several leaves. "Dr. St. John?" Waite asked. As he drew closer, Gareth saw his face was whitish green, and he seemed to have trouble focusing. "Mr. Grenville? I'm afraid I've gone a bit astray."

———

Alarming as Waite's initial appearance was, when Gareth took a look at him, he seemed to be suffering nothing more than a sick headache. A little of his power took care of that quickly enough, and tea helped considerably as well.

"You're lucky we met when we did," he said, looking sternly across the drawing-room table at the boy, "and that you didn't break your neck beforehand, wandering around the forest in the state you were in."

"I didn't, sir," Waite said. "Or not much. Oh, I got lost, that's for certain, but I didn't get the headache until I tried scrying for the way out. The way you taught us, ma'am, in our third lesson."

"Ah," said Mrs. Brightmore, her voice carefully controlled. She didn't look at either Simon or Gareth. "And what happened then?"

"As far as I can tell, someone stuffed a map of all England into my head for a few minutes," said Waite, grimacing. "Looking back on it, ma'am, I think I pronounced one of the words wrong. I did get out, though. I probably could have got to Avalon itself, if I'd wanted to."

Simon's lips twitched. "That's a rather *dramatic* version of a beginner's mistake," he said. "I only turned my fingernails purple for two weeks the first time I tried a spell."

"You were lucky," said Mrs. Brightmore, relaxing.

"Not so lucky. I was at school just then, not a school that taught magic, mind, and one of the masters had some words with me about fooling around with dangerous chemicals. I couldn't contradict him, really." Simon made a face. "Took my meals standing for two days, as I recall."

"Must have been jolly hard for both of you," said Waite looking from Simon to Mrs. Brightmore when everyone had finished laughing, "learning on your own, I mean."

"Not entirely, or not in my case," said Simon. "I had teachers. Only sometimes, and they were…various degrees of reputable…but they did help."

Mrs. Brightmore smiled. "The disreputable ones as much as the others, I'd imagine, otherwise you wouldn't know what to avoid." She leaned back in her chair, reaching for a biscuit. "That's been my experience."

"And how did *you* learn?" Gareth asked. "I'd think it'd be even more difficult for a woman."

Even before Simon lifted his eyebrows, Gareth knew he'd spoken out of malice. The question had come from anger at Mrs. Brightmore's obvious ease, envy of the shared experiences Gareth had never really wanted before now, and the simple desire to make Mrs. Brightmore pay attention to him. Unworthy impulses, all of them, especially the last, but the words were out, and Waite was listening with obvious and eager curiosity.

It was a shade too late for regret.

Besides, he told himself, someone would have asked sooner or later.

Mrs. Brightmore smiled thinly back at him and answered without hesitation. "I bought a book," she said, "because it looked interesting. I tried a spell, which worked. After that, I thought I should find someone who knew more."

Her eyes glittered at Gareth, daring him to press her on any point of the story. Given that, the flush in her cheeks was probably anger, but it was quite attractive all the same. She was a passionate woman, for all her outward calm.

He wished he hadn't thought of that.

"How did you do that, ma'am?" Waite asked.

"I started with the man who'd sold me the book," she said, "and went from there. It took me a little while."

"I think we've wandered a bit from our point," Simon said. "Waite, scrying aside, why *were* you in the forest?"

Waite flushed. "I went in as a bit of a lark at first, sir, just to see what was there. I didn't mean to leave the path, but I saw this stag. Pure white, big as anything. I didn't have a gun, and it didn't seem the sort of thing you shoot, but I thought I'd follow it."

"And?" Simon asked.

"It vanished, sir. Went around a corner and just disappeared." Waite shook his head. "Should have expected that, I suppose."

"I don't see why," Simon said. "I didn't."

"It's happened before," Mrs. Brightmore said thoughtfully. "One of the old women in the village mentioned hearing stories when she was young. Strange animals. Strange lights. She didn't give them much credit."

"And now it seems we have to," said Gareth. "Wonderful. What do you intend to do about this?"

"I don't see the need for anything dramatic just yet," said Simon. "A few apparitions are common enough, I hear. I'll tell the staff and the rest of the students not to go in, *again*, and I'd certainly like to take a look when I can. In the meantime, though"—he sighed—"I'm afraid I have more mundane concerns to deal with."

Chapter 12

"A DINNER PARTY?" OLIVIA SET HER SPOON DOWN IN THE remains of her breakfast porridge. "Here?"

Across the breakfast table, by now mostly empty of food and guests, Mrs. Grenville produced a sardonic grin and lifted eyebrow. "It's not such a bad place."

A few weeks' acquaintance had left Olivia familiar enough with Mrs. Grenville to take the comment lightly. Nevertheless, she shook her head and replied, "No, not at all. I apologize. I meant no slight on Englefield. It's a lovely house…" before going on, "It's just that…it *is* a school now, and while the students are coming along quite well, I haven't been making any of them ready for Society."

"Of course not. Why would…Although all that can be useful." Mrs. Grenville laughed briefly, though Olivia wasn't sure what amused her. "Wouldn't be a bad idea if you have the time. We'll get someone else in eventually, when we have money for another teacher. Or when Eleanor gets back."

"I know a little," said Olivia. She looked down at the linen tablecloths, remembering other breakfasts in other houses. Gray as the sunlight was on the fall morning, the tall windows still let in plenty, and the china was brightly painted and uncracked. She realized she was smiling for no reason, and spoke again. "But it's rather out of date, I think, where the best people are concerned."

Mrs. Grenville shrugged. "A start's something. As for the immediate problem, I don't see it. Woodwell probably stands up to company better than I do, even when I'm trying, and the others, except Waite, are kids."

"The youngest three certainly wouldn't be old enough for company," Olivia agreed, "though Arthur would do well enough."

Only a second, though, and then she waved a hand, accepting and dismissive at once. "Yeah, it'll look good to have a couple of the students around. The others can eat earlier in the kitchen or their rooms."

That would've been the case if they'd been at home. Fitzpatrick was perhaps getting a little old for such isolation, but Olivia thought he'd endure one more time well enough. She picked up her mostly empty cup of tea and took a sip. "Who will the other guests be?"

"Depends," said Mrs. Grenville. "Assuming nobody gets sick at the last minute or has other plans or just throws the invitation on the fire, it'll be the vicar and his daughters, the village doctor, a friend of Simon's, and us. Lots of locals, but I wouldn't ask about the forest. I don't want to give anyone reason to go looking until we've had a chance to explore it, and I don't want to bring rumors back to life. This dinner's only to show we're not running around naked and sacrificing goats up here."

"I assure you," Olivia said, pretending to be sober as she set down her tea, "I hadn't thought of it."

"Of course not. I don't know where you'd even *find* a goat." Mrs. Grenville looked thoughtful for a moment. "Can't say I've actually ever seen one."

"Nor have I," Olivia said after a moment of thought.

"Or not up close." There'd probably been a few on the tenants' farms when she'd been growing up and she'd taken baskets around from time to time, but she could dig up no particular memory connected with the word. "What will we be…? You cannot mean to openly—?"

"No," said Mrs. Grenville dryly, "and neither does Simon. Each of us for different reasons. We'll be a spiritualist institution. Try to look vague and idealistic. Talk about Great Destiny and High Callings, if you can. One of us should. I don't think Woodwell will manage it, and I know I can't."

Indeed, the thought of Charlotte pretending to be dreamy and spiritual made Olivia smile. Mrs. Grenville would be an even less likely candidate. "I'll do my best." She picked up her spoon again, stirred it through the porridge, and then let it fall. Mrs. Grenville—"

"Oh, for the love of…everything, call me Joan," the other woman said. "*You're* not a servant or a student or a man, so it shouldn't make anyone faint."

"Thank you, and you must call me Olivia." The words dropped automatically from her lips. Not that she regretted them, but it was strange how such phrases came back. It had been years since she'd used the first name of anyone who might have cared. Not that she was sure Joan did. "When are you planning to have the party? I don't know for certain if Charlotte or Arthur have brought the right kind of clothes."

"In a week or so. Take them to the village if you need to, but don't worry about it too much. Woodwell came with two trunks, and Waite's the sort who looks good in evening dress and knows it, so I'd bet he has something."

Olivia giggled, then took a bite of her porridge.

There was something about the way Joan looked at a half-full bowl, she'd discovered, that made one reluctant to waste food. In some respects, she'd have made a marvelous governess.

As she ate, Olivia was conscious of Joan's eyes on her, and of an unexpectedly awkward look on the other woman's face.

"Er—" Joan finally began, "how about you? Sorry. Simon really should be the one handling this, but he can't talk about women's clothing, idiotically enough. Just…you *didn't* come with two trunks."

"No," said Olivia, thankful she'd thought to make the trip to Mrs. Simmons, "but I should have something in time."

"Good," said Joan and drummed her fingers against the table. "That's all of us but St. John. He's about Simon's size, with a little taking in. I'm going to let him be Simon's problem."

"That generally does seem the wisest course of action," said Olivia.

Joan lifted her eyebrows. "Oh, he's not so bad. Not when he forgets you're a woman. Simon's a better choice for trying to drag him out of his cave, though, and someone will have to. I don't think the good doctor's gone anywhere but his office and his room for the last three days."

"Not entirely," said Olivia after swallowing the last bite of her porridge. "He does watch my classes."

—◊◊◊—

In time, it might stop seeming odd to have a class in the middle of sofas, stuffed chairs, and end tables, just as it might become normal to see symbols chalked on floors that had once held flawless lacquer and Oriental rugs, or to smell incense and scented candles mingling with tea and bread. Theoretically, it was quite probable.

Gareth suspected such an adjustment wouldn't happen for quite a while, if ever it did. Not for him. The students were younger and therefore more malleable. Even Simon and his wife were younger, if only by a year or two. He thought he'd used up his allotment of broad-mindedness some time ago.

All the same, he was sitting on one of the chairs.

It made sense for him to be there. That was what he'd told himself a few days ago when he'd first taken a seat, and it was still true now. His leg ached, there was plenty of space, and he was starting to feel damned strange standing in the back of the room like a government inspector. Gareth felt obligated to be there. Therefore, there was nothing wrong with being comfortable.

Not that Mrs. Brightmore had given him any additional reason to feel obligated. In all the time he'd been watching her with the students, she'd never been less than honest.

Then again, perhaps that had been because he was watching her.

"Mrs. Besant would call it an 'aetheric body,'" she was saying now, "and I think there are some Oriental sources who'd talk about *chi* or *chakras*, though I'm not at all sure it's the same thing. I'd dearly love to have a proper translation some day."

Here she gave Miss Woodwell a smile, and that young woman grinned back but held up a hand. "It works only if I hear it said, I'm afraid. I'm merely mortal where writing's concerned, and I've never studied any Chinese. Seemed a tricky sort of a language. Get a monk in here for tea and mysticism, though, and I'll jump to it."

"I'll see what I can do," said Mrs. Brightmore. She waited long enough for the general chuckle to die down and then went on to talk about the energy within each person, how people with natural talents could use it and how magicians could affect those people. "The energy, you might say, is closer to the surface in them," she said with a graceful gesture of her hands. "There's less of a shell there. But normal people and animals and nonliving things aren't as easy to reach."

"Not impossible, though, is it?" Waite asked from under half-lidded eyes. He was leaning back, doing his utmost to occupy a whole sofa, but his voice betrayed more interest than his posture.

Mrs. Brightmore shook her head, smiling again in that almost lopsided way. "Not at all impossible, only more complicated. You have to make a connection in the physical world to what you're trying to affect. William, give me an example, please."

"One of those dolls," he said promptly, "the kind witch doctors and people stick pins in."

"Correct. That's the first of the two laws of magic: a connection between a person or an object, and something that looks like it. The other is a connection between a thing and a part of that thing.

"Another example, please. Elizabeth?"

Elizabeth lowered her hand. "Blood," she said. She didn't look at her classmates, but she sounded certain of herself, which was more than she'd done at first. "And hair, maybe?"

"Yes and yes. That's the second law. Any part can influence the whole. In a way, working with energy is using that law too. That's part of someone." She looked around the room, her face becoming solemn though without the sense of purpose it had held on the first day. "There are ways to protect yourself from such things, there are remedies once they happen, and nobody can guard against everything a magician might use to harm them. As far as you can, it's best to be very careful."

"Make sure you trust your servants, I assume," said Waite.

"That's a good idea no matter who you are. You can read Shakespeare if you doubt it." The students laughed. Mrs. Brightmore didn't. "But all of you risk a great deal more than minor blackmail or missing spoons. Those of you who end up working for the school to help fight these dark forces will put yourselves in danger. If you don't, danger may find you in any case, just because of what you know. If you remember anything of these lessons, remember that."

Gareth watched Mrs. Brightmore. She still looked like a respectable young widow, not the sort who'd know anything about danger, let alone hostile magic. The impression lasted until he met her eyes.

She was good at deceit. Gareth knew that. He knew there could be multiple layers to trickery, and Mrs. Brightmore could be pretending to worry about her students and pretending to not quite hide it. He knew those things, and yet he couldn't bring himself to think that the fear he saw was anything but real. It was a species he knew too well not to recognize.

Part of him had been surprised the blood ever did come off his hands.

"What about words?" he asked, remembering her half-whispered voice the first time she'd gotten Elizabeth down from the ceiling, and how she'd spoken in a language he hadn't recognized.

For a second Mrs. Brightmore stopped, blinking. "Words?" she repeated and cleared her throat. "Words are both, in a way. A word describes a thing, 'chair'"—another motion with a slim hand—"or 'apple' or 'boy,' but it also becomes part of it, in a way that's a bit hard to explain. Words have considerable power, and more so the older the language, or if people don't use that language for daily life."

Having found her rhythm, she continued, gesturing and smiling and drawing metaphors to a trail with many scents being harder to follow. She'd been startled at first, off guard, and Gareth smiled a little at that, but he found his satisfaction didn't last as long as he would have thought.

Instead, he found himself leaning forward, listening. Interested.

Chapter 13

WHATEVER THE LAST FEW YEARS MIGHT HAVE TAKEN FROM Gareth, they'd somehow left his ability to tie a formal necktie. God, it seemed, had a sense of humor.

The provenance of his clothing was further proof. Gareth had brought evening dress overseas with him, not knowing how long he'd stay, doubting the social life but certain he wouldn't be able to find a tailor in the event someone did call on him to attend a party. No such thing had happened, and neither jacket nor trousers nor shirt had emerged from the bottom of his trunk for the duration of his service. When Simon had informed him of the dinner party, complete with awkward mention of a spare suit in case he hadn't thought to pack one— "And really, why should you have? Silly idea of mine, I know…" Gareth had doubtfully said he *might* have something.

He'd expected to find moth holes or at the minimum, the smell of mothballs, but there had been no such thing. The clothes were fresh and in good repair. Gareth suspected Helen, whose sisterly inclinations had always overcome her respect for his privacy, of doing both mending and washing when he'd been home. He'd handed the clothing over to one of the servants, had it taken in, and thought no more about it until the night of the dinner party.

Looking at the altered suit that night surprised him.

He'd never been plump, and he'd thought he'd been recovering his frame quite well once he got to Englefield,
but all the same, it was a jolt to see the seams, just as
it was to look at his face in the mirror. The young man
he'd last seen above the white collar and dark coat
seemed very far away.

Gareth made one final adjustment to his tie, straightened his shoulders, and went out to face the evening.

Over the last few weeks, Gareth had not had much occasion to be in the parlor, and his strongest memory of
the room was of Fitzpatrick's panic about Elizabeth and
of his own brief conversation with Mrs. Brightmore.
That was probably why she was the first person Gareth
noticed when he walked through the door.

Granted, her dress helped in that regard

It was deep red satin, the color of good red wine or
old garnets, with a slim skirt and a square neckline. Not
low cut. Nobody but the most old-fashioned of Puritans
could have accused Mrs. Brightmore of immodesty. And
yet it made a man very much aware of the fullness of her
breasts, of the way what skin she did expose looked like
satin, and of the long, graceful line of her neck. After
the first glance, Gareth did the gentlemanly thing and
kept his eyes above her neck, but that was almost worse.
Surrounded by a loose cloud of chestnut hair, her face
was almost luminous, and her eyes shone brightly.

He thought of fine sherry held up to light.

Then he wondered why he was thinking of metaphors
for Mrs. Brightmore's eyes in the first place.

Gareth bowed politely, saw her curtsy in return with

what seemed like an inborn grace, and then noticed
Simon and his wife standing nearby amid a small crowd
of other people. "Good evening," he said and felt more
than saw their eyes on him.

Fortunately, if he'd been standing there like a dunce
for any length of time, everyone was too polite to notice. Mrs. Grenville came forward briskly and made the
introductions. The tall, stocky man was Dr. Gardiner. A
younger and less-rectangular-looking one was Simon's
friend Mr. Desmond. The plump and balding one was
Reverend Talbot, and the plump, brunette girls in pale
dinner dresses were Miss Rosemary Talbot and her
sister, Miss Elizabeth. Gareth *thought* Miss Rosemary
was wearing blue and Miss Elizabeth lavender but he
wouldn't have wagered any amount of money on it. He
would have wagered on Waite composing bad poetry to
the one in the violet gown before the evening was out,
judging by the way the boy was looking.

Luck wasn't with Waite that night. Mrs. Grenville
took the vicar's arm when they went in to dinner, Simon
the arm of his blue-gowned daughter, and Mr. Desmond
the one in violet. To his credit, Waite made some effort to disguise his regret as he offered an arm to Miss
Woodwell. That young lady, far from being grateful, returned a sardonic elder-sister grin and a whispered comment that made Waite look like he'd swallowed a frog.

That left Gareth with Mrs. Brightmore. He turned
away from Waite's predicament to look for her, and
found her a fellow spectator, with one corner of her
mouth turned up enough to suggest suppressed laughter.

"Youth," she said in a low voice when Gareth drew
within hearing distance. Then she did laugh softly. "No

matter what the poets say, I cannot think it a great tragedy that it passes."

"Some aspects of it, yes," said Gareth. After all, he could offer his arm to her without stammering or feeling vaguely ill: a decided benefit of maturity. At seventeen, he'd either have fallen over himself, regardless of Mrs. Brightmore's past, or done something hopelessly adolescent to rebuke her for it. "Do you look forward to old age, then?"

"Say rather I'll be happy if I reach it," she replied, smiling up at him. "And I'm disinclined to try for physical immortality."

Her lips were remarkably red. Part of Gareth wanted to think it was rouge, but, probably not. Not for this company. The woman knew her audience. "It's good to know," he replied, "you have scruples in *this* area. I'm quite reassured."

Mrs. Brightmore's cheeks flushed. Embarrassment? Anger? Both? Neither showed in her voice. She laughed again, tilting her head back a little. "Practicality, sir, I assure you. No good end has ever come to those who sought the Fountain of Youth, or none I've ever heard of. I'd rather not waste my life trying to prolong it."

"One might ask how you consider a life best spent," said Gareth. He should probably stop trying to provoke the woman. He wasn't sure why he'd started in the first place, except perhaps to remind himself he shouldn't be considering metaphors for her eyes.

"One might indeed," Mrs. Brightmore replied smoothly as they reached the dining room. Chandeliers and candles blazed with light there, reflecting on old silver and throwing little prisms out of cut glass. She paused a moment, out of appreciation, he supposed, then let him help her to her seat and glanced down the length of the table. "Indeed, I might consider it an eminently suitable topic for our guests." She spoke loudly enough to catch the attention of Reverend Talbot, who was sitting on her other side.

"If you think so," the vicar replied, turning toward her with a smile, "you'd best lay it before us. I know I'll be too curious to pay proper attention to my food otherwise."

"Man's purpose in life," said Mrs. Brightmore. "Or woman's."

"A weighty subject for dinner," said Mr. Desmond, eying Mrs. Brightmore across the table. There was more than intellectual appreciation in that look, Gareth saw. "Do you often discuss such things?"

Mrs. Brightmore nodded. "Someone in my profession is obligated to consider these matters, I believe, almost as much as someone in the reverend's." She glanced very briefly, almost imperceptibly at Mrs. Grenville, and then added, "And I believe all of us have a duty to attend to certain higher callings…and to better prepare the next generation for the world that is to come."

Conversation rose around her, as if she were the moon calling the tides, and Gareth let it carry him along.

—∞∞—

"And I hear you've come up from London to serve this calling of yours, Mrs. Brightmore?" Desmond was eying her with a lifted eyebrow and the hint of a grin. "You must have been very sorry to have left so much society."

The evening, as far as Gareth could tell, had been

quite a success. The conversation had flowed along smoothly, from ideals to art to the state of the government, never stopping too long on any topic that might create too much controversy. At his end of the table, Mrs. Brightmore had always seemed aware whenever anyone hesitated or frowned, and had chosen that moment to inquire about the state of the crops or ask one of the Misses Talbot if she played or sang.

Even he had found it enjoyable. True, he'd neither eaten nor spoken as much as any of the others, but the mutton had been good, the soup better, and the company more interesting and less irritating than Gareth had been anticipating. He'd even brushed the dust off some memories to talk about boating with Desmond, who'd turned out to be the younger son of Simon's nearest neighbor, pressed into service to make up an even table.

The man had conducted himself creditably, under the circumstances, and had even had a brief discussion of Morris with Reverend Talbot and Mrs. Grenville. Still, he knew little of the school, lacked some of the motives for investigation which propelled Talbot and Gardiner, and had seemed more than a bit lost in some of the more philosophical turns in conversation. His question was no surprise.

Mrs. Brightmore shook her head and smiled. There was nothing furtive in her face, no hint of tension or of guilt. "Society can be wearying after a time," she said, "and I never moved in any particularly eventful circles. I'm quite glad to be in the country."

"Oh, I see," said Desmond. Clearly attempting to be subtle, he glanced at Mrs. Brightmore's hand and the gold ring there.

It was the only jewelry she wore, Gareth noticed now. No earrings danced when she shook her head; no onyx or rubies rested around her neck. Not like the other women. He glanced around and was certain of it. Even the Misses Talbot had small pearl beads made into necklaces and hair ornaments, Mrs. Grenville wore gold and sapphires, and emerald earrings dangled above Miss Woodwell's lace-covered shoulders.

Now that Gareth came to think about it, Mrs. Brightmore's dress seemed rather plain too. Granted, her neckline was lower than the one on Mrs. Grenville's blue velvet gown, but higher than on either the Talbot girls' dresses or Miss Woodwell's. He didn't know much about fashion, but all the others also had ribbons or lace or both.

Maybe she'd decided she would look more responsible without ornament, or maybe simply that she'd look better.

And if there was another reason, if necessity rather than choice had guided her, what of it?

"I was raised near Kent," Mrs. Brightmore said, breaking into Gareth's observation, "and came to London only once I'd married. So, you see, it's a bit like coming home for me."

"You must have married very young," said the blue Miss Talbot, impervious to her father's warning look.

Again, if the comment disturbed her, Mrs. Brightmore didn't show it. "I was seventeen," she said. Wistfully? Perhaps. Gareth couldn't be sure. She was still smiling. "At the time, I think I believed myself quite mature."

Reverend Talbot chuckled. "And so do we all, I suppose." He gave his daughters a fond glance.

"Did your husband live in London, then?" asked the same Miss Talbot. She sounded a little wistful herself, though, Gareth guessed, for reasons very unlike Mrs. Brightmore's. "It must have been quite a change."

"Yes and no," said Mrs. Brightmore. "Or not at first. He was a lieutenant. His regiment was quartered near us for a time. They departed shortly after my wedding, and, naturally, I went with them."

As far as Gareth could tell, she spoke the truth. Indeed, he had no reason to doubt her on this particular point, or to care. A woman could invent a husband, or a hundred if she wanted. It was nothing to him. He'd never really stopped to consider whether she had any right to the "Mrs." before her name.

Yet hearing her speak of it was somehow strange. Gareth could connect Mrs. Brightmore and Madame Marguerite without too much difficulty. It was far harder to connect either of them with a schoolgirl roaming around Kent or a young bride on the arm of a man in regimentals or, for that matter, a new widow in London.

He would almost have preferred to believe her husband a fiction.

Chapter 14

TAP.

Olivia came half-awake at the sound, surfacing from confused dreams of swimming in purple seas and reaching for flying fruit. Had she dreamed the sound too? She hoped so. It had been a very long day.

Tap. Tap.

No. There it was again. Now she was awake enough to recognize that someone was knocking at her door. Olivia bit back a curse, opened her eyes, and let the moonlit shapes of her room resolve themselves. "Yes, all right," she managed through a mouth that felt like something had been living in it, "I'm coming."

Olivia couldn't tell time by the moon, and she had no clock in her bedroom, but if it was before midnight, she would have been very surprised. The fire had certainly died down, and a chill had set firmly into the air. The cold woke her up quite efficiently—there was a silver lining in most things, she supposed—and she managed not to squeak. Her hands found her dressing gown and pulled it on, while her mind shook itself into awareness.

A late-night disturbance, particularly at Englefield, could have meant almost anything, but Olivia had spent the past few weeks dealing with one specific cause. When she saw Charlotte's face on the other side of the door, hair mussed and eyes half-closed, she was unsurprised. She did permit herself a sigh. "Again?"

"Afraid so," said Charlotte and stepped back to let Olivia out into the hall. Sleepy as she looked and sounded, she managed a grin. "Pity you can't keep a pot of tea around overnight."

Olivia felt it was too late to be circumspect. "Much more of this, and I'll be able to sleep right through the whole process."

They opened the door of the girls' bedroom and stepped inside. As expected, Elizabeth was floating again. She had looked particularly eerie the first time, her nightgown white in the darkness and her hair streaming down below her, but now the sight was almost commonplace.

"She's not going as high as she was at the start," Charlotte said, trying to be encouraging.

Olivia nodded. "She's at least three feet from the ceiling. It's certainly a good sign." Good signs were important just now. "Thank you for getting me. You can go back to sleep now."

"Luck," said Charlotte and promptly cocooned herself in her blankets again.

Olivia watched her enviously for a moment, then stepped back and cleared her throat. A series of words in Enochian projected her voice to the girl's ears, as if she were in the bed and Olivia leaning over her. "Elizabeth," she said, quiet and firm. "Wake up now. And don't scream."

Elizabeth didn't scream, though she did squeak and look down wide-eyed at Olivia. "Oh, *no*. Not *again*."

That was a fair summary of Olivia's thoughts, but she didn't feel that saying so would help anything. "You're awake," she said and took a seat in the chair she'd first collapsed on when she'd come to Englefield. It had, in the nights since, become an old companion. "Now get yourself down."

"But—"

"I told you last time," said Olivia, holding up a hand. She tried to keep an edge out of her voice, to remember the girl was very young and she hadn't asked for this power. "You're quite capable of descending on your own now. Moreover, the more you control your own power, the fewer nightmares you'll have, and the less likely you'll be to levitate during them."

Elizabeth blinked down at her a few times then shook her head and wailed, "I can't! I'm too scared!"

Her levitation was probably fortunate just then. Olivia had never struck anyone and had no intention of starting with a frightened child, but she could feel her nerves fraying. "Lower your voice," she said through gritted teeth, "and breathe deeply. I am right here. I will not let you hurt yourself. But, by God, you will get yourself down under your own power, or we'll both be here all night."

Something in her tone must have convinced Elizabeth, because she gulped and took a few breaths. Olivia muttered another phrase in Enochian and watched the flow of power within the girl, ready to intervene if anything did go wrong. It wasn't likely Elizabeth would fall hard enough to break her leg, and less likely she'd send herself up through the ceiling, but both were possible.

Elizabeth shut her eyes. "All right," she said. Although Olivia couldn't see her face, she could imagine the look of concentration there.

A moment passed. Then another. Then, finally, Olivia

saw power begin to subside within Elizabeth's body. Not flowing out, the way it might have with a magician like herself, but shrinking and calming, like flame dying into embers. The girl floated down a few inches.

It was working.

That was almost worth getting up at whatever ungodly hour it was. Almost.

Getting Elizabeth down under her own control was even slower than helping her to do it, though. By the time she reached her bedclothes again, she was yawning, and she was asleep a few seconds after Olivia tucked her in.

Olivia had no such luck. Her dressing gown was heavy wool, the nightgown beneath it thick cotton, but the night air had done its work quite soundly earlier, and the strain on her nerves hadn't helped. From past experience, she knew quite well all her bed held was a few miserable hours half dozing.

Also, Olivia realized as she turned quietly away from Elizabeth's bed, she was hungry. Perhaps a slice of bread and jam, and even a cup of tea, if she was lucky and the kitchen was simple, would help her bed do its work when she returned.

Closing the door carefully behind her, she slipped down the hallway and then descended two flights of the back staircase into another hall. The floors were neither carpeted nor polished here, though they were clean and well kept, and they were cold under her bare feet. Up ahead, Olivia could smell hearth smoke and tomorrow's baking. Her stomach rumbled.

The dim light coming from the kitchen didn't surprise Olivia. Her youthful memory held a vague recollection of scullery maids who were supposed to keep the fire going. One of them could probably tell her where the kettle was, she thought, unless the girl started screaming. In any event, nobody was likely to mistake her for a burglar.

With that thought, she stepped into the kitchen and blinked.

There *was* someone in there, but not the half-grown girl whom Olivia had expected to find drowsing by the fire. Instead, a tall male frame in a dark green dressing gown sat by the long kitchen table, the makings of an impromptu meal in front of him and his sharp chin propped on one fist.

"Dr. St. John," she said, surprised into speech.

"Mrs. Brightmore?" St. John jerked around to face her, his face a study in surprise.

For a moment, they stared at each other. St. John's eyes looked very dark, and the firelight threw shadows across his angular features, making him look rather like some ancient image on a coin. Then he started to get up, keeping one hand on the table, and the resemblance passed.

"Oh, don't stand on ceremony," said Olivia. "Not at whatever ungodly hour this is." Quickly, she found a chair of her own and sat across from him.

"Help yourself, in that case," said St. John. He actually smiled at her, weary but genuine, with nothing unwilling about it. "I'd say it was a token of my thanks for not making me rise, but it's not actually my food."

It was good food, and there was plenty even without what St. John had already taken: a few thick slices off a roast, half a loaf of bread, a wedge of cheese, and an apple. He had a glass of wine in front of him too. "I can't offer you the bottle," he said when he saw the direction of Olivia's gaze, "or yet another glass. I don't mind sharing, though, if you're willing to be a little primitive."

"We're in the kitchen, and it's past midnight. I think 'primitive' is rather inescapable at this point." Olivia glanced around and located a plate.

"A decent point. May I, er, serve?"

"Please. Some of everything." Confronted by food, Olivia was surprised to discover how hungry she actually was. She watched St. John load her plate. He moved quickly and efficiently, natural enough given his profession, and his fingers were long. Graceful, if one could say that about a man. "You must know your way around the kitchens, if you found all that by yourself."

"I know whom to ask," said St. John. "I made arrangements when I came." Handing the plate back to her, he relaxed into his seat. Their eyes met again, and he shrugged again, but more defensively this time, as if trying to free himself of something that had settled on one shoulder. "I'm not used to eating at regular hours. Or large meals. Not these days."

"No," said Olivia, breaking her bread into small chunks, "I suppose you wouldn't be. You mustn't have had a very settled sort of life over there."

His eyes narrowed. "Where?"

"I'm not entirely sure. I'd guess Egypt or Afghanistan, but I could be wrong. Lord knows I wasn't paying as much attention to those things as I should have been." Olivia ate a chunk of bread. "This could use butter."

"I didn't know I'd have company."

"And you don't like butter?"

"Not particularly. It goes bad too quickly."

"Ah."

St. John took a drink, put the glass down, and looked at her. "Egypt. Yes. Was it the suntan or the leg?"

"Both, among other things. The leg could be anything. You could've been kicked by a cow in Yorkshire."

"I don't have the right accent." The edges of St. John's mouth had started to twitch upward.

Olivia felt an answering smile creeping onto her face. "You could've moved there. That would probably have explained the cow's reaction."

"How provincial of it."

"Very." Olivia cut her meat and popped a slice into her mouth. It had stood up better to age than the bread had, and was still rich and juicy. She swallowed. "As for your complexion, you could've just returned from a pleasure trip to Italy. But then you wouldn't have the leg wound."

"Unless I'd been stabbed in Italy." St. John was definitely smiling now. "A jealous husband, perhaps."

"Don't you think that's a little conceited?"

St. John shook his head, his hair falling over his forehead. He flicked it back with a careless gesture. "It's no compliment. Jealous husbands tend to be jealous of anything male."

"In your wide experience," Olivia said dryly.

"In my wide experience."

A clock nearby struck, and Olivia started. The sound wasn't up close, but it was very loud in the still, dim kitchen. She glanced back over at St. John, embarrassed, and saw the same sort of rueful look on his face. Together, they listened to the bells: *one, two, three, four.*

Olivia groaned. "Worse than I'd thought."

"Mm. Why, if I may be so bold"—St. John glanced around the empty kitchen with a faintly ironic air—"are you here? Trouble sleeping?"

"Not me," said Olivia and sighed. "Or not at first. Elizabeth's still having nightmares."

"Ah. Can't you "—St. John circled one hand vaguely in the air—"shut her down for the evening?"

Olivia shook her head. "Not truly. I can make levitation harder for her, but I don't want to do that when she's not conscious. If she exerts herself too much in her dreams, I don't know what would happen."

"I can hazard a guess or two," said St. John and also shook his head. "No, you're right. Hard on you, though, waking up for it."

"Hopefully it won't go on too much longer. Besides," she said, "I really shouldn't be talking. You're as awake as I am, and you don't complain."

His lips tightened. "All I took away from Egypt was a limp and a tendency to scavenge at odd hours. I don't particularly feel I can complain either." St. John looked at her as if waiting for some reaction— anger or pity or shock—Olivia didn't think she had the energy to give.

Instead, she asked, "Was it your first, um, tour of duty?"

"First and last, yes." Finished, he pushed his plate away and propped his arms on the table, leaning forward. His eyes caught hers in the firelight and held them. "You know a few military terms, then?"

"I *was* married to a soldier," she said mildly.

"At seventeen." St. John's gaze brushed downward over her face and neck, taking in her unbound hair and the collar of her dressing gown. "You know, I find it quite difficult to imagine you as a schoolgirl."

The air around Olivia felt warmer, although she was quite certain the fire hadn't come back to life. She leaned forward as well, smiling. "I'll take that as a compliment, I think, though a rather unusual one."

"Do, if you like." He reached one hand across the table and trailed his fingers down her cheek. Olivia's skin flamed to life where he touched, and her nipples went hard. Two layers of fabric lay between them and St. John's eyes, thank God. "You're a rather unusual woman, Mrs. Brightmore."

They had risen from the table almost as one and moved toward the end without thinking, so Olivia was almost surprised when she could step forward and slide her hands up to St. John's shoulders. "Given the circumstances," she said, "I think you can call me Olivia."

She wasn't sure whether she rose up or St. John bent down, but the next thing she knew, his hands were splayed against her back and his mouth, hot and seeking, had covered hers. Her lips parted easily, eagerly under the pressure. The world swam around her.

This was not wise. This was anything but wise. But it was four in the morning, and St. John's tongue was meeting hers. His chest was firm where it pressed against her breasts, and she could feel his manhood rigid against her stomach. Olivia couldn't make herself care very much about wisdom. She melted into him, half surprised to hear a small, desperate sound coming from her throat.

St. John dropped his hands and stepped back. As Olivia blinked at him, trying to figure out what was happening now, he caught his breath. "I'd rather not use your name, madam," he said. Clearly he was trying to sound cold. The thickness in his voice didn't do much for the attempt. "After all, I've no way of knowing if it's really yours."

As icy baths went, the two sentences worked very well. Desire became embarrassment became fury. Olivia drew herself up, gathered the neck of her dressing gown around her, and lifted her chin. "I assure you it is, sir," she replied and was proud her voice didn't tremble. "You may use it, or not...or go to the devil. I truly don't care which."

Chapter 15

SHORTLY AFTER THE WOMAN WALKED OUT, GARETH REALIZED two things. The first was that, regardless of what he'd said, he could no longer think of her as Mrs. Brightmore. The name *Olivia* had gotten a grip on his consciousness, and he couldn't pry it loose.

The second was that he'd been more than a bit of a bastard.

Oh, he hadn't taken advantage of the woman, whatever Society's standards might be. Nothing was wrong with Gareth's memory. Olivia had responded quite willingly to his kiss, willingly enough to make Gareth flush and harden even when he thought about it afterward, as much as he regretted the whole incident. And she hadn't flinched or drawn back from his advances beforehand. She was no innocent girl either. She'd known what she was doing.

So had he.

Half a glass of wine wouldn't have begun to muddle his judgment, not even now. The late hour and the seclusion of the quiet kitchen had certainly helped to lower a few barriers, though. So had their attire, particularly Olivia's. Her dressing gown had been golden-brown wool, nothing that would have even whispered at seduction, but it had outlined the smooth curves of her body in a way her dresses never did. And her hair had hung rippling down her back. Watching her eat, seeing her tongue touch her lips occasionally—

It was a wonder he hadn't acted sooner.

He'd relaxed his normal suspicions under the surprising ease and comfort with which they'd talked, the simple rather than morbid curiosity Olivia had turned on his time overseas. Then he'd wanted to change the subject, and Olivia had mentioned her marriage. It had been a short jump from there to thinking of her with men...with a man...with him.

Everything after that had seemed almost inevitable.

Still, Gareth knew he could have stopped himself. If he was no seducer, neither was Olivia a second Salome. He'd wanted her, he'd showed her as much, and she'd responded. There were men who might have blamed her for that. Gareth had never liked them. He'd remembered her past too late, and he'd turned his anger on her. Whatever she'd been, she hadn't deserved that.

Once she'd walked out of the kitchen and he'd recovered enough of his mind to think properly, Gareth knew he'd been wrong.

The next morning, he wrote her a short note: *I sincerely apologize for my conduct on our previous meeting. I give you my word that it will not happen again.* One of the maids, Violet, presumably brought it to her room. Olivia didn't respond. Gareth hadn't really thought she would. He wondered if she'd go to Simon or his wife about the incident, but the day passed without either of them bringing it to his attention or even acting strangely around him.

Olivia's silence on the matter was a relief, but Gareth couldn't feel any surprise about it, or any real gladness. She hadn't seemed the type to pretend a man had taken advantage of her, and she apparently wasn't, which spoke well of her. But anything that spoke well of her increased his guilt.

If she *hadn't* wanted him, she might still have kept silent. It would have been Gareth's word against hers, after all. Simon was his friend. Olivia was an intelligent woman, and not, from all evidence, a wealthy one.

That line of thought was even more unsettling. Gareth still didn't think she'd let him kiss her out of fear or desperation. She hadn't *let* him kiss her at all. But he didn't like to consider why she might not have complained about his presence in her classes, or how she must have felt when he'd gone off to tell Simon about her the first time.

If Olivia hadn't spent her life making a profit from people's grief, he reminded himself, she wouldn't have had anything to worry about in the first place.

Gareth started taking his meals in his room over the next few days, and he no longer went to Olivia's classes. If she wanted to teach the students confidence tricks, Simon had already said he'd allow as much. Gareth could no longer tell himself she'd corrupt them in other ways, not after he'd seen the fear for them in her eyes. There was no need for his presence.

From time to time, he did see Olivia in the halls or on the grounds. They nodded politely on those occasions and passed a few civil words, as any adults and colleagues might do. Gareth didn't let his eyes meet hers or even linger anywhere on her person. He did wonder if she looked at him.

When the first frost came and the ground turned hard, he started walking, ignoring the pain in his leg, so he could get out of the house and away, in some fashion, from his thoughts. He toured the gardens, dead as they were, and he inspected the stables, feeding a few purloined apples to Simon's horses. The forest was too far, particularly as Gareth didn't know the place. If something did go wrong in the school, it was best if he was on hand.

The dormitory had walls now, if no roof. It stood stark against the green-and-brown landscape, a redbrick square that was no more cheerful for its solidity. Gareth walked around it, tried to imagine students actually inhabiting it, and found his imagination unequal to the task. Ludicrous, when his mind was equal to so many unwelcome things.

In the late afternoon, Gareth was studying a doorway when he heard someone behind him. It wasn't Olivia, he told himself sternly, doing his best to prevent dread and hope alike.

When he turned, Mrs. Grenville gave him an almost grudging nod. She stood with her arms folded across her chest, surveying Gareth or the building or both. "Not bad."

"The dormitory?" He didn't give her time to answer. "It seems to be coming along. Not that I'm any judge of architecture."

"It'll hold," said Mrs. Grenville. "It'll probably look good too, eventually. Simon's hired someone impressive, and I've seen the plans. But it'll hold, and that's the important thing."

"How many students do you think we'll get?" Gareth asked. When Mrs. Grenville turned sharp hazel eyes on him, he realized he'd said *we* and cleared his throat. "It's an unusual school."

"And I don't know how many unusual people there are in this world, let alone unusual people who want to learn. Powers forbid we find a lot who're willing to *pay*." Mrs. Grenville looked back toward the building. "But we can use the space. Classrooms. Practice rooms. Things like that."

"Like Simon's room upstairs? The one he uses for 'fencing practice'?"

Mrs. Grenville snapped her gaze back to Gareth and, for just a second, her posture changed. She didn't stiffen, not exactly, but Gareth had seen men preparing to fight. The bright green-and-blue striped dress she wore should have made the pose, or her narrowed eyes, ludicrous. It did not.

Then she relaxed, deciding, apparently, he was no threat. "Something like that," she said.

Gareth hastily revised certain opinions he'd held considering Simon's adventurous nature or lack thereof. Marriage to this woman would be like keeping a half-tamed tiger in one's drawing room. Beautiful, in a way, benevolent, in a way, but...*better you than me, old man.*

"We have," he said, attempting to smooth things over without being too obviously conciliatory, "known each other quite a while."

"So he said." There was a quick smile. The claws retracted. "Sorry. I get twitchy where he's concerned. Especially with old friends."

"From what I hear, you have reason."

Mrs. Grenville made a noncommittal sound at that, and studied Gareth for a moment, with the frank consideration another woman might have turned on a hat or a cut of beef. He drew himself up and straightened his shoulders. There were limits, even with terrifying foreign women who'd married his friends.

If she asked to see his teeth, he was leaving.

"You should start teaching your own classes," she said, which startled him nearly as much.

"On what?" Once again, he forgot his manners. Once again, Mrs. Grenville didn't look as if she'd even noticed. "I can't teach anyone else to use my talent, and I don't know anything about magic."

"You know medicine. They're going to need that. Especially field medicine. How to stop bleeding and set bones. Cautery. What to do about poison. Whatever they run into, it's not likely to catch them near a hospital. Anatomy too," she continued before Gareth could ask any of the questions that occurred to him. "I do a little in combat training, but it's probably better to be really sure where the kidneys are. At least in human beings." A pause. "Well, most human beings."

The possible questions started with *What?* and went on from there.

Gareth took a breath and tried to organize his thoughts. He did know what the students would likely be doing with other people's kidneys. Anatomical knowledge *was* useful for self-defense. The implication that human beings would not be the only sort of adversary...Olivia had hinted at similar things. He would *not* think about the library. And Simon had shown him an image or two back in university days. Besides, Mrs. Grenville's meaning was self-evident.

That left only one reply. "I've never taught anyone."

"Neither have any of us." Mrs. Grenville laughed, a short and sharp sound that somehow had a hint of fondness in it this time. "Not mostly. Besides, you should do new things. It keeps the mind fresh. It also might make you stop glaring at the servants and prevent you from throwing something through a window one of these days."

"I have no intention of throwing anything through a window."

"Most people don't. Windows get broken all the same." Mrs. Grenville eyed him much as Helen had in his boyhood, those times when she'd seen his scrapes and muddy clothes before their parents had. "I don't know what your problem is," she said. "Not right now, not in general. I'm not a…I mean, your feelings aren't my business. The school is. You've done a good job so far. Keep doing it."

"Thank you," said Gareth, not sure whether the praise or the warning unnerved him more. "I will."

Then Mrs. Grenville coughed and, in a considerably less firm and more embarrassed tone of voice, added, "If you'd like to talk about anything, that's fine. I'm sure Simon feels the same way."

"No," he said hastily. At university, he and Simon had often discussed women, but none of them had been a colleague. Gareth couldn't imagine bringing up the subject of Olivia with Mrs. Grenville, who was even now letting her breath out in what sounded like relief. "Thank you. I should be going. I'll talk with you tomorrow about scheduling the classes."

Mrs. Grenville nodded. "Be well," she said.

Gareth had taken a few steps toward the house when he stopped and turned back. "I'm sorry—" But Mrs. Grenville waved a hand at him: *go on*. He did. "You said…whatever they encounter? Do you know—?"

"What's likely to be a problem?" Mrs. Grenville shook her head. The wind made the blue-dyed plumes of her hat dance, a merriment quite at odds with the knife-edged purpose in her face. "No idea. Might not even be anything. But if something does come up, we'll damn well be ready for it. Whatever it is."

Chapter 16

"They're coming along nicely," said Mr. Grenville, looking out at the brown-and-gray expanse of the main garden and the students who were wandering through it. " As far as I'm any judge."

"*Someone* must be," Olivia replied, smiling. "You're the best qualified by far, and so I'm gratified to hear your good opinion." Lightly as she spoke, she'd felt her shoulders lift at the praise, and the brisk day seemed a little warmer as she glanced over at the students.

In that moment, they could have been young people anywhere. Charlotte was laughing with Michael and William, pointing out some feature of the statuary with brisk and exaggerated gestures. Nearby, rather to Olivia's surprise, Arthur was talking with Elizabeth, both looking very interested in a group of now-dead plants. As Olivia watched, Arthur reached over and tweaked one of Elizabeth's red braids, and the younger girl actually giggled.

"Be gratified if we all survive the winter. That's all *I'm* asking. With all of us in one house, I wouldn't dare tempt Fate by requesting more."

Olivia laughed. "More people have endured with less room, I'm certain. You must have been at school yourself. I know my cousins were, and their dormitories were far more crowded than we'll be. Have a seat," she added, gesturing to the expanse of stone bench beside her.

Obligingly, Mr. Grenville sat down "They were. And ships at sea have less room still. Neither school-boys nor sailors can command the storms, though. Not for the most part."

"I'll keep an eye on Michael, and keep him busy, as much as I can."

"Oh, Joan and I will do our parts," said Mr. Grenville. "Have no doubt of that. Gareth, too, if he's amenable."

Olivia kept her face pleasant and calm. She hadn't spoken to St. John in days, except for a few chance and formal encounters in the halls or on the grounds. When she'd gotten his note, she'd torn it to small shreds, dumped the shreds into the fire, and then wondered which aspect of his conduct he'd meant.

"How's he managing now?" Mr. Grenville asked. "Delaying the storms, that is?"

"I—oh. Michael?" Olivia cleared her throat. "Not badly. His moods still disturb the clouds a little, whether he's intending to do anything or not, but now he's able to make contact without making it rain immediately. It's very encouraging."

A most unmanly yelp broke the air. Olivia glanced over to see if there was cause for alarm, and saw Arthur clutching at the back of his neck while the other students succumbed to various degrees of laughter.

"A spider, I think," said Mr. Grenville cheerfully, "and Fitzpatrick as the agent. I shouldn't worry about it. Boys, you know."

A few words crossed the garden to Olivia's ears: *perfect beast* and *get you for this*. However, there was laughter in Arthur's voice, and she thought Mr. Grenville's advice was for the best. None of the other students, after all, looked alarmed.

"Do you know," Olivia said, "I think nothing we teach can do as much good for them as putting them here together. Showing them that other people have special abilities and can learn too, so they needn't either feel freakish or put on airs. That sort of thing."

"Where they're concerned," said Mr. Grenville, "I think you're quite correct." He smiled when he spoke, but there was a slight emphasis that reminded Olivia of the second purpose of Englefield and its students. "Certainly in cases like Elizabeth's. We can be of more benefit to her than the other way around." He added with a fond smile, "Joan would say we're probably helping the world that way too, by preventing whatever damage could result from Elizabeth's power going untrained. But Joan thinks she must see the bigger picture whenever possible."

"Someone ought to," Olivia replied and then laughed. "And I suppose traditionally it should be one of us. Cosmic vision and so forth."

Mr. Grenville chuckled. "I'll endeavor to develop some."

"Once we survive the winter?"

"Indeed. Or perhaps you'll step in and save me the trouble."

Olivia laughed again and shook her head. "I think cosmic vision has to be cosmically *small* as well as cosmically big," she said, half-seriously voicing thoughts she'd never quite said aloud before. "Whatever form of it mortals have. In any case, I'm quite satisfied now that

Elizabeth's not shooting up into the air once a week and nobody's getting lost in the forest."

Also as long as she was getting a regular salary, she reminded herself, and more-than-decent room and board. One didn't say such things, certainly not in front of one's employer, but they were important to keep in mind. Olivia wondered at herself, briefly, that she hadn't thought of her finances earlier in the conversation. Perhaps she should ask for more salary if they made it through the winter unscathed.

Don't count your chickens.

"Is she still having nightmares?" Mr. Grenville asked.

Olivia shook her head. "Or if she is, she's getting down by herself. I'm quite relieved."

"For a number of reasons, I expect."

"Oh?" she asked, a little higher than she meant to.

There was no knowledge in Mr. Grenville's face, though, and he simply shrugged. "I'd imagine you're fond of a good night's sleep."

"Yes, rather" Olivia laughed and tried to make her heart stop racing. Guilt hadn't thrown her off in *years*, for heaven's sake, and now she was acting like one of the students caught at mischief.

The mischief in question didn't bear thinking of. Certainly not here and now. Olivia shifted uncomfortably on the bench and cleared her throat. "I haven't found anything in your books about the forest," she said.

"I would expect as much," said Simon. "Eleanor and I aren't the first to spend more time away from Englefield than here. Father's position keeps him and Mother abroad most of the year, and has done so ever since I can remember. You might talk to some of the servants," he suggested.

"Only if you wouldn't mind," said Olivia.

Mr. Grenville shook his head. "Not in the slightest. I'd be glad to find out, and I fear I don't have as much time for research as I used to."

That evening, as Violet was putting away her clothes, Olivia remembered the earlier conversation and turned from her mirror to look at the maid. She was young, sixteen, as Olivia had found out during one of their brief conversations, and the woman in the village had been old. All the same…"Violet, did you grow up here?"

Violet turned, one of Olivia's skirts still hanging from her hand. "Yes, ma'am. I've never been anywhere else, not really."

Olivia hadn't expected a different answer. Over the last few weeks, as Violet had acted the part of not-quite-lady's-maid, she having other duties and Olivia not needing much help except for the dinner party, they'd had a few brief conversations. Mostly, these had consisted of Olivia making some friendly overture and Violet asking a myriad of questions before she remembered propriety. Questions about London, about Kent, about any place other than Englefield.

Now that the tables were turned, Olivia felt rather awkward. "Ah, did you ever hear about the forest? The one here?" she added unnecessarily.

She wasn't sure what reaction she'd been expecting. A stifled laugh certainly hadn't been among the possibilities, though. "Ah—" Olivia began again.

"I'm very sorry, ma'am," Violet said, sobering up at once. "It won't happen again, I promise. It's only…I should have expected one of you to ask before this, given…" A sweep of her skirt-bearing hand took in Englefield as a whole.

"I didn't know the place was that infamous."

"Oh, it's not, not really. Just old stories and that. Nothing…nothing bad. Violet bit her lip, her forehead wrinkling. "My grandmother used to talk about a child or two who disappeared there, but that's what *her* mother had told her, so like as not, she was just trying to get us to behave."

"And children do go missing, even in quite normal forests," Olivia agreed. Carefully, she plucked a pin from her hair and set it on top of her dresser. "Especially back in those days, I'd imagine. It must have been wilder then. What else did your grandmother say?"

"Not her," Violet replied. "Not exactly. But there was an old lady in the village. Mrs. Colton. She died when I was just a girl," she added with all the sage and wintery hindsight of sixteen. "But she said if you gathered wood from the forest when the moon was full and brought it to her, she could look into the fire and tell you who you'd marry."

"Did it work?"

Violet shrugged. "I suppose so. My friend Patience's older sister said it did. The way Patience tells it, Mrs. Colton just said Kitty'd marry a dark-haired man, and any girl 'round here would have her pick of those."

"They aren't very rare, it's true," said Olivia, smiling. She'd had her palm read once when she'd been around Violet's age. The crone, or pretend crone, she thought now, knowing the tricks that could make a healthy, middle-aged woman seem ancient and raddled, had said Olivia would go over water to live. When she and Tom had crossed into London, she'd probably been fool enough to think of prophecy too, the number of creeks between her father's estate and anywhere else notwithstanding. "And men have seen things there, I hear?"

"Any man hunting in the forest, ma'am, would as like as not have been in a state to see anything at all," Violet said with unusual crispness for her. "It's Mr. Grenville's property, after all." She hesitated.

"But Mr. Grenville wasn't here for years, or any of his family. I'm sure anyone who went into the forest when they were gone was just doing so out of…service. Keeping the population down and so forth."

"Well," Violet said, drawing the word out. "I did hear about animals that talked sometimes. But I never gave it much credit. Not until—"

She stopped. No matter. Olivia was fairly certain she could finish the sentence on her own. "It is strange," she said, "having one's point of view so suddenly expanded. A bit like the first time on a boat."

"I've never been, ma'am. But you seem to have your sea legs well enough."

"In some matters, yes," Olivia said. She thought of St. John's lips and of the way she'd forgotten about her salary for a bit that afternoon, and sighed. Her hair, free of its pins, went tumbling down her back. "Less so where other things are concerned, I fear."

Chapter 17

FIVE PAIRS OF EYES WATCHED GARETH. FIVE FACES TURNED toward him, curious and amused, expectant and nervous. All were attentive for the moment. Gareth suspected it would be no mean job to hold that attention, eager though the students were.

Olivia had always managed it. Olivia was at home on a stage, and if he wasn't, that was a point in his favor under most circumstances. She also had flashy magic tricks to her advantage. The magic might have been real, but the tricks were still flashy. Showmanship. Gareth had knowledge, and therefore would need none of that.

Besides, he was trying not to think about the woman.

"Good afternoon," Gareth began. "At Mr. Grenville's request, I'll be teaching you the basics of medicine"—he gestured to the table in front of him, where he'd laid out some neatly rolled bandages and straight pieces of wood—"and anatomy. Miss Donnell?" She was too young, really, to be a "Miss," but he wouldn't make her the only one in the class he addressed by first name. "You have a question?"

"Will we be learning about diseases and poisoning too?" she asked, eyes serious and steady in her freckled face. "Or mostly broken bones and cuts and things?"

"Internal and external both," said Gareth, trying not to look as surprised as he felt. "Of course, this will not qualify any of you to practice medicine under any normal circumstances, nor will we particularly touch on surgery. Not most types. I'll be teaching you what the late Major Shepherd called 'first aid': the immediate care of a wounded patient."

He saw recognition in Miss Woodwell's face—hardly surprising, given her father—and, more curiously in Fitzpatrick's.

The others didn't seem to know the term, but Waite and Fitzpatrick exchanged a look before the older boy raised his hand. "In adverse conditions, I assume, sir?" he asked when Gareth called on him.

Long after midnight, and a wind that did nothing to cool anyone, particularly the men who tossed and turned on their beds, but had managed to put out half the lamps. Screaming. Crying. The smell of blood, the cleanest smell in the air.

"Yes," said Gareth. "As far as we can manage them." He cleared his throat. "Today, however, we'll begin with theory. The major arteries in the human body…"

Words and theory could make a wall when he needed them to. Gareth had discovered that some time ago. Overseas, his construction had often been slapdash and hasty, but it had served him well enough. Now he built carefully, brick by brick, speaking of the jugular and the carotid, the femoral and the radial, naming things so he would picture them less vividly.

"Some of you, I am sure, are wondering about supernatural healing. Hard not to, I'd imagine, given your presence here. It exists. I'd be a fool to deny it." Gareth allowed himself a small smile at that. "By and large, though," he continued, "I intend to stay focused on the normal aspects of medicine. Tell me why. Mr. Fairley?"

"Magic's still easier if you know what's going on, sir."

Gareth nodded. "That's part of it. You can pour all the power you want into a broken leg, but if you don't know how the bones are supposed to line up, your patient's likely to end up worse off than before. To put it lightly."

He'd come into his power early, too early to remember his first experiments very clearly at all. Nevertheless, he did recall what he'd been able to do at fourteen and how clumsy it had been in hindsight. Medical school had taught him what to reach for and what to avoid, and Gareth thanked God he hadn't tried anything really serious beforehand. Broken bones, at any rate, were reasonably straightforward.

"That's one reason," he said. "Another reason is that most of you won't use it."

He noted the reactions: Miss Woodwell's skepticism, Fitzpatrick's disappointment. Elizabeth, he noticed, seemed not to care very much one way or the other. She'd been more interested in the pulmonary arteries. Fairley didn't look particularly surprised either. It made sense. They, out of all the students, might most easily have figured out what Gareth was about to say.

"Supernatural healing is an inborn talent, like controlling the weather or floating on air. I have this particular talent. Had it most of my life." Gareth cleared his throat and repressed the urge to run a hand through his hair or to pick up a pen and toy with it as he spoke. He'd never spoken of his abilities so bluntly before, and the words dropped like lead weights onto the floor. "There may well be other people with the same talent. As far as I'm aware, none of you have it. Therefore, there's not much use in talking with you about magical healing."

He stepped back, letting them digest that, and Miss Woodwell raised a hand. Gareth nodded at her.

"Natural talent isn't the only method, though. Sir," she added with a half-rueful grin for which Gareth couldn't fault her. She did make a very odd schoolgirl. "There must be ceremonial magic for healing. It's such a basic sort of a need. I'd bet you anything there are spells in some of the books here, at that."

"It's quite possible," he admitted. "I wouldn't know. I don't have much to do with magic, but I would imagine everything I just said still applies. There is, after all, likely a reason the Grenvilles asked me to teach this class."

Miss Woodwell dropped her eyes. "Of course. Sorry, sir." She looked embarrassed but not cowed, which would have been a relief had Gareth been at all concerned about intimidating her. He thought a cavalry charge would find the task difficult.

It seemed he was to live out his days surrounded by headstrong women. If his sister had ever shown the least interest in magic, Gareth would have suspected a curse.

"Quite all right," he said. "Honestly, as long as you also pay attention here, you could do worse than find those spells. Especially if—" Gareth hesitated, looked at Elizabeth, and then remembered some of the faces he'd seen white with pain and how young they'd been. "Especially considering what you've signed up for. I'd ask Mr. Grenville about them, if I were you."

"Or Mrs. Brightmore," said Elizabeth thoughtfully. "Thank you, sir."

"Yes," said Gareth. He did work with Olivia. There was no changing that, not without treating her badly or leaving himself, neither of which he would do. Therefore, he was not about to flinch whenever anyone spoke her name. "Now, if you and Miss Woodwell would come up here, we can begin the practical part of today's lesson."

As the girls rose, he heard footsteps approaching in the hall outside.

They were light. Probably female. There were a number of women in the house. The person approaching could have been Mrs. Grenville or Mrs. Edgar or one of the maids. However, he was in the room where Olivia had taught, now sitting in the chair he'd started occupying when he'd listened to her, and he couldn't help but wonder.

The footsteps grew closer then stopped just outside the door.

She could come in. Gareth had never said anyone should stay away from his classes. Olivia would make a seventh person, which would let Gareth out of practice-dummy duty, and she could even, perhaps, answer some of the questions about healing with ceremonial magic.

It would be rather nice, actually, if Olivia did decide to join them. Gareth would have the opportunity to prove he could work with her, that he was enough in control of himself to treat her as a colleague without any question of either incivility or...

Outside, the footsteps began again. Whoever it was passed the door, headed down the hall, and was gone.

Gareth fought back the urge to swear.

Chapter 18

MICHAEL OPENED HIS EYES AND RELAXED. "DONE, MA'AM."

Looking out of the large window, Olivia eyed the gray clouds overhead. They were considerably thicker and darker than they'd been ten minutes ago, but no rain was falling yet. "Good," she said and smiled a little. "Again."

"You learn quickly," said Joan, rising from her chair at one end of the ballroom. She eyed Michael for a second, fingers toying with the rose-colored cotton of her skirt. "Do you always work indoors?"

"Mostly, ma'am," Michael said. Under her scrutiny, he'd stood up a little straighter and clasped his hands in front of him.

"Why?"

"Never wanted to get caught out in the rain, ma'am."

A smile flickered across Joan's face. "Sensible. But now it doesn't have to rain, so…" She shrugged. "Ever been around animals when you used your power?"

Michael frowned in thought. "We had a cat," he said slowly. "When I was little. She never minded, not as far as I remember. I was in the stables once or twice too."

"Did you ride?" Joan asked. When Michael nodded, she made a brief thoughtful noise and then turned to Olivia. "Can you?"

"I—yes," Olivia said. Once, it had come as naturally to her as walking. That had been before Tom, before London, before Lyddie or Hawkins or Madame Marguerite. "But it's been quite some time."

"That shouldn't be a problem. Take him out and have him try a few things on horseback. One of the advantages of natural talent," Joan went on, "is you can do things quickly in a variety of situations. Or you should be able to."

"Absolutely," Olivia said. For a moment she was simply relieved she could put Michael on a new path before he got bored with the old one. Then she realized what she'd agreed to. "Ah," she said, "I don't—"

"I'll lend you some clothing. You can get more made in the village later, but this is sudden, I know. I'd do it myself, only I've apparently got to deal with Society for a few days"—Joan made a face—"and I want to move quickly."

"I can't say I'm surprised," Olivia couldn't resist saying.

Joan laughed. "No, I didn't think you would be. Let me know how it goes, and good luck."

A day and a half of hasty alterations and severe second thoughts followed. Ten years, Olivia realized fairly quickly, was a long time. She didn't have the reflexes she'd had at sixteen, nor would her bones mend as quickly if she took a fall. And she would have to divide her concentration between riding and observing Michael.

More than once, she considered making her excuses, but this was her job and she *could* ride and everything would more than likely go smoothly. Besides, if Joan had to deal with Society, chances were good that Mr. Grenville would be busy too, and the only possible substitute for Olivia would then be St. John. She'd be damned if she let him know she was unsure of herself.

Therefore, she showed up at the stables on a cold and clear morning, wearing a coat and scarf that thankfully covered the worst alterations to Joan's riding habit, and allowed one of the grooms to help her onto the back of a small gray gelding.

Once seated, she found to her great relief her body remembered the right pose. Memories came back along with it. Once she'd cantered down the paths of her father's estate, leaving cousins and governesses behind. Once, she'd ridden up hills and across streams with no more thought than she'd given to pouring tea. That had been ten years ago, but Olivia thought now she was equal to a calm walk down the flat paths by the gardens.

Michael sat his bay pony with ease, helped considerably, Olivia suspected, by the fact that he was also sitting astride and wearing breeches. He showed an inclination to trot at first, which Olivia thought best to indulge for a bit. She sent him off to "let the horse get some exercise" and took the opportunity to accustom herself a bit more to her own mount, not to mention her clothing. Joan's habit had been taken in considerably in some places and let out almost as much in others, and it was still uncomfortably snug across her breasts.

After a slow walk around one of the fountains and a few deep breaths—not too deep, considering the circumstances—Olivia felt considerably more equal to the task ahead of her. The scenery was an unexpected pleasure too, for all that it was late autumn. The hedges were well kept, framing the graceful fountains and statues in rich dark green. She could smell wood smoke in the air, a cozy, comforting sort of scent.

A few minutes later, Michael returned, reluctant but not as much so as he might have been in other circumstances. "Do you want me to start now, ma'am?"

"When you feel ready," Olivia said. "See if you can make it more or less overcast." The sky above was mostly blue, the clouds floating across it puffy and white. It was a pity to change it, really. Clear days were rare enough at this time of year, but business was business, and it would clear up afterward if everything went right. "Still no rain, though."

"You don't have to tell me, ma'am," said Michael cheerfully. "I'm out here, aren't I?" As Olivia laughed, he looked up at the sky and began to concentrate. The horses, to Olivia's relief, showed no signs of panic. Both stood still, tails swishing, and Michael's bent its head to sniff at one of the fountains.

Overhead, the puffy clouds bloated and grew. It was happening much faster than it had in the past, Olivia thought. Being outdoors did help, then. Not really surprising, given the nature of Michael's power. She glanced back down at him—

And saw his face go rigid with fear.

"Michael?" She spoke calmly, or tried to. His eyes were open now, but Olivia didn't think he was seeing her. She wasn't sure he was seeing anything. His stare was glassy, and his face still turned upward.

The clouds were huge now, blotting out half the sky, and almost black. Around them, the wind picked up, clutching at Olivia's scarf and hat. The horses' manes and tails streamed. The horses shied, particularly

Michael's pony, aggravated by its rider's sudden tension. Somehow, unconsciously, he clung to the saddle.

Rain began to fall, a rain so cold and stinging Olivia almost thought it was hail at first. Within a matter of moments, her hat and coat were soaked, and the gelding was whinnying in distress. Olivia nudged him in the side, trying to get him over toward Michael and keep him calm at the same time. She wished Charlotte were there.

The wind was howling now. "Michael!" Olivia raised her voice and let it take on an edge. "Michael, send it away. Now!"

She saw it in Michael's eyes when he came back to himself a little. "Mrs. Brightmore," he said, and his voice was slurred. "Trying…too much…too easy."

"Let go, then." Somewhere in the distance, people were shouting. There might have been figures running toward them. The wind snatched her hat off, sent it whirling away. "Just let go." God willing, Nature would right itself when Michael wasn't trying to clutch at it.

He gulped and nodded, and then screamed. "Move!"

Instinct alone made Olivia respond, since she had no idea why or, for that matter, where she was supposed to be going. She dug her heels into the gelding's sides again, dimly feeling the hairs on the back of her neck stand up, and the horse bolted forward—

Then the world went white.

Some part of Olivia's mind retained enough control to think *lightning*, and to know that she and Michael had escaped the bolt. The rest of her just sat, numb, as the gelding reared and bucked. She didn't have time to feel either fear or pain as she fell, not even when she landed and something snapped in her ankle.

She simply lay there, in the cold mud, with white and violet spots dancing in front of her vision, and wondered what had happened.

Chapter 19

THE RAIN WAS GARETH'S WARNING AGAIN.

If he hadn't known about Fairley's powers, he might have started to believe in omens. This one would have been particularly bad. The sky had been blue one minute and pitch-black the next, and freezing rain had fallen in a sudden downpour that made Gareth pity anyone caught out in it. As prophecy, it would probably have meant war or some other great disaster.

As a manifestation of Fairley's will, it didn't bode very well either, though the damage would likely be confined to Englefield. Gareth still didn't like it.

He was halfway down the hall when he heard a sharp crack. At first he didn't recognize the sound. Then, as a loud boom followed it, he blinked and thought *thunderstorm*. Not too surprising, given the clouds. Very surprising, given November. Surprising even for Fairley.

The boy was supposed to be getting better. Olivia was supposed to be keeping him under some kind of control. And his power had never gotten away from him as Elizabeth's had. Gareth shook his head at the empty hallway then started walking again, his boots loud on the polished floors.

One of the maids was crying somewhere in the neighboring rooms, and the footman Gareth passed looked considerably white around the lips. Someone certainly needed to have a word with Fairley, perhaps a harsher word than Olivia had managed.

He strode into the front hall, ready to round the turn to his office and slam the door behind him, and then stopped. Froze, really.

There was a small clump of people coming through the door. Michael was near the front, and Gareth dimly noticed he was paper white, his eyes huge and frightened. Perhaps there was more to this storm than temper, then. The thought was vague. Other things pushed it to the background. Mostly Olivia.

A man, one of the stable hands, Gareth thought, was carrying her. Rain and mud had soaked through her clothes, her wet hair hung down around her face in dark strands, and most importantly, her face was as blanched as Michael's. There was pain in her expression, not just fear.

"What happened?" He was speaking even as he stared at Olivia and moving at the same time to open his office door. "What's wrong?"

Michael and the stable hand began to speak at once, looked at each other, then hesitated. For a second, Gareth thought he might give a black eye to one or both.

"I think my ankle's broken," said Olivia. She sounded breathless, but she kept her voice fairly level. The effort that took was obvious. "I'll explain the rest of it later."

"Damn the rest of it," Gareth snapped and cast a quick look over Fairley. "Are you well?"

The boy swallowed. "Yes. Sir."

"Not really," Olivia said and then winced, and went back to biting her lip.

"You shouldn't be talking," said Gareth. Somehow

they'd made it into his inner office. "Waste of strength when you're injured. Fairley, get dried off and have something hot to drink. I'll take a look at you later." The boy left, moving at half his usual speed but neither limping nor bleeding.

Olivia grimaced, though Gareth suspected it was as much a reaction to pain as to him. "It's just a broken ankle," she said sharply. "They're not usually—*hssst*—mortal."

It was best, Gareth decided, not to dignify that with a response. He gestured to the long couch against one of his walls. "Put her down there, please. Gently," he said to the stable hand. Then, without thinking, he stepped forward and slipped his arm under Olivia's knees. "More stable with two."

"Sir," the other man replied. He didn't sound as if he understood entirely, but he moved, which was the important thing.

"Thank you," Gareth said once they'd gotten Olivia settled. "You may go now."

"You've been very helpful," Olivia added. "Thank you." She glanced at Gareth as the stable hand left, closing the door behind him. "I can talk, you know."

"Well, don't," said Gareth. "It's distracting." He knelt to examine her ankle, getting both skirt and shoe out of the way without concerning himself with propriety. Olivia didn't seem inclined to scream or faint, at any rate, not for reasons of etiquette. She did flinch when he touched her ankle, though. "Sorry. You know I'll have to set this."

He didn't look up. Her quick intake of breath was enough to stab him in the heart and so was the forced steadiness in her voice when she spoke. "Best do it quickly, then."

It would have been better, in a way, if she'd cried and carried on, or gotten demanding and petulant.

Gareth turned his attention firmly to the ankle, trying to consider the injury separate from the woman: one fairly simple fracture, no complications or puncturing of the skin, no apparent blood vessels severed. He took a breath, reminded himself he'd once been used to doing far more complicated and dangerous injuries daily, and brought the ends of the bone in line with each other.

From further back on the couch, he heard nails dig into fabric.

He switched his vision then, almost automatically. The lines of force that made up Olivia in Gareth's magical sight were a warm amber color, mostly. Gareth could spot the rising bruises, oddly enough, paler than their surroundings when he looked at a person this way. And, most importantly, the snapped lines around her ankle. Nothing tangled. He'd done his work well there.

As he'd done so many times before, he reached with his power for the loose ends. They came to him more easily than he'd expected or he'd remembered from other times and people. Perhaps it was long practice. Perhaps it was that Olivia had more control than most over her response. Perhaps she knew what he was going to do and didn't fear it. Any or all of those factors could have explained the newfound ease.

None of them really accounted for what happened next.

Connection was the only word Gareth could think of for it, particularly in that instant, when he almost froze with surprise. He reached to tie his energy in to Olivia's, only to find no tying was necessary, no effort. Her life force reached to meet his. His mind interpreted the contact as an unexpected warmth. The whole sensation was like extending a hand for a stiff greeting and finding himself in an embrace.

Most such embraces, in the real world, would have been uncomfortable. Gareth easily saw how the magical equivalent could be so—worse, likely enough, if the other party lacked scruples. Half-remembered stories came back to him, mentions of succubi and vampires. He'd given his vital energy dozens of times, and the worst he'd ever suffered was three days of lethargy, but he'd always been in control of the process. If Olivia pulled on the connection…

But she didn't.

As close as he was to her, Gareth was certain she wouldn't. She didn't give him her own energy either, and so he thought the situation was probably as unexpected to her as it was to him. For a little while they stayed still, simply joined.

Best not to let his mind dwell on that fact too long. The last thing he needed was to start considering symbolism. He had a job to do. They could sort the rest out later.

Although Olivia didn't give him any energy directly, her participation, half-conscious as it might have been, was surprisingly helpful when the healing actually began. There was no sensation, as there usually was, of reaching or pulling, of coaxing uncooperative elements along or nudging them out of the way. Everything went quickly and easily, until Gareth blinked back into normal vision and found himself kneeling by the couch, feeling far less drained than was generally the case for far more trivial injuries.

To make sure he'd done everything right, he took another look at Olivia's ankle. It lay straight and unswollen, and the few bruises he could see had already begun to fade.

Without thinking, Gareth let his gaze travel up the straight, slim line of her leg. Her disarranged and rather badly fitting riding habit left it well outlined, particularly as she lay on the couch. The fabric clung to her, in fact, clearly showing the curve of her hips. It took a moment for Gareth to realize it was damp, and to remember Olivia's condition when the stable hand had brought her in.

He was a beast, really. Normally healing would have left him too tired to notice a woman's figure. He'd have to be careful now. Gareth cleared his throat. "I'm sorry. You must be cold."

"No." Olivia sounded surprised and a little dazed. "I should be. I was, but not anymore." Then she laughed and started to sit up. "Abusing your furniture horribly, though, I suspect, and probably anything but presentable." She pushed back her hair absently.

The laugh had been almost normal, perhaps a little high, nothing at all obvious, but her hand was shaking. "No, stay there for a moment," Gareth said. Without thinking, he reached out to stop her. His hand landed on her leg just below the knee.

Beneath his palm, her bare skin was warm and very soft. They held still for a few seconds, though Gareth's hand ached to move, to glide up and under the hem of Olivia's disarranged skirt. His cock just ached.

Gareth started to back away. He moved too late and too slowly to pretend he was anything but reluctant to stop touching her, even if his body had let him. Still, he knew he should. Then Olivia leaned forward and reached out. One slim hand skimmed up Gareth's chest, found the lapel of his coat, and pulled him to her.

The idea of resisting didn't cross Gareth's mind until much, much later. He went willingly, bending over her, finding some space on the sofa and getting one arm behind her head. She'd moved, she had to have, but he neither knew nor cared about the exact logistics. Then he took her mouth. It was as hot and as silky as he remembered, and Olivia arched upward against him when they kissed. If it hadn't been for her damn corset, he could have felt every inch of her through her clothes. As it was, she was soft and sweet and warm, and his erection was right against the juncture of her thighs, all quite enough temptation.

Then she wriggled against him, caught her breath at the sensation…and did it again.

Gareth thought he might have sworn, or maybe just growled. He knew he spread one hand over Olivia's bottom, pulling her closer, yet even as his hips jerked forward, and he heard her moan deep in her throat when he ground against her. Her legs parted, as much as her skirt would allow, and she rocked back up against him, finding his rhythm and matching it

There were many buttons on the top of Olivia's riding habit, not to mention everything beneath it. Too much to handle just then, far too much. So Gareth simply cupped one of her breasts in his free hand, hating the layers between his skin and hers, pressing gently and then a little harder as the sounds coming from Olivia's mouth continued to express pleasure. He brought his other hand up to do the same and rubbed, small circles, just as he rubbed his cock between her thighs—

Until she stiffened, suddenly, and cried out into his mouth, and a wave of color swept over her face and neck. Her hips jerked against him once, twice, then again, and Gareth nearly spent himself then and there.

He pulled away from her again. Not much. Just enough to start undoing his trouser buttons with one hand, the other pushing her skirt up, sliding over her leg like he'd wanted to do in the first place. Damned distracting, trying to do both at once, but he felt no inclination to stop touching her, particularly as she showed no inclination to stop him. She was breathing hard in the aftermath of her climax, and watching the rapid rise and fall of her breasts was enough to make Gareth yank the rest of the buttons open, hearing threads break and not caring. His fingers reached her thigh, slid farther up to feel wetness and soft hair, and Olivia made another of those maddening noises in her throat.

And then there was a knock at the door.

Chapter 20

NONE OF THE WORDS GARETH USED WERE EXACTLY NEW TO Olivia, not after ten years in a not-precisely genteel neighborhood of London, but she hadn't ever heard them in such close proximity. One had to give the man credit, though. He kept the profanity under his breath. Given the circumstances, Olivia wouldn't have blamed him if he'd sworn at the top of his lungs.

She found the idea rather tempting herself.

Nonetheless, she didn't say anything, only lay still and managed not to protest as Gareth drew his hand out from under her skirt then got to his feet. Several of his trouser buttons had come off, and his arousal was still quite apparent behind the ones that remained. She felt another pulse of heat between her legs, an echo of her earlier crisis and the excitement that had been starting to build again.

Another knock.

"Yes?" She and Gareth answered as one, and neither of them sounded particularly patient.

There was a longish pause. Then: "Um. It's Violet, sir, ma'am. Mrs. Grenville asked me to come and see if Mrs. Brightmore was all right."

Olivia raised herself gingerly from the couch, supporting herself on one of the arms until she found out her ankle would bear her. She didn't look at Gareth. "Yes, thank you. Dr. St. John's been very helpful."

At least she'd remembered to call him by his title and last name when she spoke. Her mind, apparently, had decided it was absurd to keep thinking of the man that way, considering what had just passed between them. Considering what had just passed between them, Olivia told herself, was a horrible idea just now.

After a moment of silence, Violet continued. "Oh. Um, in that case, she says you're to join her and Mr. Grenville in the drawing room. In about an hour. Mrs. Brightmore, we've some dry clothes upstairs, if you can walk, and we're running a bath."

"I'll be right out," she said.

"Let the Grenvilles know I'll join them shortly," said Gareth. Olivia couldn't resist glancing over her shoulder at him, and saw he was sitting at his desk and staring fixedly out the window. His hands were flat on the top of the desk pressing hard. She didn't want to think about the urges he was resisting.

Really, she did. That was the problem.

Olivia made a few quick adjustments to her dress and opened the door. The accident would explain any lingering disarray.

It was a good thing she did have an appointment downstairs, or she might have lingered in the bath, retracing the path of Gareth's hands on her body and remembering the moments of mindless pleasure she'd felt when she'd rubbed herself against him.

Needless to say, Olivia told herself, she hadn't entirely been in her right mind to begin with. She'd heard of great fear producing certain reactions afterward, excess energy and survival instinct and all that. She would have responded the same way to any halfway attractive man, probably, and she'd found Gareth handsome as soon as they'd met. Fortunately, and a little amusingly, he was also the least troublesome of the men at Englefield in a way, being neither married nor too young nor a servant.

Besides, there'd been that odd connection when he'd mended her ankle. It hadn't been sensual at the time. She'd been in too much pain to register anything like pleasure, but she'd been aware of the contact between their energies. That had probably played into the attraction she'd felt.

There were explanations for everything. Moreover, they'd been interrupted, thank God, before anything more could happen, and it wouldn't happen again. So there was nothing to worry about.

That is, nothing except looking him in the face next time they met.

Olivia rinsed her hair, toweled off, and told herself not to be a ninny. Gareth was a man of the world and a man of some experience, obviously, and she was no debutante. She bit her lip at the memory of his hands, knowing and firm and urgent. Things had happened. Life went on.

She'd made paying audiences think she could summon the dead and float crystal balls around. Keeping her countenance around one man should not, would not, be a problem. Even so, she chose the plainest of her black skirts and a high-collared shirtwaist in dark gray and pinned her hair up in the primmest knot she could manage.

At times like these, a woman did need some armor.

—◆◆◆—

Everyone else was already in the drawing room when Olivia walked in: the Grenvilles on one of the couches, Gareth straight-backed on the edge of a chair, and Michael, whom she hadn't expected, perched on another. Michael and the men rose as Olivia entered, and everyone looked at her.

The Grenvilles, to her relief, seemed only polite and curious. Gareth met her eyes soberly and squarely. His hands moved slightly on the arms of his chair, fingers flexing, but his face was a very careful blank. Michael, on the other hand, let out what sounded like an hour's worth of held breath, then gulped and flushed and looked down at his shoes.

While Olivia found a seat, everyone was silent, her footsteps on the carpet were the only sound, and then the rustle of her skirt as she sat. Even such small noises seemed obtrusive. The atmosphere felt solid and fragile all at once, like cut glass.

"Well," she said and smiled at Michael. "Nobody's come to any great harm, it seems, and now we know something we didn't before. Not a bad afternoon on the whole, I'd say, though I hope none of the horses were hurt."

"No," said Mr. Grenville. "A little frightened, but that's all."

"An apt description for everyone involved, then," Olivia replied.

"I'm sorry, ma'am," said Michael, dragging his head up so he met her eyes. "I didn't mean to. I'd *never* have meant to do anything like that."

Olivia reached over and patted his shoulder. "Of course you didn't," she said briskly. "I saw you, remember? If you knew what you were doing, you'd have to have been a remarkable actor indeed to have looked *that* scared. Furthermore, I told you to—"

"And I told you," said Joan.

Mr. Grenville smiled. "Perhaps Gareth's the only one of us who shouldn't be castigating himself this afternoon."

Briefly, Gareth's fingers tightened on the arms of his chair. "I'm sure I can think of something to regret," he said and did not look at Olivia.

The door opened again before anyone else could speak, and hopefully before anyone but Olivia noticed the slightly husky tone in Gareth's voice. One of the footmen came through, carrying a silver tea tray. Pouring and serving broke some of the tension. Michael in particular seemed heartened, though whether that was due more to the words or the sandwiches and cakes, Olivia couldn't say. For a thirteen-year-old boy, it was probably a fairly close race.

"The question is," Mr. Grenville said once the footman had left, "what exactly happened, and why? Michael, how much do you remember?"

"Most of it, sir. It's…a bit hard to put in words, though." Michael toyed with one of his crusts.

"Do your best," said Mr. Grenville. "We'll figure out the rest of it."

Michael took a deep breath. "All right. I started to try to reach the clouds, like Mrs. Brightmore told me to do. And I did. Only I went…too far, maybe?" His forehead wrinkled. "It was like I meant to whisper and wound up shouting instead. Only it took me a bit to stop shouting once I realized I was doing it, and then I'd, um, woken things up."

"Was it you shouting?" Joan asked, leaning forward. "Or was it something acting through you?"

"Me, ma'am. I didn't really know what I was doing, but it was me." Michael looked down at his plate again.

Joan relaxed back against the couch. "That's something."

"Gareth," Mr. Grenville said, "have you had a chance to look at Fairley?"

Gareth nodded. "Shortly before we came in here. There's nothing physically wrong with him. He's in excellent health."

"Good," said Mr. Grenville, and Michael looked considerably relieved as well. Mr. Grenville hesitated for a moment and then went on. "I can think of a few reasons someone might use more power than he intended. Splitting his attention between the magical task at hand and controlling a horse, for example, one of the things we were originally attempting to test. You're looking doubtful, Fairley."

"It didn't feel like being distracted, sir," Michael said.

"Distraction doesn't always," said Mr. Grenville slowly, "but that's certainly a point away from the first theory. Another factor could be, well, your age." He coughed and picked up a sandwich. "That may be something you should discuss with Gareth when the ladies are gone."

A brief, awkward silence ensued, in which Joan rolled her eyes, Olivia tactfully pretended to consider her teacup, and Michael turned red again.

"The third possibility," said Mr. Grenville, "is location. Have you worked outside before?"

Olivia shook her head just as Michael replied, "Not

here, sir. At home, once in a while, but not most of the time. Nothing ever happened there."

"It might not," said Olivia, looking over at Mr. Grenville. "We talked about the forest before, you know. The gardens are tolerably close, and if there's any kind of effect, the rest of the land might share in it to some degree. Magic doesn't have terribly strict borders most of the time."

Mrs. Grenville lifted her eyebrows and shrugged. "Could be," she said and then smiled. "I hear men see strange things there."

"On occasion," said Mr. Grenville with a smile of his own. Olivia decided to pour herself some more tea and noticed Gareth seemed to need another biscuit as well.

She looked across the table at Gareth, intending to be businesslike, and ended up noticing the line of his neck, almost golden against his white collar. "Have you," she asked, trying to keep her voice brisk, "ever been in places where it was easier to use your talent? Or harder, I suppose?"

"I haven't exactly kept records," Gareth said, immediate and curt. He looked slowly from Olivia to Mr. Grenville to Michael, then, and sighed. "But there might have been a place or two. Possibly. Nothing as showy. Then again—"

"You have a great deal of practice in not being showy," said Mr. Grenville.

"Right," said Gareth. "And it wouldn't have manifested. I mean, healing is self-limiting."

"Sometimes," said Joan. "You got off lucky that way." She grimaced, and the others followed suit as unpleasant alternatives came to their minds.

Olivia finished off a sandwich, her third, but it wasn't exactly a formal party, and she was unexpectedly hungry. Terror and lust, she supposed, would do that. Certainly Gareth had put away most of a plate. "It seems to me," she said, "we should try a few tests. Only, less dangerous tests."

"How?" Joan asked. "Fairley's dangerous. Donnell'd be worse, floating off the way she does." The room collectively shuddered at the thought. "And Woodwell's talent isn't internal and wouldn't increase in power even if it was. I guess you could always cut yourself and see how much it takes out of Dr. St. John when he heals you."

"Perhaps as a last resort," Mr. Grenville said while Olivia blinked and Gareth coughed.

"I was thinking perhaps ceremonial magic rather than natural talents," Olivia said. "If there's a thinning in the world in the forest or a nexus point of power, it should influence all sorts of magic. Ceremonial's much easier to control. That is, it's easier to find spells that won't do much damage if they do get away from the caster."

Mr. Grenville nodded. "At the very least," he said, "I think it's time to more seriously investigate the forest. You and I, St. John, and Mrs. Brightmore." He said to Joan, "If you don't mind keeping the students in line while we're out." She nodded briskly. "Perhaps, Miss Woodwell as well. The wild beasts might know something we don't. We'll set out tomorrow, weather permitting."

"Meanwhile," said Joan, "keep any experiments indoors. Nobody's died from that so far."

Chapter 21

"DAMN."

Olivia hadn't expected profanity from Mr. Grenville, and certainly not at the breakfast table. Neither had almost anyone else. There had been only the one word, and it had been quiet, almost a whisper, but it had nonetheless made most people catch their breath. Even the footman paused for a second. At the other end of the table, Joan was watching her husband too, but she didn't look at all surprised.

Worried, yes. Olivia couldn't blame her.

Mr. Grenville was staring at a buff-colored slip of paper: a telegram. His lips were a thin line with a little bit of whiteness around them. Olivia wasn't certain he knew he'd sworn, or spoken at all, for that matter.

Bad news. Urgent *bad news.* Olivia thought of death, of disgrace, of financial ruin, and glanced quickly across the table to Gareth before she realized what she was doing. He'd started taking breakfast with her and the Grenvilles in the last few days, for some reason, though he never talked much. Now Olivia was glad of it. He knew Mr. Grenville far better than she did.

But Gareth looked back with as much confusion as she felt.

It was late fall, almost winter, and the wind whistled outside. The sunshine was deceptively bright through the windows. The silver was old, and the food was rich, but Olivia remembered a small flat in London and the taste of dry toast. She'd left a piece half-eaten when the doctor had come downstairs to inform her of her husband's death. It had been summer then.

Very carefully, she put down her teacup.

"Simon?" Joan's voice was both steady and steadying. "What's wrong?"

Mr. Grenville looked up and let out a breath, only now seeming to focus on his surroundings. "Nothing. Nobody we know. It's from Gillespie." He glanced over at Olivia, who held herself very still, then back at Joan. "He wants us to come up to London."

Joan lifted her eyebrows. "I'm guessing not a social visit."

"No. Not at all. It's that business in Whitechapel."

The stillness around the table changed, transmuted into something both less and more fearful, relief that the news wasn't worse, dread of what might yet happen. Even out at Englefield, the papers had been very informative. The previous day's in particular.

Olivia picked up her teacup again, mostly to have something to do with her hands. She didn't realize where she was looking until she met Gareth's eyes again. No answers waited there, nor had she expected any, but there was comfort in his gaze nonetheless. It helped to know she wasn't the only stunned bystander in the room.

"I told you before," Joan said, forehead wrinkling, "I don't recognize anything in this Ripper but a madman who's managed to find some easy targets in an awful neighborhood. What does Gillespie think we're going to find?"

"Perhaps nothing. Perhaps he wants only to confirm that we *are* dealing with a human here and not one with any particular powers. Or, perhaps not." Mr. Grenville smiled a little, without much humor in it. "It's rather difficult to read a man's mood in a telegram, you know."

"So we'll have to wait until we get to London. Which means I'd better start packing." Joan rose from the table, glanced over her shoulder, and added, "St. John? Olivia? You'll have to manage the forest without us. Woodwell should be able to get you in and out if the maps fail."

"We could wait—" Gareth began.

"You shouldn't," said Joan.

"It's probably best not to take any chances," Mr. Grenville added, "given what's already happened. If anything out there could affect this household, we'll need to know."

"We'll head out today, then," said Olivia. She picked up her tea and drank but didn't taste anything. Responsibility felt like a lead cloak on her shoulders.

———

"It should take a few days. A week at most. I'll certainly write if we're delayed any longer." Simon prowled the library, three volumes in his arms already, and frowned dubiously down at a fourth. "You can write as well. Brooks has my address."

As he turned to cross the room again, Gareth stepped to the side, then took refuge against the windowsill. His leg wouldn't permit much more dodging. Neither would his dignity. "I doubt I'll have to," he said.

Simon paused. "I don't know what's in that forest

or what Michael's display yesterday afternoon might
have awakened. I do know I'm leaving you and Mrs.
Brightmore with five students and the servants to
keep safe. The killings in London are likely the fault
of a human, probably without any magic at all, and
I very much doubt there's anything human in the
forest other than a few poachers. And they won't be
the danger.

"If women weren't dead, I'd much rather stay here
and keep a watch on Englefield."

Gareth sighed and shook his head. "No. No, that's
fair. I just wish you'd more information going in than
three lines from some...who is this man?"

"Gillespie?" Simon chuckled. "It's somewhat difficult to describe him. He's a bookseller, let's say, and
a magician. He was the one who recommended Mrs.
Brightmore to us."

A month ago, Gareth would have made a snide comment: *That's certainly a mark of distinction*, or something similar. He could feel the shape of it now in the
back of his head, but other things seemed more important. "Oh? How does he know her?"

"She was his student for some years. Other than
that, it's not my business to tell. You could ask Mrs.
Brightmore about it, if you're curious."

"You assume she'd tell me," said Gareth.

Simon grinned suddenly, a man who'd found a welcome distraction, if a momentary one. "Oh, I think she
would, at the right moment," he said. "You get along
very well when you forget to dislike each other."

<p style="text-align:center">~~~</p>

"I don't think we'll have too much trouble," said Olivia, trying to sound like she believed it.

Not just for her own image. The Grenvilles did a decent job at hiding their feelings, Joan a little more so than her husband, but Olivia had spent enough time reading strange faces that familiar ones were easy. She saw worry there, and while she couldn't do anything about what they went to face in London, she could ease their minds about what they'd leave behind.

"I'm sure you'll all live," said Joan, "and I don't give a damn about anything else. Will you be leaving after we do? For the forest?"

Olivia nodded. "Mrs. Edgar's watching Elizabeth and Michael, and the boys are old enough to be left by themselves for a few hours. Charlotte's out at the stables, waiting for me and Dr. St. John."

"Be careful," said Mr. Grenville, "but you know as much as I do, more in certain areas, and I wouldn't be leaving if I didn't think you could cope with the situation. I thought you should know that."

"'Be bold, be bold, but not too bold,'" Olivia quoted. Even so, hearing Mr. Grenville's opinion lifted some of the invisible weight that had settled on her shoulders and in the pit of her stomach.

The three of them stood in the hall, the Grenvilles wrapped tightly in winter travelling clothes, the servants bustling around them with baggage. Most of it was gone already. There wasn't much time left. Olivia couldn't think of anything she'd forgotten to ask about, or to say, but she was certain there was something.

"Just send the students into the ballroom for combat training," Joan said. "Waite, Woodwell, and Fitzpatrick at one, Fairley and Donnell at three. Look in from time to time to make sure they haven't actually killed one another, but they know what to do."

The door behind them opened. Olivia heard the sound and knew Gareth would be coming out, but she couldn't keep herself from glancing over her shoulder to make sure. Their eyes met for a second. Olivia expected the challenge she found in his expression, but was surprised to see camaraderie as well. *We're in this together*, his face seemed to say. *I'll do my part as long as you can manage yours.*

Gareth crossed the room quickly, long legs covering a great deal of ground even with his limp, and came to stand beside her.

"Good luck," he said to Mr. Grenville, holding out a hand. "We'll keep the place standing for you."

"Good man," said Mr. Grenville and shook hands heartily. "Remember what I said."

In some ways, Olivia thought, the parting was ludicrous. The Grenvilles would be gone less than a fortnight, and yet they, as well as Olivia and Gareth, were acting as though it would be months before they returned. An observer would have laughed.

An observer wouldn't know what took the Grenvilles to London or what sort of danger might wait for them despite all their protestations. Even Olivia didn't know precisely. She'd seen glimpses of places and creatures when scrying, read cramped and obscure passages in books. She'd heard a few very dark stories. Nothing very probable, perhaps, but the possibilities were bad enough.

What waited in the forest might be worse.

"Have a safe journey," she said at the last, not knowing what else she could say. "And a safe trip."

A few more parting words, a few more bows and handshakes, and then they were gone in a flurry of November wind. The door closed behind them.

Olivia took a breath, turned back, and looked up at Gareth. "Well," she said rather inadequately. "We should probably meet Charlotte, shouldn't we?"

Chapter 22

WHILE THEY MET AT THE STABLES, IT WAS JUST A CONVENIENT place. They didn't ride. "I'm not risking another incident on horseback," said Olivia, "no matter what you can tell the horse in question, Charlotte."

"Oh, I can't tell them anything if they're too scared," Miss Woodwell said, shaking her head and rolling her eyes in a way that was almost equine itself. "They're a great deal like people, you know. Have you ever had much luck telling a man not to be stupid if something's frightening him?"

"I can't say I've tried," Olivia said.

"I have," said Gareth, not letting himself dwell on that particular memory, "and you're right. Shall we?"

Miss Woodwell grinned. "Absolutely. Except…will you be all right, Dr. St. John?"

Gareth lifted his walking stick. "I should be, with this. Quite possibly better than I would be riding."

Olivia was carrying a stick too, but hers would never have done for walking. It was slim, polished, and about the length of her forearm. There were symbols carved along its length, letters that looked somehow Arabic and runic at the same time. *Wand* was the appropriate word, probably.

"I never saw you use that before," said Gareth.

"I generally haven't needed it. Or any other tools. Words and patterns have mostly sufficed for anything that's come up here."

They walked down the road toward the forest, with the wind plucking at their coats and hats and the sun bright in their eyes. Gareth turned his head a little, which also gave him an excuse to watch Olivia. He wasn't sure if that was an advantage or not.

He'd tried not to think about her, not to remember the taste of her mouth, the way her body had felt against his, soft and firm, or the sounds she'd made at the height of her passion. Sometimes he succeeded. Mostly he failed, particularly at night and in the morning, when he surrendered to memory and the partial relief of his hand.

Now he looked across at her, her face flushed and shining above her brown cloak, and felt desire and, more dangerously, simple admiration. Particularly when she turned her head and smiled.

"I forgot how pleasant it could be," she said, "wandering about in the autumn."

"Oh, rather," said Miss Woodwell and laughed. "My nurses never liked it as much. I used to sneak out. To tell the truth, I used to slip my leash any chance I could get, any season of the year. But I always liked autumn best."

"It must have been different outside of England," Olivia said.

"Autumn, yes. Me, no. I never really reformed, you understand, just outgrew the bonds after a while. Englefield's pleasant enough to make me behave, though. I couldn't ask for anything better, except maybe the sea."

Olivia nodded. "You were born on the coast, you said."

"Born and raised on *some* coast or another. Near Millbay, and Cairo, and then Ramsgate. Now Ramsgate,

I suppose…This boarding business makes it deuced difficult to say where you do live, doesn't it? But I've always been near the water till now. You too, I suppose."

"Yes. Not the sea, but some sort of water." Olivia turned toward Gareth a little, guarding her eyes from the sun. "And you?"

"Not growing up. My father always said God made the sea to try men's courage. My mother said he meant his constitution." Gareth smiled, remembering. "Her brother was in the navy. I'd imagine a woman could hate the sea on that account, but she always seemed rather fond of it. On holidays and such."

"Was your father religious," Miss Woodwell asked, "or just, um, poetic?"

"Both, I think," said Gareth. "He was a vicar. Still is, I suppose. He's getting ready to step down."

That had caused another moment of dislocation when he'd gone home. Of course men did retire, even men of the cloth, and of course it had been some time. Gareth hadn't expected the man to go on eternally, changelessly preaching on Sundays and frowning over his sermons on Saturday nights. It had just been…odd to have proof he wouldn't. Odder than his own changes, in a way. He'd accepted he was no longer the young man he had been, but he'd been unprepared to find changes in his world as well.

"And you were in the army," said Olivia, thoughtfully. "That's three of us with some connection."

"Common enough for younger sons, certainly," said Gareth, "even in this day and age."

Miss Woodwell cocked her head, sparrowlike, and peered at Gareth. "I'd no notion you'd served too, though I should've guessed. Somewhere rough, was it?"

"Egypt," he said, "and then the Sudan. Trouble enough, even for a surgeon, and I saw the worst of it only secondhand."

"Bad enough, I should think! Papa got reassigned before things got very bad, but we heard plenty of stories. How about you, Mrs. Brightmore? Foreign lands and interesting chaps trying to shoot you?"

Olivia shook her head. "I might have gone with my husband," she said. Her voice was no longer cheerful but matter-of-fact and brisk. "But he never went himself. He fell ill shortly after we came to London."

"Oh," said Miss Woodwell, looking chagrined. "Should've put a bridle on my tongue, shouldn't I?"

Again, Olivia shook her head, the fabric of her hood rippling around her face. "I brought it up, really. Besides, he's been at rest for years now." She smiled. "At my age, one is bound to have lost a few people. It's neither a shock nor an affront when I find them connected to the conversation."

"You've got about thirty years to go before you're allowed to start saying 'at my age,'" said Miss Woodwell.

Olivia laughed. "Spend enough time around Mr. Fairley and anyone will feel decrepit," she said. "Not that the rest of your fellow pupils are much less disturbing on that account."

"The lady speaks truth," said Gareth. He didn't intend his words to have a double meaning, but Olivia's gaze was wary for a second when she looked at him. "As a gentleman and the oldest member of the party," he added, "I suppose it's my duty to grow a long white beard now and provide relative comfort to both of you."

The women laughed at that. "I'd prefer you didn't,"

said Olivia. Gareth thought only he saw her relax a little. He was almost certainly the only one to feel relief when she did.

A few more steps on a narrower road, and the forest enclosed the three of them.

———ᴥ———

Nothing about the forest *felt* different to Olivia. The shade made it even chillier than the road had been, a chill balanced somewhat by the fact that the trees shielded them from the wind, but that was all. She couldn't see anything that would have been out of place in any other forest, certainly neither lightning nor strange animals, nor could she hear anything strange, though they walked in silence for a quarter hour.

Then, when Olivia could barely make out the path behind them, she stopped to dig out the map Mr. Grenville had given them. She glanced quickly at Gareth and Charlotte, but their faces held only the same blank look she suspected was on hers. Olivia shrugged, half responding to them and half to herself.

"After all," she said quietly, "if strange things happened here all the time, the place would have much more of a reputation. All the same, Charlotte, perhaps you should start making inquiries?"

"Glad to, as soon as I see something that looks talkative."

Olivia nodded and frowned down at the map. She could see the path they were on. It would fork soon unless the map was out of date. Paths got overgrown in places like this, didn't they? She wished briefly she'd spent any time in the wilderness.

"Here," said Gareth. He reached out a hand but didn't snatch the map as a younger man might have. When Olivia looked up at him, he lifted an eyebrow. "I *can* read a map," he said, "and the two of you have other duties, as I understand it. Speaking of which…"

"After the first turn, I was thinking." Olivia surrendered the map and began to walk again. "Far enough to be really inside but still some way away from the center."

"And what exactly do you plan to do? No, not exactly, I don't think I want to know details."

"I can simply draw energy, if I need to. Usually one puts power into something, a ward or a weapon or a good-luck charm, or disperses it back into the ground, as I did with Miss Donnell. But I believe it's possible to hold it and then release it."

"And you know how much is typical? How much"—Gareth waved his free hand around, map and all—"effort for how much power, and that sort of thing?"

"For here, or for London, yes. I've done enough work to have some idea. I generally get some sense of my environment at the same time, magically speaking. Furthermore, given what happened before, I'd imagine any change will be…dramatic." Olivia grimaced.

"We'll be on the watch for fireworks, then," said Charlotte. "You've already taken one bad spill. Any more, and you might decide we're more trouble than we're worth."

Remembered pain flickered through Olivia's mind, but only for a moment. The memory of pleasure afterward was far more vivid and far less willing to retreat. She hoped the gloom would hide her sudden flush.

"Right," said Gareth. Was his voice a little thicker than it might otherwise have been? Olivia couldn't tell.

"Wait!"

Charlotte, frozen in her tracks, hissed a whisper toward them. She gestured with one hand toward the edge of the path, then spoke again, at normal volume but not in her normal voice. Her words had the same not-quite echo Olivia had heard before. "I see you there, but you don't have to run. We'd like to talk. I promise we won't harm you." She knelt down, heedless of her dress hem falling into the dirt.

Something moved in the shadow of the trees, slow and close to the ground. Olivia spotted a dark muzzle, then shiny black eyes, and then a small, round body covered in prickles.

The hedgehog took a few more steps out, peered at Charlotte, and snuffled a few times. Rather large for a hedgehog, Olivia thought.

Charlotte blinked. "Charlotte Woodwell," she said. "I'm a...student...over at Englefield. These are my teachers." The hedgehog made a few more noises. "Yes. I don't see why not." She glanced back over her shoulder. "She wants to come back with us."

"Ah." Olivia turned to stare at Gareth, who just stared back. Finding no help there, she turned to Charlotte again. "She likes you?"

"She doesn't *know* me," said Charlotte, clearly finding the question absurd. "She wants to live around people, better food and less chance of being eaten. Says she's done it before."

"I...yes, for my part." Olivia said. "I don't know what the Grenvilles will say when they get home."

"Oh, they won't mind," Charlotte said, waving one hand airily. She turned back to the hedgehog. "You can come with us, but we're staying out here for a bit yet. The more you can tell us, the sooner we'll leave."

"I see" said Gareth in the tone of a man who wasn't at all sure any of this was really happening. "If she's coming with you, perhaps you could chat while we walk?" He glanced around the forest. "Best to keep moving, I think, before it gets darker."

"Might as well," said Charlotte and then glanced back to the hedgehog and held out her hands. "Will you?"

The hedgehog trundled obligingly forward and let Charlotte, rather gingerly, pick her up. She didn't make much noise as they walked along, or not much that Olivia could hear: a few grunts, squeaks, or snuffles. Charlotte seemed to be listening intently, though. From time to time, she'd ask questions in a quiet voice or nod. Mostly, she just looked curious.

"To put it briefly," she said, looking over at Olivia after a little while, "you're right about the place being strange. A couple times she's seen the colored lightning you mentioned, and the white birds, though she hides from the bigger ones. There's a white deer somewhere around here too, or was a few years ago."

Olivia blinked and peered at the small creature in Charlotte's arms. "A few years? Must have been half her life."

"That's another thing. The beasts here are normal for the most part, but every so often a few of them are born different. Bigger, smarter, longer lives." Charlotte shrugged. "She says she's seen ten years, she thinks, and she doesn't feel old. She also says she went wandering for a bit when she was young and lived with a boy for a while."

"Does she know why creatures are different here?" Gareth asked.

Charlotte snorted and shook her head. "Doesn't know or care. She's still a hedgehog, after all."

"Right," said Gareth and sighed as he looked ahead. Olivia followed his gaze and saw the path forking, the branches trailing off farther into the forest. "I suppose we'll go ahead with the rest of this outing, then."

Chapter 23

HONESTLY, OLIVIA WASN'T SURE SHE WAS MUCH MORE pleased than Gareth about what lay ahead. Curious about the forest, yes. She would eagerly have read a book on the topic or listened to any number of lectures. Attempting to work magic there herself was, at best, something of a mixed pleasure, particularly considering what had happened with Michael.

Nothing she'd heard had mentioned anyone getting hurt, but nobody had been poking at the place. And there had been those missing children.

Violet's grandmother had probably made those up. If she hadn't, they'd gone missing a long time ago. And missing wasn't exactly the same as hurt…or killed.

Nonetheless, when Olivia spotted a clear patch just past the fork in the path, her emotions were decidedly mixed, and there was far more wariness in them than excitement. Not so for Charlotte, who stared with avid interest as Olivia stepped forward and began drawing her circle in the dirt.

Neither she nor Gareth spoke. Even the hedgehog seemed to have fallen silent, and it was too late in the year for many birds to sing. Olivia told herself the quiet wasn't at all that unnerving and turned her attention to the task at hand.

The shape of the circle came first, a wide sweep with the wand. She didn't get it as exact as she could have done indoors, another reason to be nervous, as if she needed more, but she thought it would serve. She was using the first part of a minor warding spell, the sort she'd used to protect herself from pickpockets in London, and those spells were generally rather gradual and undramatic.

She took a deep breath and drew another circle inside the first. Now a shiver ran down her spine. Power, or just nerves?

Olivia knelt inside the double circle. The plea came first, power for protection against those who would work by deceit and stealth. She reached out with the wand, drawing the first few symbols...

A rush of power streamed up her arm, as if she'd plunged to the shoulder into a warm bath. Olivia caught her breath, paused for a second, and then slowly kept writing.

As happened at such times, the world around her shifted. She could see the things of the earth: the trees, the ground, Gareth and Charlotte, the hedgehog, but she could see the power inside them too, and the true nature that lay under their physical forms. Usually, in the past, that sight had been only a faint translucence, a dim, many-colored fire inside everything.

Now the fire overwhelmed the forms. The trees were rays of steady light, green and brown mingling. Charlotte was a brighter apple green that shifted and flickered, the hedgehog in her lap aswirl with dark green and white and gold. And Gareth was a shimmering bronze. Olivia couldn't even make out features, just vaguely shaped bits of light.

She realized, then, the world she saw was only one of many.

There were layers here, like an onion, or maybe like sheets of paper in a book. Olivia couldn't see them, exactly, but she knew they were there. She'd spoken of worlds that followed different rules. Now she felt she could almost reach out a hand and touch one. The temptation was enormous.

And God, perhaps very literally, knew what would follow.

She drew her mind back from that edge. As she focused, something else caught her attention, a pale radiance, not immediately around her but nearby, off a little way down a narrower path. She wasn't surprised it had taken her so long to notice it either. The light was almost part of the landscape. Olivia had never seen that sort of light so still before or so strongly tied to such a comparatively large area, but she knew the phenomenon very well.

There was a ghost here.

Power was still rushing into her, filling her with a warmth and energy not unlike strong drink. The metaphor held on more than one level, Olivia managed to think, and changed the symbol she was drawing, adding a line through it to close off the channel she'd opened. She gestured around her with the wand, to Gareth and Charlotte and herself, and saw lit versions of the symbols she'd drawn rise up and wrap around them.

The power went from her with that action, flowing into the symbols. Olivia released a breath she hadn't known she was holding, broke the circle with a few more gestures of the wand, and stepped back.

"I think," she said and heard the breathlessness in her voice, "I've found the first part of our answer."

—∿∿—

Watching Olivia cast the spell had been both slightly boring and rather nerve-wracking at the same time. On the one hand, wards were invisible, and Gareth had no idea what any of the symbols Olivia traced actually meant. As far as he could tell, she might have been simply drawing in the dirt. On the other, he knew Olivia could cast spells, he knew the forest did strange things where magic was concerned, and he thought there was a not-very-faint possibility everything could go horribly wrong.

He'd come along for that reason, of course. Except, it occurred to him as he watched Olivia work, that while he could almost certainly handle the aftermath of an emergency, he would have no idea what to do *during* one. Miss Woodwell might. He hoped so. He tried to forget the girl had all of three months' training.

When Olivia froze and her eyes widened, Gareth felt a jolt of…something. Probably simply fear, he told himself later, rather different from previous occasions, but then so were his circumstances. He waited, hearing Miss Woodwell's quick breathing beside him, and watched Olivia's face.

She did go on. The spell, whatever it was, went through, and Olivia broke her circle, stepped back, and spoke. Only then did the half-electric feeling along Gareth's nerves subside.

"What answer?" He didn't recognize his voice at first.

Olivia bent and carefully brushed away the symbols she'd drawn. Her face was a little whiter than Gareth would have liked, and she kept it turned toward the ground as she spoke. "First of all, I don't think anyone will try stealing from any of us for a year or two. So there's that." She laughed. Her voice was a little too high and none too steady.

Gareth took a step forward, reaching a reassuring hand toward her shoulder...and stopped. Best not to distract her just now.

"Someone's spirit lives here, for one thing." Olivia went on after a moment, concentrating on the most mundane of the not-very-mundane discoveries she'd made. "I'll try and talk to him or her and find out more. We need to know more. The world's...thinner here. I don't know why. I don't know that there's a mortal man or woman who could explain it entirely, but it's easier to go beyond the physical here. Easier to access power. Easier to access other things as well...and for them to reach us."

Miss Woodwell whistled, long and low. It sounded like a bird call.

As responses went, it was neither ladylike nor mystical, and therefore steadied all of them. Olivia laughed again, but she sounded more normal this time. "Quite so," she said. "Exactly so. I'm only glad I picked the spell I did."

"Because it doesn't do very much?" Miss Woodwell asked.

"That," said Olivia, getting to her feet, "and because the only things I called on were the elements. Nothing with real personality. You actually have to *try* to drag up elementals."

Gareth stared at her for a moment. "As opposed to demons, I suppose?"

"Neither Mr. Grenville nor I would summon demons," Olivia said crisply, "or nothing that *really* fits the name. There are dark things out there, but there's no danger of any spell we use calling on them. Some do invoke spirits, though, and that would have been trouble enough. As I said. Some would have been worse."

"Worse?" Gareth asked.

"Archangels," said Olivia, "and gods."

"Angels wouldn't be a problem, would they?" Miss Woodwell asked. "Good sorts, from everything I've heard—"

"Good doesn't mean harmless," said Olivia, "not at that scale. You can invoke something that powerful, but you don't ever want to catch its attention. Not unless…Well, if that's your best option, you're in a great deal of trouble anyway."

She looked off, down a small trail Gareth just then noticed. "And now," Olivia said, "if you'll follow me, I'll see if I can find the second part of the answer."

Chapter 24

"BLOOD SACRIFICE?" CHARLOTTE ASKED. "YOU COULD HAVE asked. We'd have brought a chicken."

She was mostly joking, or sounded like she was. The path Olivia had found was rocky and overgrown, choked with fallen branches and the thorny briars of some very persistent plant or other. Winter clothing served decently well as armor, but Olivia had acquired a scratch or two across her face after they'd been walking for a few minutes, and she didn't think the others had fared any better. At least the hedgehog had armor, of a sort.

She wished she could have sent them back. The ground was too uneven particularly for Gareth, though there was no way to phrase that tactfully, and she wasn't certain what she was going to find at the end of the path or how successful she was going to be at speaking with it.

That said, if anything *did* go badly, Olivia knew she would need someone around. As much as she hated to admit it, having Gareth there was some comfort aside from his healing abilities. He was a teacher, he was an adult, and they'd worked together in some respects before, even if she tried to avoid remembering that most of the time.

Olivia took a breath, pushed aside a few more briars, and led Gareth and Charlotte out into what had once been a clearing. The trees had crowded in now, and the undergrowth had taken over, so there was barely room for the three of them to stand.

"I'm sorry about this," she said as she took as even a stance as possible over what had once been a grave.

"Oh, you should be," said Charlotte cheerfully. "Next time you see a ghost, be sure you set fire to the place before you try and speak to it. I'll help if you like."

"I'll try to avoid that being necessary," said Olivia. "If you'd be so kind, please do remember anything I say. I'm never sure whether or not I will."

She closed her eyes, took a deep breath, and began.

In London, Olivia had almost always used candles when she called up the dead, but she'd known toward the end she didn't really need them. Most of the time, all it took was opening her mind in the right way, like focusing on a picture until she saw the hidden image. The bells and candles she'd started with had been there only to show her the way.

In theory. In practice, she was standing in the middle of the forest, trying to contact a spirit that had probably been dormant for years and which might not be very pleased at the intrusion.

Olivia tried not to think about that.

Instead, she pictured the border between the mortal world and the world of the dead, and saw it becoming thinner in a small ring around her, fading like smoke into air. It vanished alarmingly fast compared to what Olivia was used to, and she was glad there weren't more ghosts out here. "O spirit," she said, fumbling in her memory for the words to use when she didn't know a name, "thou hast here a mortal vessel, which shall be pleased to serve thee in speech and in knowledge. Come and speak, if thou art willing."

Olivia felt a presence in the back of her mind. It moved slowly, almost groggily forward…

Then she slid backward, a passenger in her own body, and the other slipped down in front of her. Most spirits she talked to had been urgent in that procedure, eager or sad or enraged. This one was…respectful. Courtly, almost. Olivia got the distinct sense of a bow.

"A fair day to you, good sir and lady," said her mouth.

It spoke English, but a very old version. Olivia could see Gareth's brow wrinkling. Only the spirit's presence in her mind let her understand what it said.

"Good day," said Charlotte, and the echoes about her voice told Olivia she was using her gift to translate. She paused, then shrugged and went on. "I'm Miss Charlotte Woodwell. He's Dr. St. John."

"I am Brother Jonathan, late, very late, an' my wits deceive me not, of Englefield Abbey. What do you here, you and your enchantress companion?"

"It's probably best to tell him the truth," said Gareth when Charlotte gave him a questioning look.

Olivia sensed the spirit's amusement. Gentle amusement. He'd been a kind man in life, she sensed content with his books and his gardens at the abbey. "Lying *is* a sin," she heard her voice say and was glad of her detachment from her body. She might have blushed, otherwise. She certainly couldn't have met Gareth's eyes. "So I will commend your wisdom and your virtue both, sir. And still I would have answers. Why have you come?"

"It's the forest," Charlotte said. "Strange place, you know."

"What else would keep me here so long since my appointed hour? And yet I am not enough and will not be."

"Enough?" Gareth asked after a moment to figure out what the spirit had said.

Brother Jonathan sighed using Olivia's lungs. She never quite got used to that feeling. "Enough to prevent. Enough to balance. Enough to keep the water behind the dam should people keep taking away rocks."

"Nobody *means* to," said Charlotte.

"And good intentions pave the road to hell," Brother Jonathan shot back just as quickly. "For the most part, I can repair such damage as has been done, but this place is…fragile. 'Tis easy to break, as my vessel has seen. With only one guardian, and I so far from living, I cannot make it stronger."

"Should we leave, then?" Gareth asked. "That is, there's a school here—"

"I know," said the spirit. One of the annoying parts of being a medium, Olivia had found, is the spirits tended to get a lot more of her memories than she got of theirs. "And 'twas an abbey in my day. No great harm came of it, and some good. In times of great need this place may be useful, and 'tis better to have those here who have some idea what they do"

Using Olivia's memories, Brother Jonathan was adapting his accent. This time, it didn't take Gareth very long to figure out what he'd said, and he looked quite relieved when he had figured it out. "Thank you," he said.

"You'd want a living guardian?" Charlotte asked.

"More than one would be best. This forest…'Twill never be ordinary, but mortal minds and mortal strength can help it become a refuge or a threat."

Charlotte nodded. "What would they have to do?"

"Heal. Balance. Shape. Stay and watch lest the tides turn again, lest something slip through the borders."

"Stay at Englefield? All the time?" Charlotte, who had been lifting her chin and doing her best inspiring-statue impression—though the hedgehog on her arm would have been an incongruous detail—suddenly took a step backward, almost running into a stump in the process. "Forever?"

Gareth reached out and put a steadying hand on her arm.

"Not forever. Mine is a strange case. Had anyone taken up the role, I would have gone to my rest long since. And not in the house at all times. 'Twould be best if they did not venture very far, though."

"Oh," said Charlotte and gulped.

"It need not be you, child," the spirit said. Olivia felt his amusement as well as his growing weariness. He would not stay much longer. "And it need not be just now. Let it be soon, though." The spirit looked out of Olivia's eyes at Gareth and Charlotte, and his grim sincerity was clear to all of them. "There are deep waters here. I cannot keep the tide back, or the sharks, do you bleed. And they will come. My strength, such as it is, will not last."

"We'll be careful," said Gareth, his voice hard. "I give you my word."

"Then God go with all of you," said Brother Jonathan, "as I cannot."

He had enough strength to give Olivia something like a bow. Then he was gone, dormant again, and the three of them were alone in the forest.

Gareth was the first one to speak. "We'd better get back," he said and looked to the west. "The sun's going down."

Chapter 25

IT WAS SHORTLY AFTER TEATIME, AND THE CLOUDY SKY beyond the drawing-room drapes was already quite dark. The younger students were practicing self-defense, the older ones were studying or talking on their own, and Olivia had shut herself in with the piano. She thought she deserved as much.

They'd come back from the forest in almost complete silence. She and Gareth certainly hadn't spoken much, and Charlotte had mostly been talking to the hedgehog. Olivia had gotten through her classes somehow, though she'd felt shaken and numb the whole time.

On the one hand, it was good to know there was no immediate danger. On the other, the forest was much stranger than she thought, and the need for a guardian—she'd have to speak to Mr. Grenville about that as soon as he came back.

What was "much longer" to a ghost? A year? A month? A day?

For the moment, there was nothing she could do, so she sat and played Gibsone, "Sigh of the Night Winds." Someone, possibly Miss Grenville, had left the music, but it was much faded. Between that and the rusty state of Olivia's skills, she was concentrating rather thoroughly after the first few bars.

She didn't even hear the door, let alone footsteps.

"You play well." Gareth's voice dropped, sudden and

close at hand, into a pause in the music. Olivia's hands froze on the keys, and she snapped her gaze upward to find him almost at her shoulder, coatless and with his shirtsleeves rolled up, looking at her with an unreadable expression that turned to apology as she watched. "I didn't mean to scare you."

"Only startled," she said, "I assure you." Her heart was racing, but Olivia couldn't pretend that was all surprise. Not when she also felt considerably warmer than she had a moment before. "And thank you. I'm rather out of practice, actually."

"As am I, then, as a listener." Gareth tilted his head slightly to look at her, eyes glinting green in the lamplight. "You must have been very good once."

"I flatter myself I was. Not a genius, simply an accomplished young lady, but...I found it restful when I was young. And then Charlotte persuaded me, and I found I still do." She smiled despite herself. "It's rather amazing how some things come back."

"Some of them," said Gareth. "Some are...more difficult. At best."

"Yes," said Olivia. Her voice was a little sharper than she intended, so she tempered it with another smile. Although, if he'd come in just to be Byronic, a little sharpness was warranted. "That's why what does return is so remarkable."

His lips twitched, acknowledging the point. "And why one occasionally makes the effort to seek out lost things, I suppose. Sea change or not."

"I would say so." He smelled pleasantly masculine. She shouldn't have noticed, but she did. She went on quickly. "Particularly things that gave us pleasure."

That had definitely been the wrong phrase to use. The words had not been magical, not in the sense Olivia usually understood, but they might as well have been Enochian for their effect. In a second the room shrunk down to the two of them. Gareth's eyes, fixed on Olivia's, darkened, and then his gaze dropped, first to her mouth, then lower.

"Pleasure," he said, and his voice was rough. He started to reach out to her then took a quick breath. "That isn't what brought me here."

"What did?" Olivia asked, not knowing whether he meant the drawing room or Englefield as a whole. She wasn't sure she cared. The tension in his long, lean frame was obvious. Observing it was sending waves of desire through her body. If conversation would help, she'd grasp whatever she could of it.

"I had questions," he said and cleared his throat. "About the forest."

"Did you?" It would be sensible to look away, back at the piano or over at the door or anywhere besides Gareth's face.

That would also be backing down. Running away. He could avert his eyes, if he wanted to. He didn't.

"Yes," Gareth said and swallowed. "Questions about danger. About the...origins of the place. About many things."

Olivia lifted her eyebrows. "If I thought we needed to do anything about it, or could, just now," she said, trying to keep her voice steady and ignore the curve of his mouth, "I would've said so. And I don't know. I've told you everything I know."

"Yes," said Gareth again. He reached for her a second

time. This time his fingers skimmed the line of Olivia's throat, tracing a band of fire from behind her ear to just above her collar. She caught her breath. "I realized that a moment or two ago."

"Only then?" Olivia moistened her lips. "Pity. You could've saved a trip."

The hand on her neck moved lower, down over her shoulder, fingers caressing her skin through the thin cloth. "I should agree with you there," said Gareth. Somehow he'd settled himself beside her on the bench. There was really no mystery to it. "But oddly enough, I can't regret my presence here just now."

"Glad to hear it," said Olivia. Then Gareth's wandering hand found the upper slopes of her breasts. She had to close her eyes for a moment, and she shifted her weight in a vain attempt to ease the pulsing ache between her legs.

"Of course," Gareth continued, leaning forward now and sliding his other arm around her waist, "if I'm intruding, or unwelcome..."

There was a little too much triumph in his voice for Olivia to ignore, even half dizzy from lust. She opened her eyes, steadied herself as best she could, and shook her head.

"No," she said, "you're not intruding at all." She reached out her hand, settled it on his leg just above his knee, and then stroked upward. Gareth's breath went out in a rush, and he held very still.

She'd surprised him, then. Among other things. Olivia couldn't resist smiling, but she couldn't stay smug for very long either. The emotion drowned in sensation, heat and rigid muscle beneath her hand with only a layer of cloth between her skin and Gareth's, and a look on his face of barely restrained hunger. Without thinking, she leaned toward him, into his touch, and liquid heat spread through her.

It seemed she couldn't tease him without tormenting herself as well. Perhaps she should have regretted that. She didn't.

Breathing again, though somewhat raggedly, Gareth drew his hand away from her breasts and back up toward her collar. Olivia bit her lip. She would *not* protest, she told herself, and she certainly wouldn't let herself make any disappointed noises.

"This is probably very unwise," said Gareth, his breath hot against her ear. "You do know that."

His fingers unfastened the button at her collar.

"As well as you do, I'd imagine," Olivia managed. "And yet here we are." She let her hand glide farther upward, though not inward. Not yet. She brought her fingers to a rest just below his waist, looked into his eyes, and smiled. "Fancy that."

He leaned forward and kissed her then, his mouth quick and seeking. Olivia wound her free arm around his neck and pulled him toward her, seeking the friction and the heat she remembered…and then the piano keys clanged dissonantly as her back hit them.

They sat forward quickly, but they were laughing as they broke the kiss. Gareth hadn't taken his hands away from Olivia's shirtfront, and one of her hands was still at his hip, the other grasping his shoulder. A month ago, they'd have broken off for much less interruption.

Now he was undoing her second button.

She felt she should reciprocate—she rather *wanted*

to reciprocate—and she was trailing her free hand down Gareth's chest, feeling his firm body beneath the irksome layers of shirt and waistcoat, when she felt air hit her bare skin. Gareth had managed a third button. Now the opening of her shirtwaist was large enough for his hand to slip through.

He brushed his fingertips against Olivia's breasts, and this time she couldn't help moaning, just a little. Gareth swallowed hard when he heard the sound. The response clearly wasn't one-sided.

Even so, Olivia made herself speak. "There are. Umm—" Gareth dipped his fingers beneath the edge of her corset, and she briefly forgot what the next word was going to be. "Better places."

"Probably." Gareth muttered. He brushed his fingers over one hard nipple, and Olivia arched helplessly into his touch, not caring where they were or what he was saying as long as he didn't take his hand away. He didn't, but he did pause, wretched man, and looked at her with half-lidded eyes just long enough for her to regain a little coherence before he said, "If you'd like to cry off now…"

In answer, she lowered her hand and traced her fingertips over the hard ridge that strained at the front of his trousers. The organ in question leapt at her touch, and Gareth made a thoroughly satisfying noise in his throat. So she did it again, lightly at first and then more firmly, finally cupping her hand over his erection and stroking the length of it through the fabric.

Some years had passed since Olivia had touched a man, so she was aware, briefly, of a hint of uncertainty she'd never have admitted to Gareth. His response banished it both quickly and thoroughly in any case. He gasped and thrust himself against her palm, and the hand on her breast tightened most enjoyably.

"God," he said, a quick hoarse whisper, and caught at her fingers, though he showed no inclination to remove her hand from its current location. "You can't...I won't...I need..."

Olivia would have laughed, but in all honesty, she didn't think she could have managed to be any more coherent just then. His meaning was clear enough, and she squirmed just thinking about what was to follow.

"The couch," she said. Desperate or not, she had no wish to be taken on a piano bench or the floor.

They rose in the same moment. Gareth put a hand on the small of Olivia's back, as if to guide her, and while she needed no such urging, she welcomed the contact. It took the better part of her self-control to walk instead of sprinting.

Then midway across the room, Gareth stopped. Olivia turned to look at him, puzzled and halfway bracing herself for another chilling comment...

But the look on his face wasn't sardonic. It had nothing to do with arousal either. He looked like a man who'd taken a blow to the head.

Olivia took hold of his shoulder to steady him now rather than to inflame. She would have plenty of time to be frustrated later. For the moment, she shoved desire to the back of her mind. "Gareth?"

"Something's wrong," he said, putting a hand to his temple. "Something close. Don't ask how I know, but..."

There was a loud crash from somewhere nearby. Then someone screamed.

Chapter 26

FOR THE SECOND TIME, GARETH HURRIED FROM THE drawing room to meet some form of disaster. He had no idea what he'd find this time, but it would likely be worse than Miss Donnell's power. The disturbance throbbed sickly in his head like a rotten tooth: not simply pain, but a feeling of…wrongness. Something was twisting. Something had broken or was breaking.

He managed to walk. He even managed to walk quickly and to focus on the hallway in front of him.

"Can you tell where?" Olivia asked from beside him.

Gareth shifted his focus, the way he did when he prepared to heal, and then winced. The disturbance was much stronger to his left, and much more painful to examine on the spiritual plane. "Ballroom," he said between gritted teeth. "That direction."

"All right."

Olivia said another of those twisty, more-foreign-than-foreign words, and the hand on his shoulder suddenly felt cool, even through the fabric of Gareth's shirt. The pain and the twisting feeling didn't vanish, but they retreated.

That was good enough for him.

As they turned into the corridor that would lead to the ballroom, another scream split the air. Female, Gareth thought with the detachment that had let him calmly ask for sutures and make diagnoses in the midst of blood and sand. Terror, at the moment. Not pain. That was good. That was something, at any rate.

Nevertheless, he dashed the last few yards, not caring how much his leg would make him pay for it later. He was half-conscious of Olivia at his side, holding her skirts out of the way, and the thought crossed his mind that he should be doing something to protect her.

Then they stepped through the ballroom door, and the notion seemed absurd.

Disconnected images flicked before Gareth's eyes. Violet, screaming, huddled against the wall with the ruins of a tea tray on the floor in front of her and her hands held out in a vain gesture of aversion. Fitzpatrick and Waite stood in the center of the room on opposite sides of a circle whose chalked symbols were glowing a lurid red. In the center…

In the center was a shape as high as a man that glowed the same bright red as the symbols. Some veil yet lay over it, or perhaps it wasn't fully formed yet. Gareth couldn't make out details, but he saw enough.

The thing in the circle was not human. From the neck down, it might have been. The proportions of its limbs and torso were slightly off, in a way Gareth couldn't quite understand, but it might have been a deformed man below the neck.

But it had three heads, and only one of them looked anything like a human head. The others were horned. All three had red eyes.

Now he heard a humming in the room, not quite like the sound bees or flies would make. More unified. Less animal. Less natural, or less natural to the world Gareth knew. It blended with Violet's screaming, making a sick counterpoint, and the feeling in Gareth's head twisted again.

Spirits and demons, Olivia had mentioned in the forest. Archangels and gods. The thing in the circle looked like no angel Gareth had ever heard of, but…

He would have sworn, but he didn't know what the words would do.

"Everyone hold still," Olivia snapped in a voice miles away from its normal silky quietness. There was ice and iron about it now. "And keep *quiet*."

Violet shut her mouth then clapped a hand over it to be sure. It would have been funny at any other time. The humming kept up, though. It might even have been a little louder.

Olivia turned to the maid. "Get me a candle and matches, some salt, and something silver. Anything. Run." As Violet scrambled to her feet, Olivia turned toward the circle.

Gareth took a step toward her then caught himself. She knew what she was doing, and he had only the vaguest idea what was happening here at all. Anything he could do would only make matters worse. He knew that, and yet it was almost physically painful to stand and watch as Olivia stepped closer and closer to the circle and to the thing that was coming through it.

The veil was a little lighter now. Gareth could see one of the non-human heads was that of a bull, the other that of a ram. All three had fangs.

Halfway between Waite and Fitzpatrick, Olivia stopped. The shape towered over her. It was taller than any man now. Shadows flickered and danced in the red light of its body. Olivia held up one hand.

A word poured out of her mouth, twisting and sinuous, and Gareth saw her free hand clench at her side as she spoke it. The shape spun toward her then, and sullen light flared out around it.

"O thou spirit," she said, and now her voice filled the room. "Thou hast diligently answered unto all commands. Now I do here license and abjure thee to depart. Go now unto thy proper place—"

All three heads opened their mouths and roared. Gareth felt heat brush past his face, and the stench of sulfur was very strong.

"Unto thy proper place," Olivia continued, her body rigid against the onslaught, "without causing harm or danger unto man or beast. Let the peace of the greater order and the powers that serve it be upon thee, insofar as thou may receive such blessings, and let there be no debt or enmity between thee and me. Depart then, I say, in the name of—"

More words. Gareth could understand none of them, but they seemed to strike the thing in the circle like darts, and then like arrows. It writhed and snarled, twisting its form around. For a moment, it rose up almost to the ceiling.

And then it shrank down, man-height again, and smaller, and smaller still. The veil fell back over it, making it a shape and then a shimmer of red light. Gareth saw a shadow stretch out from behind it. It might have been a part of the demon, but it didn't look quite connected. A tail? Another arm? A tentacle? Then again, he could barely see straight.

The twisting in Gareth's head lightened and began to make sense at the same time, as if he'd pulled back far enough to see a picture rather than splotches of paint. Now he saw the hole in the world the thing had come through, saw it the way he saw wounds and illnesses in the human body. It was closing even as the thing retreated, knitting up behind it with remarkable ease.

Smaller. The shape Gareth had seen was gone now. Perhaps it had never been there in the first place.

Smaller.

Gone.

Violet came dashing back in, breathless, with a candle, a shaker of salt, and a silver fork, all nearly falling from her hand. "Ma'am...I..."

"It's all right," said Olivia, stepping back from the circle. She was breathing heavily, and her forehead was wet. "It turns out they weren't necessary. Thank you."

"You should sit down for a little while," Gareth said. This, in any case, was something he could handle. "Have some tea, yourself, and a little brandy in it. You've had a nasty shock." He looked at the girl, who was white and wide-eyed but didn't seem in any danger of fainting. "I'll walk you back to the kitchen, if you'd like."

"Oh, no, sir," said Violet, shaking her head. She eyed Gareth and Olivia with much-warier respect than Gareth had ever seen on her face. "I mean, no, thank you. Thank you. I'll be going now."

In her haste to leave the room, she forgot to curtsy.

Watching her go, Gareth wondered if he'd actually done anything to frighten the girl. The pain in his head might well have found expression on his face, but perhaps it was enough that he'd come in with Olivia. Perhaps it was enough that they were connected to the thing in the circle, if only by dealing with it. Violet wouldn't have been the first to make such an association.

He glanced back to Olivia, several questions on his mind, but she wasn't looking at him. She was studying the no-longer-glowing chalk circle instead, a detached and somewhat scholarly expression on her face.

The door clicked closed behind Violet. Olivia looked up, not at Gareth but at Waite and Fitzpatrick, still standing rather dazed on each side of the circle.

There was nothing detached in her expression now.

—⁓—

"Balam." Olivia folded her arms across her chest and looked from William to Arthur. "An interesting choice. Were the two of you after invisibility or prophecy? I couldn't let myself hope for wit, however clearly you need it."

The room filled up with silence for a minute. Olivia didn't let it last any longer. If she didn't keep talking, she thought she'd start shaking, either with fear or anger. "Mr. Waite," she said, "I was not talking to hear my own voice. What were the two of you seeking?"

He met her eyes, but his face was flaming. "Invisibility, ma'am," he said. No muttering either. Someone had taught the boy manners at one time. "Thought it'd be a lark."

"Of course you did," Olivia said. She turned to look at William, who was staring off ahead of him. "Calling up dark powers is *precisely* the way to amuse yourself on a dull afternoon. I'm surprised it's not in the *Boy's Own Paper*."

From behind her, Gareth made a noise suspiciously

like a stifled laugh. Olivia ignored him. Best not to think about either his presence or what the summoning had interrupted. Thank God she'd managed to button her shirtwaist on the way.

"Can either of you," she asked, "give an account of this matter that involves anything but complete and utter stupidity? Mr. Fitzpatrick?" William began muttering at his shoes. "So we can *all* hear you, please?"

He jerked his chin up. "They're not *really* demons. Not really. Summoning them doesn't make you bad. Mr. Grenville said so, and so did you."

Olivia closed her eyes for a second. She was going to have a world-beating headache when all of this was over, she knew. "Yes," she said, putting every ounce of patience she possessed into her voice. There wasn't much. "That's true. I did say that, unlike the case with other beings, it was possible to deal with the Ancient Lords and retain both your mind and your soul. *Possible.* Did I, at any point, say it was safe?"

"No, ma'am," Fitzpatrick admitted.

"Did Mr. Grenville?"

"No, ma'am."

"I can't speak for Mr. Grenville, but I seem to remember saying exactly the opposite. In case I was mistaken about your presence at the time, let me make myself clear now." Olivia took a deep breath. "The Ancient Lords have no love for humanity. They respect power and will. They have no mercy for inexperience or weakness. They will trick you if they can. They will kill you if they can. They've done both to older and wiser men than you. Am I clear, Mr. Waite?"

He swallowed. "Yes, ma'am."

200 ISABEL COOPER

"You do *not* call them up for a good time, for idle curiosity, or for anything less than dire need. Especially not here."

"Here?" Fitzpatrick asked.

"You've heard about Michael. This place is…different. I don't suppose you thought about *that* either."

Fitzpatrick shrugged. "Mr. Grenville said the house was safe."

"Mr. Grenville didn't mean you should start summoning demons here. The house is *warded*, and all homes have some protection, but neither protection nor wards count when you open a door in the middle of the house. With the forest right outside, we're lucky you got one demon instead of the legions of hell. Now," Olivia said, "you will both clean this up. Thoroughly. Ask one of the housemaids for soap and hot water. Add the salt, and sage if they have any in the kitchen. I will stay here and watch you, as it's obvious I can't trust you alone together. One of us will also search your room before you go to bed tonight, and you will *stay* in your room, for the next week, when you're not in class or otherwise supervised."

Fitzpatrick didn't say anything, but he gave her a thoroughly mutinous look, in response to which Olivia glared right back. To her surprise, Waite simply nodded. "Yes, ma'am. Ma'am?"

"Yes, Mr. Waite?"

"What would have happened?" Fitzpatrick turned his scowl on Waite, who ignored the younger boy and went on. "If you hadn't come in, I mean?"

"I can't say for certain," Olivia said. "If you'd drawn the circle well enough to hold Balam, and if nothing else had gotten through, he'd have given you what you wanted, in some fashion. Generally a troublesome one, he might have made you invisible with no way to turn back, for instance. In the process, he would have tried to get one of you to break the circle. If you had, or if the circle hadn't held in the first place…" She shrugged. "We would have been fortunate if only the two of you had died."

"Oh. I see." Waite scrubbed the back of his hand across his mouth, looking faintly green. "Right, then."

Olivia nodded. "Go get what you need, both of you. Be quick about it."

She waited until they were gone, then dropped into one of the chairs against the wall. The headache had, indeed, started to make itself known, and that reminded her of Gareth, who was still standing near the door when she looked up. "Feeling better?" she asked.

"Hmm?" Gareth then seemed to realize what she was asking. "I…suppose. Something still feels off, but I'd imagine that will pass."

"I'd wager you've never been around an attempt at demon-summoning before," Olivia said dryly.

"I can't say I have."

"It's a new experience for both of us, then. Or all five, probably. We'll all be feeling the aftermath for a while. Which reminds me that one of us should see to Violet."

"I'll do it," Gareth said, crossing the room as he talked. "I'm not certain my training covers this, but it's close, and you have to stay and supervise, don't you?"

"It seems the least I can do." Olivia grimaced. Not all of her anger, she was realizing now, had been for Waite and Fitzpatrick. "I thought I'd taught them better. I really did."

Out in the hall, the clock began to strike seven. Olivia listened to the chimes, letting the rhythm soothe her mind a little.

Then Gareth was in front of her, smoothing the loose strands of hair back from her forehead. "You did," he said and shook his head a little, helplessly. "Young men are idiots. They're idiots no matter what you tell them. Getting them to their majority alive is a small miracle."

Olivia looked up at him and laughed briefly. "I shouldn't find that reassuring, should I?"

"I wouldn't have said it otherwise," said Gareth.

Their eyes met again. Even exhausted as she was, Olivia felt a brief resurgence of her earlier desire. More than that, there was a quiet comfort in his face and the touch of his hand. She could almost feel her nerves re-settling themselves.

"You should go talk to Violet," she said. "Thank you, though, and for getting me here faster."

"Thank you," he said, "for keeping us all alive."

He fell silent and bowed. Before he turned toward the door, Olivia saw the startled look on his face, as if he was surprised to say the words or to mean them.

Chapter 27

"ANY INJURY CAN BE MORE SERIOUS THAN IT LOOKS," Gareth said. "Any injury can be less so. I've seen a man die from taking a punch to the stomach, and I've seen a man recover after being shot in the head." Young Lewis had possessed a singularly thick skull in more ways than one, and Gareth had entertained a few suspicions about the quality of his enemy's powder. "You have to consider not just the visible injury," he went on, "but also the possibility of hidden damage, not to mention infection, shock, and the patient's general condition. Miss Donnell?"

"Sir," the girl said, lowering her hand slowly, "you said last week we often wouldn't have time to think very much."

"Yes," Gareth said. "I did. And it's true. Decisions about treatment and triage usually require significant thought. You...you five, especially, of all people, will almost certainly need to make them in moments, perhaps seconds." He felt a wry smile cross his lips. "Mr. Grenville and Mrs. Brightmore ask you only to learn the unlikely, Miss Donnell. We're attempting the impossible in this class."

Uneasy laughter followed. Miss Woodwell exchanged a glance with Fitzpatrick, who was sitting next to her on the couch. Waite and Fairley just looked a bit blank. Elizabeth curled the end of a braid around one finger. Gareth remembered how young she was and had the urge to say something comforting.

There was no comfort to give. None that would be doing Elizabeth or her fellows any service

Gareth sighed. They were *all* so young, really. None of the faces turned toward him bore any wounds, any marks of great grief or fear. He didn't doubt there'd been pain in their lives, but it had been the pain of any half-normal childhood. And he and Olivia and the Grenvilles, were sending them into…he couldn't even say what.

It was no wonder, in some ways, Waite and Fitzpatrick had come up with their particular form of idiocy. No excuse, but they'd likely get over being young and stupid. From the exasperated look Miss Woodwell had given both of them when they'd come to class, the story had gotten around the student body, and embarrassment might help as much as punishment.

Waite was more attentive than usual today, and Fitzpatrick, though sulky, gave his answers fairly readily. They were raising their hands at practically the same times, Gareth noticed, and glancing at each other whenever one got an answer right, one in triumph, one in annoyance.

Whatever the private aftermath of their summoning had been, it had not resulted in closer friendship.

Gareth, who had dreamed uneasily all the night before and had spent the day with a strangely diminished appetite, couldn't find much sympathy for them.

"Few lives go by without hasty decisions," Gareth said now, looking down at the seated students. "I doubt any of them will be yours. Luckily, knowledge helps whether or not you have time to think. There's a point where theory and practice becomes reflex, just as it does in riding or shooting."

"But it's never certain, sir?" Fitzpatrick asked.

"We're in the wrong world for certainty, Mr. Fitzpatrick," Gareth said. "The best huntsman takes a toss every so often, the best shot can miss when the wind or the light is wrong, and the human body is far more complicated than either."

He stopped and looked around the room again. All of the students were watching him now, nervous and earnest and waiting. He had planned to give them certain facts, basic and practical and perhaps somewhat dry. The rest, Gareth had thought, they could get from Olivia or the Grenvilles…or from life.

But neither Olivia nor the Grenvilles had likely been in certain situations, and life might break the unprepared.

Gareth cleared his throat. "You *will* be wrong. Each of you. All of you. If you deal with injury and disease, and, I suspect, with everything else you're training for here, there will be times when you get bad information, when you lack the proper supplies, when you've had little sleep and less food and you make the wrong decision. There will be times when you know that. There will be times when you don't. There will be times when there's *no* right decision."

The room was silent.

"Sometimes," said Gareth, making himself simply speak and not remember, "there isn't anything you can do. Nothing that will make a difference. And sometimes you don't know if there might have been."

"What then, sir?" It was Fairley who asked, the only

one young and blunt enough to voice what was probably on the others' minds. "I mean, how do you—?"

"Cope with it?" Gareth asked when the boy was obviously lost for words. "Different men have different methods."

Prayer, strong drink, or bad women, one of Gareth's teachers had said, but they'd both been men, and Gareth had been of age.

"Religion is an aid for some," he said now, and the words were stiff and awkward in his mouth. His father would have put it better, but also wouldn't have said *some*, and Gareth had seen too much to say *all*. "Sometimes music is a comfort, or art or the company of friends. And some," he added, honesty forcing the words, "turn to other distractions. I'd recommend the less dangerous sort. Particularly if you think you'll need your wits about you the next day."

Ordinarily, even such a veiled reference would have gotten a knowing smirk from Waite and Fitzpatrick. That they still looked serious reassured Gareth. He was making something of an impression.

Gareth just hoped none of them asked about *his* experience with self-destructive forms of comfort. He'd been lucky enough not to end up craving drink, and he'd never touched opium, but he couldn't pretend to have been completely temperate either.

"That," he said, "is what you can do afterward. Beforehand, you prepare as well as you can, and you do the best job possible. That's as much as anyone can manage."

He didn't speak for a minute, simply watched them. Elizabeth's lips were pressed tightly together, and her face was pale. Waite was frowning, but abstractly so, as if considering a problem. Fitzpatrick was studying his hands. Miss Woodwell just looked determined and businesslike, and Fairley chewed on his lower lip.

"In that spirit," Gareth said and reached for one of his rolled-up charts, "let's consider the human leg."

He'd told them as much as he could. The rest *would* be up to life.

———

"Dr. St. John?"

Gareth hadn't expected the voice. He'd turned away as soon as he'd dismissed the class, and started to straighten up the place. In truth, there wasn't much to do. He'd brought a chair up and some charts in, and the servants really would have done it all, but old habits died hard.

Old reflexes too. He'd turned before the voice, male, young but broken—therefore Fitzpatrick or Waite or a footman—had gotten more than halfway through his name.

Waite stood in the middle of the empty room, hands in his trouser pockets. At Gareth's sudden turn, he blinked but didn't step back. "I hope I'm not bothering you," he added. "I was wondering if I could ask a question."

"Any number of them," said Gareth, tucking one of the rolled-up charts under his arm. "I might even answer a few."

"Ah." Waite smiled a little uneasily, remembering some of Gareth's earlier lectures, perhaps, or that Gareth had no reason to be particularly patient with him just then. "More in the line of a favor, really."

"A favor," Gareth repeated flatly.

"That's right. Not my day for it, I know. Only…" Waite extracted one long-fingered hand in order to run it through his hair. "Say a student wanted some more-advanced lessons than the rest of us do."

Gareth lifted his eyebrows. Waite had done decently well in his classes, but he'd never excelled, nor had he seemed to find the subject matter particularly enthralling. Still, he wasn't inclined to discourage anyone who sought after knowledge. "Say one does," he said and kept his voice neutral.

"Would that be the sort of thing you'd do? Assuming you had time, I mean."

"That depends," Gareth said, "on how the student was doing elsewhere, for one. I'm not the only instructor here, after all."

He expected to see Waite flinch at that reminder of Olivia, but the boy just shrugged almost impatiently. "Quite well, from everything I know, though it's not like you give us marks here, sir."

"No," said Gareth, "there's a reason for that."

He glanced around, making sure he'd gotten everything. Now the room could have been a model or the background in a painting: pale yellow walls, darker furniture, thick carpets, wide windows. There was no sign left of five students, whether lounging and listening or applying bandages to one another, and nothing of the charts they'd studied or the notes they'd taken. Only Gareth and Waite.

The boy was still there, standing straight and looking earnest. And he did need something to keep him out of trouble.

"Was there any particular aspect of medicine that caught your attention?" Gareth asked.

"Oh. It's not me, you see." Waite gave him a rather sheepish grin. "It's Lizzie. Miss Donnell. Wants to learn surgery and all that…" *Don't ask me why* was all through Waite's voice, but he had the good sense not to speak it. "I said I'd have a word with you."

Elizabeth made more sense than Waite, but…"Why didn't she ask me herself?"

Waite coughed and looked down for a second, for the first time in the conversation. "A bit scared of you, sir," he said apologetically and added, "You know how girls are sometimes."

"Not really, no," Gareth said. His life since leaving home had sometimes involved women, rarely involved ladies, and hardly ever involved girls. Not until the last few months. "I'm hardly *frightening*."

"No, sir," said Waite politely.

Gareth chose not to pursue that particular line of questioning any further. "I'd be glad to teach Miss Donnell," he said, "but I can't imagine the classes will go very well if she's too intimidated to talk to me."

"Oh, shouldn't be a problem, sir. Not when she's not asking you a favor." Waite waved a hand. "Besides, Miss Woodwell said she'd go along, at least until Lizzie gets used to the whole thing."

"How kind of Miss Woodwell."

"Oh, rather," said Waite. "She's a jolly sort of a girl. Doesn't seem to mind getting a batch of younger siblings ready-made."

"Neither do you, by the evidence," said Gareth.

Waite shrugged. "I've two little sisters back home,

you know. You'll probably have them on your hands in a few years, and God help you all then."

"We'll try to be equal to your family," Gareth said. He started across the carpet toward the door, and Waite followed. "But your parents may want to keep your sisters at home. It's not by chance we have only two young ladies here." On impulse, he glanced sideways at Waite and added, "Most people think no more of female students than they do of female teachers."

"Right, sir," said Waite, looking satisfactorily uncomfortable. "Easy enough mistake, when you don't know better."

"Most mistakes are," said Gareth.

They walked toward the door together, in silence that wavered between embarrassed and companionable, until Waite spoke again. "Must have taken some getting used to on your part too, sir. Working with a woman and all. Not to mention the magic thing."

"*Teaching* took some adjustment," Gareth said. He'd meant to protest that he and Olivia didn't work that closely together, but then there'd been the day before, and the trip to the forest, and the feeling he'd gotten when Simon and his wife had left. If he put a hand out, he knew she'd catch him.

And she'd spent years falsely offering a hand to others.

Suddenly impatient, Gareth looked over at Waite. "You have somewhere to be, don't you?"

Chapter 28

THERE WAS NO OMEN OF DISASTER. IN FACT, THE DAY HAD gone fairly well. Both of the older boys, after the first bit of sulking, seemed to be taking their punishment with relative good grace, and certainly nobody had tried to summon anything *else*. Charlotte had kept Michael busy making a box for the hedgehog, which they'd named Star, after a book on Babylonian mythology had connected her species with the goddess Astarte, and Elizabeth was lost in a book.

She'd slept well for the past few nights too, or, if she hadn't, she'd managed to get herself down without waking Charlotte and thus Olivia. Olivia had followed her youngest student's example and, curling up in one of the library chairs, had immersed herself in *The Moonstone*. Reading anything fictional these days was a rare enough pleasure to occupy all her attention. If the household had experienced any alarm, she didn't hear it...

Not until the door opened and Mrs. Edgar stood on the threshold, face white beneath her cap. "You're wanted upstairs," she said. "Now, ma'am."

"Who is it?" Olivia asked irritably, yanked abruptly from Indian diamonds and drowned maidservants. If Fitzpatrick and Waite *had* tried summoning again, she would personally feed them to whatever they'd called up. Feet first. "One of the boys?"

"No, ma'am," said Mrs. Edgar, voice low and quiet.

Annoyance gave way to fear. "Elizabeth? Or—?"

"It's the master, ma'am," said Mrs. Edgar. She swallowed and shook her head. "He's home. *They're* home. And something's wrong."

———ᨆ———

Wrong didn't begin to describe it.

Gareth stood by the bed in Simon's room, looking down at his friend's still body. Simon still breathed regularly, and he'd had the strength to reach his room with Gareth and Mrs. Grenville supporting him, but he hadn't moved since he'd fallen onto the bed. His eyes didn't seem to focus on anything either. He didn't speak, and his skin had gone a shade of grayish green Gareth had never seen before and could only assume was a very bad sign indeed.

Not, however, as bad as his right arm.

Snaking up from Simon's wrist, the lines of his arteries stood out as if his arm had been a picture on one of Gareth's charts. Unlike in the picture, though, Simon's arteries from his elbow down were glowing a sick purplish black that looked like it shifted every time Gareth blinked. Like it *squirmed*.

That was mad. Light didn't move on its own. Then again, a man's blood vessels didn't glow either.

Gareth looked up. Simon's room was rather pleasant as such things went, done in shades of blue and gold, with a fire already blazing in the fireplace. Painted lamps cast their own circles of light over the bed, and a small pile of books lay on the night table. It was all very civilized. Mrs. Grenville stalked through it as if it were a jungle. If she'd had a gun, he almost would have expected her to start shooting holes in the mantelpiece.

Sensing his gaze, she spun and glared at him. "Well?"

"What *is* it?" Gareth tried not to sound querulous. He did usually like to know the normal facts about a patient before viewing him in any other way. He wasn't sure there were that many normal facts in this case, but the theory, notwithstanding, held.

"A curse. Or something." Mrs. Grenville shrugged, the first desperate and uncertain movement Gareth had ever seen from her. "On a rose, of all the stupid things. It hit the first finger on his hand. Goddamn *classic*," she spat.

He supposed it was, as curses went. Gareth picked up Simon's hand and turned it over . It felt unnaturally cold, he noted, even while he screamed his own, rather less-effective curses in the back of his mind. There *was* a hole on the right forefinger. Not large. "How long ago?"

"Half an hour. We'd just gotten into the carriage when he collapsed."

"Right. Give me a moment." Gareth switched his vision and almost immediately felt his stomach turn over in revolt.

As bad as Simon's arm looked in the normal world, it was far worse in the spiritual plane. The light that had clustered around his arteries was thicker, almost viscous, and a dark gray that brought to mind old bread dough. Gareth could almost smell the decay. That wasn't the worst of it.

When he looked at the light through his aethereal vision, it *did* squirm, growing thicker in places before splitting up again and sliding farther along Simon's arm.

Gareth could see the dark blue shape that was Simon breaking apart before it, slowly but steadily. The rest of Simon was paler—energy expended to try and fight the intruder, Gareth assumed—but nothing like what was happening midway up his arm. Gareth suspected it wasn't simply flesh and blood that crumbled.

No, dammit.

He flung power out without thinking, slamming it down into Simon's arm in a wall between the rest of his friend's body and the invading, rotting light. There was a blast of amber fire in the aether. From Mrs. Grenville's startled curse, Gareth thought something had showed itself in the normal world as well.

The rotting light…*retreated* wasn't a strong enough word. Gareth's power blasted it backward, down the long paths it had climbed to get so far, and left it midway between Simon's wrist and his elbow. *Radial*, Gareth thought absently, textbooks turning their own pages in his mind, *ulnar, brachial*. For the moment, the light's restless writhing movement halted.

It wasn't out yet. But Gareth had made a good start. He took a breath, feeling renewed confidence fill him along with the air…

Then the rotting light turned its attention on him.

———

Nobody was screaming this time. At first, Olivia found that a relief. Then, as she made her way up the stairs and down the hall, the silence became more ominous. There was carpet on the hallway floor and no way her footsteps should have echoed. They echoed in her mind anyway.

Mrs. Edgar opened the door to the master bedroom and stood back, farther back than simply letting Olivia inside would have required. There was no explosion, however, and nothing rushed out the door.

Olivia rushed in.

The room receded in her vision, its furnishings becoming faint and then almost translucent. None of them mattered except Joan, pacing the room like a caged beast, and her husband, lying on the bed and looking about three steps from a corpse.

Gareth was standing over him, holding out both of his hands. A faint golden glow had formed around them, contrasting with the rather leprous air Olivia could see around Mr. Grenville's arm as she got closer. Closer still, she saw the pallor on Gareth's face and the sweat on his forehead.

He was fighting something with all his strength. She had no idea whether he was winning.

On her way out the library door, Olivia had retained enough presence of mind to snatch up a candle and matches. She lit the wick now and made hasty gestures to the four directions, invoking all the elements to protect her in whatever happened thenceforth. It was a hasty compromise. She didn't have time for a proper shield, but she wasn't fool enough to go in without one. Not the way Mr. Grenville and Gareth both looked.

A word in Enochian brought her more knowledge, and she caught her breath with the terror of it. Now she could clearly see the writhing foulness inside Mr. Grenville's arm, insidious and persistent and awfully aware, like nothing she'd encountered and only barely like anything she'd read about. It seethed in his hand and his forearm, but a wall of dark amber power blocked its further progress.

For the moment.

The light was throwing itself at the wall, a steady stream of gray rot that, at the moment, beat itself against the power to no effect, but that didn't let the power progress any farther either. Stalemate, Olivia thought. In time, Gareth's power would weaken and so would the wall, even if he fed it with his own life force.

That was if the light didn't begin to attack him directly. Olivia could feel it in the air now. It was blind malice, but it wasn't quite senseless, and it knew Gareth was there. If the light found the link between power and man...it would be very bad. And there was almost nothing she could do. The light was magical, but it was physical. It was part of Simon's body now rather than a spell Olivia might lift.

She swallowed. "A healing spell might help," she said, turning toward the door. "I'll get the notes." Olivia tried not to think of the time it would take or how she'd never had call to use that particular sort of magic. No need, when Gareth had been there. No need now, perhaps, if he'd had enough power.

Abruptly, she turned back. A few more steps carried her to Gareth's side, just within arm's reach of him. Olivia bent and traced symbols on the ground, calling on power, and saw the world shift again. It wasn't as dramatic as it had been in the forest, but it was enough, and she bit back an oath at the roiling half shape the light took on in that view.

Warmth rose up from her feet and spread throughout her body. If working with power was enough to let her

see the light's true shape, hopefully the power itself
would be enough to defeat it. Olivia remembered the
way she'd grounded Elizabeth's energy, fixed her mind
on reversing the process…

…and placed a hand on Gareth's shoulder.

———∿∿———

For the first few seconds, Gareth wasn't sure where the
rush of energy came from, nor did he care.

The rotting light had been pressing forward relent-
lessly. He'd been holding his ground, pouring more and
more of his power into the wall, and it had held under
the assault. Only held, though. Gareth was no tactician,
never had been, but he thought trying to gain ground
might be disastrous for him and for Simon. As it was,
he had started to feel the price in his own body as the
light came onward.

The thought had occurred to him that he was in over
his head.

Injuries didn't fight back. Disease did, in its way, but
any illness he'd ever faced had been a pale shadow of
this, whatever it was, which coiled and gathered only
to surge again. The sense of its hatred for him, for all
normal life, had crept over Gareth like the faintest brush
of the power itself. Balam might have killed them all, if
he'd gotten out of the circle, but he had been straightforwardly predatory compared to the cold and slimy
thing in Simon's blood.

Gareth had been trying not to think much about that.

Then, like a drenching of cold water on a hot day—
energy. It flowed over him and into him, and Gareth
took it without thinking. The wall blossomed outward

into amber flame, driving the rotting light off, back, then out, destroying it on the way. Gareth's head was full of a high buzzing he thought was the light screaming, and he felt himself smile at the sound. Hurt, did it? *Good.*

Somewhere nearby, Simon was breathing more deeply. His hand clenched and then relaxed, fingers spreading, and the last of the light vanished.

Gareth sent his power through Simon's arm once more, scouring his veins for any trace of the curse-or-whatever, and smiled when he found none. Energy still lingered in his body. When he shifted his sight back to normal, he thought he probably looked slightly mad.

No matter. Mrs. Grenville was kneeling by Simon, her hands on his good shoulder, and talking urgently and intently in a way Gareth didn't think he should watch. Instead, he turned to see who his rescuer had been.

Deep brown eyes met his, shining with the same energy and triumph Gareth felt.

Olivia.

Chapter 29

"WE SHOULD GO," OLIVIA SAID QUIETLY, GLANCING OVER Gareth's shoulder to where the Grenvilles were talking. "They'll tell us what happened later, and…"

Gareth turned his head to follow her gaze, looked back, and spoke quickly. "Right. Yes."

He was grinning, and Olivia wasn't sure he knew it. She wasn't surprised. One never used just enough power to solve any problem. Dr. Gillespie had told her as much, and she'd found out through experience. Either one drew too heavily on reserves and ended up exhausted, or just enough remained to be energizing…and more than a little intoxicating. If Olivia was any judge, Gareth had just experienced the latter effect on top of the former.

Olivia bit the inside of her cheek to keep from giggling. Poor man. In so very far over his head. And doing quite well for all of that, she had to admit.

Outside, Mrs. Edgar and a few of the other servants solemnly watched them emerge. Olivia fought the urge to laugh again. She realized she was not exactly at her soberest either. She managed a relieved smile instead. "Everything should be fine now," she said. "Mr. Grenville's…recovering. They'll want privacy for a little while, but then some food and wine would probably be welcome." She pulled her thoughts into order. "The students—"

"Violet's sitting with the girls, ma'am, and Henry's keeping an eye on the boys." Mrs. Edgar looked between Olivia and Gareth. "Perhaps you and the doctor should sit down somewhere for a while as well, ma'am."

They should, and should also probably try to talk about what had just happened. Certainly it wasn't wise to leave Gareth alone just now. He seemed mostly in his right mind, but God knew what the remnants of outside power would do in someone with natural talent.

Now that Olivia thought about it, she realized she *hadn't* really thought about it. Not before feeding Gareth the power. She swallowed and told herself whatever she might have done was certainly better than what the curse would have done to him and Mr. Grenville.

"We'll be in the library," she said. "Bring tea, please, when you've taken care of the Grenvilles."

She smiled, turned, and walked down the hall. Walked *straight*, moreover, which was an excellent thing. Power wasn't intoxicating in quite the same way alcohol was, but the euphoria could play havoc with motor control from time to time, just as it could do the opposite. Gareth was following her with a certain graceful speed, though he still limped somewhat.

Naturally, grace was a matter of perception. Power heightened that as well.

Olivia took a deep breath and headed for the library. Hopefully there'd be plenty of distraction there.

———※———

Sitting down didn't suit Gareth. He tried it for a moment or two, long enough to fill his cup of tea, then stood up, teacup in hand, and walked to the window. It was raining outside, again. Pity: he could have done with a walk.

He could have done with a number of things.

Some of the electricity racing through his veins was mortal enough, he knew. He'd felt it on those few occasions when battle or a hard task hadn't left him completely exhausted. He was alive, the foe was vanquished, and a very primitive impulse in him said: *celebrate*.

It had never been this powerful before. Gareth felt sixteen again, though with none of the nervous clumsiness that had been his portion as a youth. No, he felt like his hands could move with the speed of thought, that he could have taken the wind itself in a footrace, that—

"There is," Olivia said, "a reason why many of us turn to opium eventually." She was trying to be crisp and sober. Her voice held amusement, though, and deeper, more sensual notes.

Gareth gripped the windowsill and didn't look at her. Power hadn't done a damn thing to enhance his self-control. "I'd imagine so," he said hoarsely.

Behind him, Olivia cleared her throat. "Do you know what—?"

"No." Gareth swallowed, put his teacup down on the windowsill, and tried to collect his thoughts. "Mrs. Grenville said it might have been a curse, but she didn't sound certain. *I've* certainly never seen anything like it," he added. "My experience of such things is limited."

"I'd imagine," Olivia said. There was a faint rustle of cloth. She was moving, not entirely at ease. "But your own talent—"

"Started when I was fourteen." This particular string

of memories was relatively safe. "Old enough to know it wasn't normal. I...tried to ask some questions, look things up, but didn't get very far. Until I met Simon, I had no real idea how the unseen world worked, not beyond me." Gareth laughed and shook his head. "And my own skills are...lacking. I taught myself. I'm bound to have missed a few points."

"Or found a few nobody would think to look for."

Gareth wondered if she'd used the same calm tone of encouragement on her marks back in London, and then if she used it on the students now. "You don't have to be kind," he said sharply. "Not to me. Lord knows I've never..."

Been kind to you were going to be the next words, but Gareth stopped himself. That sounded like apology, and he had nothing to apologize for.

A few seconds passed without a response. He could picture Olivia but wasn't certain how she looked. Had his temper stung her? Amused her? Was she wearing that carefully blank expression now, the one that spoke of being a grown woman and a professional, and so above reacting to him?

He was on the verge of saying something else when she spoke.

"I suppose you'd call healing my leg medical obligation. And my wrist. So let's assume I was speaking from professional obligation as well, shall we?" Her voice was low, firm, and closer. Not in his ear, but nearby. "I've never said anything to you out of charity, Dr. St. John. But I have no wish to insult you either." She paused for a second, did not say *most of the time*, and then went on. "Or to withhold praise where it's due."

She placed one hand on his shoulder. "You did good work up there."

Olivia's touch was light. She had probably meant only to make glancing contact, as one colleague to another. Her body was close to Gareth's, her scent light and sweet, and the energy had been building in his body for what seemed like ages. The feel of her hand simply lit the fuse.

Before she could pull away, Gareth reached up to catch her hand in his. Her skin was warm beneath his palm. He could feel her pulse racing against his fingertips.

He turned in a quick motion that felt like it took days, and pulled her to him.

In the second before Gareth's lips met hers, Olivia knew she'd been expecting that to happen.

Oh, not consciously. She hadn't *planned* it. Retreating to the library really had seemed the most sensible thing to do at the time, and it would have been unwise to leave the man alone. But given what had already happened between them? With the aftereffects of magic further eroding their self-control? Some part of her had known what would result.

Just then, nothing could have made her object.

Gareth's tongue slid into her mouth, stroking hers. One hand roamed down to the base of her spine, while the other cupped the back of her head. He held Olivia against him firmly, but there was no haste to his movements. Even through the layers of their clothing, she could feel the heat and hardness of his body very well.

No hesitance either. Deliberation, rather…and challenge.

Olivia welcomed it.

She let herself laugh, low in her throat, letting Gareth know she was on to his game. Then she broke the kiss, reluctantly at first, and then less so when she trailed her lips up Gareth's neck. He caught his breath, and his grip tightened.

Then he started unbuttoning her blouse.

That was a bold enough move to make Olivia pause, not in reluctance, but in surprise mixed with pleasure at his touch. Gareth's fingers had just grazed her breasts as he brought his hand down, but even that brief contact was enough to make her ache for more.

Not that she would ask for it.

Instead, Olivia traced the outline of Gareth's ear with her tongue, nibbled on his earlobe for a second—*definitely* a stifled gasp there, which she counted as a point to her score—and began undoing Gareth's buttons. The coat and vest parted easily enough, but she had to lean up to unfasten his necktie. That movement pressed her body very closely against his. Through her skirts, she felt his erection pushing against the juncture of her thighs.

Her own response was instant: wetness and heat and the urge to moan. Not yet, though. Not before he did. Olivia bit her lip. Acting on instinct and on the memory of their earlier encounter on the couch, she rocked her hips slowly back and forth, once and then again.

She thought Gareth gasped aloud. She couldn't be sure, because at the same time she heard fabric tear and the sound of buttons hitting the floor. Cloth slipped down her shoulders, and the air was cool against her skin, a pleasant relief in her current aroused state.

Somewhere along the line, Olivia had lost track of what she'd been doing. Gareth's tie hung open, and the first few of his shirt buttons were undone as well, but that was as far as she'd gotten. Now she moved to continue her work, but he stepped back, making a low sound in his throat that both gratified and further aroused Olivia.

So did his gaze, dark and hungry as it swept from her flushed face and disarranged hair, down to where her blouse fell open and her breasts rose out of her corset. Then he reached for her again, unfastening the little metal hooks of the corset with fingers that fumbled only a little. Medical training, Olivia decided, was certainly worth something.

Distracting Gareth would have been relatively easy just then. Olivia could tell as much from his rapid breathing, from the way his pulse beat in his neck, from the rigid control he focused on the metal hooks and eyes. He was trying very hard to keep his attention on the task at hand, and if he had to try, she could have sabotaged the attempt easily. The only problem was…she didn't want to.

Tactically, Olivia reasoned, it would do her good to let Gareth undress her. It would put her on higher ground if he acted as a servant now. Besides, the layers of cloth and metal, which she barely noticed most days, were now unbearably confining. So she stood and watched and held mostly still until Gareth unfastened the last hook and shoved both corset and blouse off her body. She didn't notice when they hit the floor.

Gareth didn't look either. His gaze lingered for a moment on her breasts, the dark pink nipples already hard and straining. Then, with a sigh of mixed relief and torment, he pulled Olivia back toward him, sliding his hands around her waist and then upward, caressing the skin he'd just exposed. His mouth met hers again just as his hands cupped her breasts, hot and slow and intent.

Biting her lip wouldn't work that time. Olivia cried out, unable to help it. She felt Gareth's satisfied chuckle even as he muffled the sound with his mouth, and she blushed, but she couldn't make herself care very much. Especially not once he started playing with her nipples, brushing them lightly and then rolling them between his thumb and forefinger. Now she was moving her hips with no conscious thought of seduction, with very little conscious thought at all, in fact, simply seeking pressure and heat and sensation.

It did help that Gareth thrust back against her and moaned. It helped that his grip was harder now and his body rigid beneath her hands. The small section of Olivia's brain that still thought about games and scores found his reactions immensely satisfying. The rest of her just burned.

When Gareth drew her down into a chair, she had no idea of resisting. She knew only that straddling him let her rub herself against his male organ all the more effectively. Her legs wouldn't support standing up much longer, anyhow, and their new position brought her nipples much closer to his mouth.

Then he took one into his mouth, and Olivia arched helplessly forward against him, lost in desire. She vaguely noticed Gareth was holding himself very still. More importantly, one of his hands was on her leg, pushing her skirt and petticoats aside and sliding upward.

She let out a rush of breath when his fingers brushed

against her sex. Somehow she didn't scream. Gareth's touch was light at first, teasing. His hand circled away, down her thighs, and then came back to cup her more solidly. One finger slid inside, then another, exploring, preparing.

Then guiding.

At some point he'd gotten his trousers undone. The head of his erection pressed against Olivia's opening, hot and hard, and, from her limited experience, rather on the large side. She caught her breath and shifted her weight, taking him just a little bit inside.

"*God*," said Gareth.

His voice came from deep in his throat, and his free hand tightened on Olivia's hip, but he made no particular move to rush things. Olivia was mostly glad of that. Ready as she was, it had been a very long time. But, she thought vaguely with what small part of her was still capable of thought, it would be nice to provoke him entirely out of his self-control sometime.

Slowly, she lowered herself onto him, and near the end the slowness was a challenge to her willpower as well as his. The feeling of fullness inside of her, of heat and pressure, was incredible, and the guttural sounds Gareth was making only aroused her more.

When they were fully joined, Olivia held still for a second. Some sensations took time to fully appreciate. Gareth's head was back against the chair now, his face tense, and he'd closed his eyes, which was both a relief and a disappointment. Olivia could still read controlled desperation as well in the rest of his expression. Looking down at him, she began to move, one very gradual circle of her hips.

She couldn't stay slow for long. Not with Gareth's body pressed against hers while his manhood throbbed inside her. Certainly not when he leaned forward and sucked at her nipple again. By the time he gripped her hips and urged her into an ever-quickening rhythm, she was more than glad to go where he led. Olivia let her head fall back, closed her eyes, and let go.

Pleasure didn't so much build as break like a storm. Everything blended: Olivia's increasingly frantic motions; Gareth arching beneath her, forcing her to take him deeper and harder; heat and sweat and lights flashing behind her eyelids.

Olivia had barely enough presence of mind to scream into her hand when her climax hit. Gareth wasn't far behind. One more powerful thrust forward and up, a long breath escaping through gritted teeth, and then a spreading warmth within her that matched the aftershocks of her own release.

A moment or two later, she opened her eyes reluctantly.

The world was still there.

This was going to be a slight problem.

Chapter 30

THOUGHT FOLLOWED FAR TOO QUICKLY ON THE HEELS OF satisfaction. Gareth would have welcomed a little more time before certain realizations sank in: that he'd just given way to lust on a library chair, for instance, or the woman he'd given way with was, Olivia Brightmore. Particularly the latter.

Briefly, he indulged in a wholehearted wish that his recent activity hadn't burned off the rest of the magical energy. A little intoxication would have been quite welcome.

Gareth forced himself to look up at Olivia. Flushed and disheveled, with her bare body rising up from her dark skirt, she was enough to quicken his pulse even then. Nonetheless, it took an effort for Gareth to meet her eyes. It didn't help either that Olivia's were still a little dazed.

Gareth cleared his throat. "Well," he said and stopped, having come to the end of his store of speech.

"Well," said Olivia. She looked around, glanced down at Gareth, and rose quickly. Gareth's body protested the loss of her warmth, but he resolutely ignored it. "We'd better get back before someone comes looking."

Her voice was crisp now, if not entirely steady. As Gareth watched, she plucked her corset from the floor and began to undo the laces, fingers moving quickly and precisely.

After a moment to rearrange his clothes, Gareth sat up, looked at the wall, and braced himself. Honor demanded certain things from him. Obligations he'd never thought to have toward a confidence woman, granted, but…

He had known Olivia's past when he'd kissed her. He had known it when he'd undressed her and drawn her down onto the chair. Gareth couldn't pretend he'd been under any illusions about her then.

When he looked back at Olivia, she was hooking up the front of her corset, her dark head bent forward. Locks of her tumbled hair fell against one cheek, obscuring Gareth's view of her face. Perhaps that was just as well.

"You must permit me to apologize," he began. "My conduct was—"

"I don't."

Her voice was quiet, and the words were a little muffled by the position of her head, but Gareth heard them well enough.

Still, he asked, "Sorry?"

Olivia sighed. "I don't permit you to do any such thing." She sounded exasperated, hardly flattering at such a time, and she jerked hooks into place as she spoke. "You took no advantage. If anything, I was in more control than you were. I'd less power affecting my mind, and I'm more used to it."

What she said was true, and Gareth couldn't deny it was a relief to hear. He hadn't really expected tears or recrimination, not from Olivia, and yet, a man could never be certain. Especially since he hadn't bedded any respectable women before, not even one with Olivia's nebulous claim to the title.

Nonetheless it left him floundering a little. "Ah…"

The last hook clicked into place. Olivia lifted her head and met his eyes, her gaze as steady as her voice. "You haven't ruined me. I was married before, if you'll recall. And…" Then she did break off and bit her lip. Color rose up her neck. "I'm in no danger of…I know how to keep from…"

"I *am* a doctor, you know," he said and then frowned. "But most methods of preventing children aren't very reliable."

"The magical ones are." Olivia turned away and reached for her blouse. The corset didn't fit at all well now, but it would stay on, or it looked like it would. "Or they're supposed to be. I'll let you know if there's any trouble."

"Yes," said Gareth, trying to get his thoughts into some kind of order. She had magic to keep from getting pregnant? He should have expected as much. He felt rather like the floor was moving.

When he reached for some sort of mental handhold, the lessons of his youth came back again, damn them. "I really think I should—"

Olivia snapped her head up. Her hair fell in dark curls against her bare neck. Glaring at him, she looked like some Olympian goddess faced with a presumptive mortal. "Well, *don't*," she snapped. "It happened, there's no going back, I'm really quite aware of all your regrets, and I give…I'd lose as much as you would if the Grenvilles found out. More, probably. So you don't have to worry about that."

"I wasn't," said Gareth, who truly hadn't thought of the possibility until then.

Some of the flame went out of her eyes. Not all,

though. "Then stop apologizing, and stop trying to work yourself up to whatever offer you think you have to make." Olivia pulled her blouse up onto her shoulders. "I assure you I don't find the idea any more enticing than you do."

While she fastened up the remaining buttons, Gareth stood silently, trying to find some words that were appropriate ones she wouldn't see through as lies. Not that she was repulsive—far from it—or even that marriage would necessarily be unpleasant, though he hadn't thought of the prospect in some years. But to let anyone so intimately into his life, and especially a woman with Olivia's past...

It would have gone against all sense.

Therefore, it must be a relief to hear there was no need for such an offer, to have Olivia reject it before the words had even crossed Gareth's lips. She was certainly a woman of the world and would understand, or should.

Yet Gareth found he couldn't simply say so.

After a little while, she looked up at him with a softer gaze, one hand full of the buttons that had tumbled onto the floor. "Really," said Olivia, "trying to live up to your name is all well and good. But I'm not a damsel in a tower, and this isn't Camelot. We both know anything that...came from this...would be horrible. As for the rest..." She shrugged. "You're a grown man, I'm a grown woman, and we had a moment of weakness after a very trying event. It's hardly the end of the world."

"One can only hope," said Gareth, seeking refuge in wryness. "Hard to know for certain around here."

Olivia laughed quickly. "I think one of the books would have mentioned something," she replied. She slipped the buttons into her skirt pocket, tugged at the front of her shirtwaist, and glanced over at him. "Do you think I can get back to my room without scandal?"

Gareth eyed her, trying to keep his gaze clinical and dispassionate. The missing buttons wouldn't be too obvious unless someone stood very close. Her hair might be a bit of a problem, though. He personally wanted to run his fingers through it, just before trailing them down her neck...

"If anyone asks," he said, "tell them you had a headache after everything upstairs, and I said your hairpins were making it worse. Other than that, I think you'll do."

She flashed him a smile, quick and almost impersonal. That was probably wise, Gareth told himself. "Thank you," she said and headed for the door.

At the last moment, her hand on the knob, Olivia turned back. "Really," she said. "Don't worry. I don't blame you, and there won't be consequences. These things happen. Now that we know, they won't happen again."

"Of course not," said Gareth, because he couldn't think of anything else.

On any other day, Olivia knew her appearance would have drawn attention then questions then probably outrage. Even Gareth's reassurance had been halfhearted, and reasonably so. Her loose hair was blatant, and once someone noticed that, they'd almost certainly be looking for other things amiss.

Take the headache a step further, she told herself, keeping to a swift but decorous pace as she climbed the stairs. She wanted to run, but that would have looked suspicious and she wasn't entirely sure her legs were up to the challenge. *I felt faint, I had to loosen my laces quickly, and I tore some buttons in my haste. Gareth was in the room with me, but he* is *a doctor. There's some advantage to that.*

She repeated the story in her mind a few times, couldn't find any noticeable holes, but still wasn't sure it would hold up. People found scandal in the most innocent things. Her mother had been very clear on that point, long ago, and there was nothing innocent in what she'd just done.

As had happened when she'd come to Englefield, a memory rose up to give her comfort: Hawkins, when she'd first started working for him. She'd asked a similar question, though not about anything carnal. He'd laughed and pulled the ends of his ginger mustache. *Human nature, my dear, straining at gnats and swallowing camels. Lie boldly enough, and a man will believe whatever you tell him. Look nervous, and nobody will believe you if you say the sky is blue.*

Remembering that helped. Regardless, as soon as Olivia made it back to her room, unseen, thank God, or so she thought, she sat heavily on the bed and let herself go weak with relief.

She knew she had been astoundingly lucky. Lucky she wasn't seen, lucky she had a handy excuse, and lucky she'd lived by herself and her clothes still reflected as much, although the idea of Gareth assisting her was diverting on a few levels. Lucky, horribly enough, the Grenvilles' return and distress had kept the household's attention.

Lucky she knew how to lie well, if it came to that.

Quickly, she stood up from the bed and began to repair the damage to her appearance. It really *wasn't* too difficult, not now that she was back in her room and not trying to talk with Gareth at the same time. Not being distracted by his attempts at propriety.

Although the apology had been a bit exasperating, and the halfhearted approach to a proposal more so, Olivia had to admit most men wouldn't have bothered with either. Not for a widow who'd been quite enthusiastic about the whole process, not for a woman who they knew had been on the stage in any capacity, and certainly not for a woman whom they held in less-than-high regard. Gareth was more civil these days, but Olivia was certain his feelings toward her were decidedly mixed, at best.

Despite all of that, she hadn't been surprised when he'd spoken. Irritated, but…Of *course* he'd apologized. Of *course* he'd felt he should offer. Anything else, from Gareth, would have been like sprouting wings or growing a second head. Perhaps even less probable, given their surroundings. Olivia knew him well enough by now.

And even though she'd meant it when she said nothing would happen again, she couldn't find it in her to regret what had already passed between them.

Chapter 31

FOR A MAN WHO HAD BEEN SO OBVIOUSLY CLOSE TO DEATH a few hours before, Mr. Grenville looked remarkably well when Olivia saw him again. That wasn't saying a great deal. He was still lying in bed and very pale, but his eyes focused when he saw her, and he smiled. Joan was actually sitting in the chair by him rather than pacing.

She still looked like she wanted to hit someone.

A bouquet of pink roses lay in her lap, wrapped in several layers of white cloth. "I didn't touch it bare-handed," Joan said when she saw the direction of Olivia's gaze, "and I don't think anyone else did. It was still on the floor of the carriage. Have a look."

With most of her remaining magical strength, Olivia invoked her sight again and peered at the flowers. To her surprise, she saw nothing overtly sinister there—nothing like the light that had attacked Simon—but the roses didn't look normal either. In the aether, they were gray shadows of themselves, bleached and drained of all vitality. When Olivia looked at them again in the normal world, the blossoms were already beginning to decay.

"They were…wrapping," she said, reaching for a metaphor. "Concealment. The spell was the package."

"Bloody good package," said Mr. Grenville, his voice hoarse. "The thorn went straight through my glove."

"Should I—?" Olivia started to rise, thinking of

defenses. "All the students are indoors and being watched, but if there's more someone should do…"

Mr. Grenville shook his head. "Not just now. The wards hold. Anyone who could get past them wouldn't have bothered with roses."

The door opened again. It could have been a maid, it could have been one of the students, but Olivia knew it was Gareth even before she glanced backward and met his eyes.

Any hopes she'd had about their attraction dying out now that they'd acted on it had clearly been vain ones. The time and place quelled some of the energy Olivia felt when she looked at Gareth, and so did her exhaustion, but it was still there, like a faint but constant whisper.

She looked down quickly, and Gareth looked past her, letting his breath out as he approached the bed. "Simon…my God, you're a quick healer."

"Mostly your doing, old man," said Mr. Grenville and then gestured to Olivia. "And Mrs. Brightmore's. So Joan tells me, at any rate. You both have my deepest thanks. I rather suspect I owe you my life."

Customers had been effusive in their gratitude sometimes. Women had clung to Olivia and wept, and men had made all sorts of melodramatic speeches. Compared to them, Simon's thanks was almost curt. But Olivia blushed and couldn't think of anything to say for a moment.

"What in the name of God *was* that?" Gareth asked even more abruptly than Olivia might have expected for such a question.

"St. John, if I say more than 'a curse,' you won't

understand and you won't want to know," Mr. Grenville replied. He reached for the glass of water on the bed stand, sipped, and went on. "And I'm afraid I don't know much more than that, in any case. We had come off the train from London, and John was just bringing the carriage around. Joan got in first. I was about to join her when someone called my name—Miss Talbot."

"*Rosemary* Talbot?" Olivia asked, though she would have found it just as hard to believe Rosemary's sister had been involved in this affair.

Mr. Grenville nodded. "We spoke a little. She—" He shook his head. "Some of the specifics are blurred now. I probably could have remembered more before I was ill. She was very friendly, very pleasant. Now I think there was something off about her, but…hindsight taints these perceptions."

"And she gave you these?" Gareth gestured to the roses in Joan's lap.

"She told me to give them to my wife," said Mr. Grenville. He spoke bluntly and without inflection in his voice, but Olivia caught the glance that passed between him and Joan.

Joan shrugged. "Doesn't mean I was the target. Young women here wouldn't give a man flowers for himself. She was very enthusiastic about something, though. I didn't hear her speak, but she put a hand on your shoulder for a second."

"That's…not usual," said Mr. Grenville and sighed. "But it's not exactly damning either. Perhaps she was eager for news of my sister. Or she'd just become engaged. I wish I could recall more clearly."

"Do you know where she got the flowers?" Gareth

asked. "Perhaps someone from London. Someone who heard you were looking into the Ripper."

"No," said Mr. Grenville. "Joan was right. There's no magic in the killings."

"That doesn't mean there isn't any around them," Joan said. "Flies gather. And we didn't keep our return a secret. Talbot makes a much better dupe than she does a magician. If someone on an earlier train gave her the flowers—"

"We'll have to talk with her," Olivia said.

She stood and went toward the window, where she could see a thin line of darkness between the blue velvet drapes. She knew about the purpose of the school. The aim wasn't simply teaching children to control their powers. However, until now, any outside threats had been purely theoretical. Her hands were cold, as if she'd pressed them against the window glass and held them there.

"I'll go tomorrow," she said to the window.

"Take St. John, then," said Joan. "He's tangled with the curse. He might be able to see its tracks. Also, he can probably shoot," she added and turned to Gareth with no apparent apology for talking about him like a piece of furniture. "Can you?"

"Barely," said Gareth.

"Better than not at all. I'd go myself, but if Simon's wrong, and that's been known to happen, something *might* try to hit us here. I'll need to be here if it does."

Any other two men Olivia had known would have protested the idea of a woman trying to fight off whatever forces were behind the curse. She didn't hear any objections, though. When she turned from the window,

Mr. Grenville was actually grinning at his wife with both affection and confidence.

Gareth, Olivia suspected, was less happy about Joan's plan, but he knew her too well to speak against it. So did Olivia, for that matter.

"Who do you think might have planned this?" she asked.

"I couldn't say," said Mr. Grenville, "not with certainty. We mostly encountered stories in London. Some of the groups we heard of may exist. Some may be as old and as bloody as people claim."

"But, at the time, there was nobody who looked like an immediate threat," Joan said and grimaced. "We'll have to revise that now, obviously. But who would've noticed us *and* decided Simon needed to die *and* gotten an agent down here before we did? We didn't even get in any fights."

She sounded almost disappointed.

"You might not have had to," Olivia said. "If someone knew about Englefield already and thought you were expanding your interest…maybe. However, it does seem odd."

She leaned back into her chair. Now, after a sort of love and a sort of war and all sorts of worry, exhaustion was creeping into her bones. She resisted the urge to lean her face against the plush and fall asleep.

"We shouldn't tire you," Gareth said. He spoke to Mr. Grenville, but Olivia thought he'd glanced at her first. She straightened up and tried to look alert. "If we can't do anything before tomorrow—"

"You can tell me what happened while we were gone," said Simon. "I think I probably have the strength to hear it."

"I wouldn't be so sure of that," said Gareth.

—៳៳—

"This place *was* a monastery once," Simon said when Olivia had finished her account of the forest. "Dissolved sometime in the 1540s, so we can blame old Henry VIII for most of our troubles. My enterprising ancestors took a heavy hand with anything that looked too connected to Rome. I think the only remnants of the original are the foundation and your monk."

"Your monk, really," said Gareth.

"I somehow don't think he'd take that well," said Simon. "I'm surprised there weren't more...dramatic events in the history after Brother Jonathan died."

Olivia, who was looking remarkably tired and re-markably lovely at the same time—rather unfair, to Gareth's mind—shrugged. "Perhaps there were," she said. "Perhaps the people responsible left, one way or another. If you couldn't exercise your powers without them getting out of control, you'd probably move away too. Or they stopped doing anything outdoors near the forest, and the land had some chance to repair itself. Then most people stopped believing—"

"Until we started a school here, full of exactly the kind of people who *would* try magic outside"—Mrs. Grenville sighed—"or ask her students to do it."

"You couldn't have known," said Olivia. "Besides, it's better that we found out when we did. Otherwise, the power out there could've fed something even worse than Michael's storms. As it was, it very nearly did," she admitted, startling Gareth with her forthrightness. "Waite and Fitzpatrick summoned Balam yesterday."

"*Did* they?" Gareth wouldn't have quite called Mrs.

Grenville's expression surprised. One didn't describe a lion as surprised when it spotted an antelope came in sight. "I see."

There was a world of promise in those words, and Simon clearly heard it. He laughed and winced at the same time. "Try not to kill our students."

"I damn near didn't have the chance. I wish I had pictures to show them. Visual aids always work better." Mrs. Grenville sighed again, directing it at the world rather than herself this time, and turned back to Olivia and Gareth. "Everything's all right, though? Nobody's hurt?"

"Nobody's hurt," Olivia said. "And I sent Balam back. I haven't really dismissed many demons. There was some strange resistance there toward the end, but I don't believe I left him a passage back here."

Gareth thought again of the shadow he'd seen. Perhaps Balam had been calling in reinforcements? He wasn't sure how demons worked, and he hadn't seen either the demon or the shadow since.

"You'll have to give me more details soon," Simon said. "I've never dismissed a demon before, not one that was incarnate physically, and certainly not one of the Ancient Lords. Well done."

"I was fortunate," said Olivia, "to get there before he'd fully manifested." She glanced over at Gareth then, subtly and just for an instant, and raised one eyebrow.

Somewhere in the last few months he'd learned to read her face. She would tell the Grenvilles what had happened. They needed to know, but she was giving him the chance to speak first, to be the one to tell his part of it.

Gareth fought back the absurd urge to take her hand.

Chapter 32

WORD GOT AROUND QUICKLY.

By breakfast time the next day, two of the maids were eying Gareth as though he were a fire-eater at a carnival, he'd distinctly heard whispering about "Mr. Grenville's health" and "strange men in London." Fairley, with the boldness of thirteen, had actually come out and asked what had happened and what Gareth had done.

"If the Grenvilles wanted you to know," Gareth replied sternly, "they would have told you, wouldn't they?"

"But they can't, sir. Nobody's seen them yet." Undeniably true. Fairley hesitated a second before drawing closer to Gareth's desk and lowering his voice. "And he was in London, and Waite says—"

"I can only imagine. Go on," he added. Since the Grenvilles *hadn't* yet come down, and he wasn't sure where Olivia was, Gareth supposed the role of authority, and the necessary quashing of rumors, fell to him. "What pearls of wisdom does Mr. Waite have in this situation?"

Fairley looked down. "He says there's Chinese magicians who can make a man's blood turn to lead, sir, or his hands and feet fall off. And Indians who—"

"If Waite's ever met a man from anywhere beyond Calais, it will be the most astonishing news I've heard all year," Gareth said. "Which is saying a good deal."

"Then people can't do what he said?"

Gareth paused. His time at Englefield and his

conversations with Simon had left him sure there *were* magicians capable of the sorts of feats Fairley described. Some of them could well be from China or India, though Cornwall or Surrey were origins just as likely. It didn't matter. He'd seen concern in Fairley's face beneath the youthfully morbid curiosity. That mattered.

"Mr. Grenville retains all of his limbs, I assure you," he said dryly, "and his blood contains no stranger elements than any man's. He *was* attacked, which he'll tell you about when he chooses, or not, but he was doing quite well last night, and I expect him to be even more recovered when I examine him this morning."

Manfully, Fairley tried to hide his sigh of relief. *Poor lad*, Gareth thought. He'd read what records Simon kept on the boy and had gained some impression of the parade of tutors and relatives' homes that had been facets in his life before Englefield. Human compassion aside, this was the first place where anyone had really been able to teach him. No wonder he'd been worried.

"You may also tell Waite," Gareth added, "that if the worst should happen, your training would continue. I'm certain Mr. Grenville has made preparations for that." If Simon hadn't, Mrs. Grenville almost certainly had. She was, in Gareth's experience, a woman willing to consider a truly frightening range of possibilities.

Not, sadly, that a husband's death was so far out of the ordinary, particularly in this case. Gareth didn't like to think it about his friend, but a man who'd set himself against the sort of forces Simon had, was a man who might not count on seeing gray hairs. Mrs. Grenville seemed aware of this, unlike many women who married into war.

Had Olivia thought of the possibility? She'd been young, younger than Miss Woodwell, and there hadn't been a war at the time. Easy enough for a schoolgirl to see the uniform and not think about what it meant.

"Sir?"

Gareth focused his attention on Fairley again. "Is there anything else?"

"No, sir. Only—"

"Only there is, isn't there?"

"Wellll," Fairley said, stretching the word out like taffy, "are we going to get attacked, sir? I mean, if someone tried to kill Mr. Grenville, maybe they might want to get us too? Not that I wouldn't fight them, sir," he added hastily, thirteen-year-old pride asserting itself.

No, you damned well wouldn't. Gareth shut his mouth over the words and banished the mental image of Fairley with his eyes dull and his throat bloody. "Mr. Grenville has told me specifically that we're in no danger," he said. "Besides, the grounds here have their own protections. Is *that* all?"

"Yes, sir," said Fairley.

If there ever *was* an attack, Gareth would personally see to it that Fairley and Elizabeth ended up locked in a wine cellar or a closet with the servants, ideally with something the size of Balam guarding it. He would have preferred such a location for almost everyone else too, but sixteen *wasn't* too old for a man to fight if he wished, which meant Waite and Fitzpatrick had a right to decide on their own, and Mrs. Grenville and Miss Woodwell were quite capable of taking care of themselves in any battle that was likely to involve Englefield.

So was Olivia.

Gareth wasn't entirely certain if it was more relief or worry to recognize her capabilities. He *was* certain he shouldn't be thinking about it, that the question should trouble him no more than that of Miss Woodwell's situation.

He was also certain he wasn't the sort of man who started drinking at nine in the morning.

Regrettably.

"Is Mr. Grenville doing well?"

It was the first thing Olivia found to say, other than "Good morning," and she managed it only after she and Gareth had left the gates of Englefield and started down the road to the village. She felt ridiculous. Ten years performing before skeptical audiences, three months teaching and working with the man, and now she was a tongue-tied schoolgirl.

He hadn't said anything either. That might have been a good sign or a very bad one, and Olivia spent the first part of the walk wondering which, before taking the plunge and speaking.

Gareth seemed to welcome her question. He smiled at any rate. "Much better," he said, "though it will probably take him a while to recover fully. I can't speak from any authority as medical school doesn't precisely cover the subject, but I'd wager it'd be good for him to avoid magic for a while, as well as any other taxing activity"

"I agree," Olivia said, thinking of the roses and shivering, "and I can take over his lessons for a while. Hopefully that'll permit him to rest for a time."

Hopefully. If the curse wasn't simply the first stage of a more thorough attack. Gareth might have been thinking the same thing, for he was no longer smiling.

"When we get to the Talbots'," she said, "I thought I would talk to Rosemary for a while. That might be enough of a distraction so you could…inspect her, I suppose. I don't know if any trace of whatever happened would show up to you, but it might be worth an attempt."

Gareth nodded. "Will you look as well?"

"I can't, really," Olivia said and sighed. "Not without being obvious. And I'd really rather not anger the Talbots if we can avoid it. I'd imagine they can make life very unpleasant for us."

They turned down a road and came into sight of the vicarage, an old stone cottage with a pleasant garden in front. As they approached, a gray-and-white cat ran out from behind the house and past them.

"It looks peaceful enough," said Olivia, bracing herself and trying to think of the least awkward way to begin the conversation again.

"Most places do," said Gareth.

The door opened even as he reached for the knocker, and Olivia and Gareth were suddenly looking into the vicar's pale face. He looked between them for a while. Then his wide eyes came to rest on Gareth, and relief tempered a little of the frantic dismay. "Thank the Lord you've come," he said. "Rosemary's upstairs."

Rosemary Talbot lay white and still in her bed, and Gareth couldn't find a reason for it.

Her breathing was shallow but regular, her pulse fainter than he'd have liked but steady. She had no fever, and when he examined her, he could find no wounds.

Certainly there was nothing about her that resembled the way Simon's arm had looked the night before.

He shifted his vision and found nothing more definite. The rose-pink threads that made up her body were faded, but that was all.

In any case, he could do something about that. Gareth put a hand on Rosemary's shoulder and carefully fed some of his own energy into her body, watching as the threads took on a brighter shade. She didn't open her eyes, but her breathing became deeper, her pulse stronger.

"She *should* be well enough," he said, sitting up, "in time, with rest." His gift usually showed anything really wrong, even if it wasn't apparent from outside.

All the same, it was best to be sure. "I'd like to speak with both of you in the hall," Gareth said to the vicar and his elder daughter. "Mrs. Brightmore, if you'd be so kind as to keep watch in case Miss Rosemary wakes up?"

"Of course," Olivia said. Meeting Gareth's eyes, she also nodded a second after she'd spoken. She'd understood his silent message. "I'll be right here."

Outside, Miss Elizabeth Talbot clung to her father's arm, while the vicar faced Gareth with somewhat less panic than he'd shown before. "I know it's Providence that brought you to us," he said, "since we didn't have time to send a message. I don't know how to thank you, Doctor. She is going to be all right?"

"She looks very much like she will," said Gareth, "though I'll want to come back tomorrow to be sure. When did this happen?"

"Perhaps a quarter of an hour before you arrived," said Miss Talbot. "She simply…collapsed."

"Had she been feeling at all ill beforehand?"

Reverend Talbot shook his head. "Not that she mentioned, but she *had* been rather subdued for a day or two. She said she was simply tired, and she went for a walk a little while before you came. Perhaps the activity was too much, and I shouldn't have let her go."

"Papa," said Miss Talbot, "it was by no means your fault. She looked well enough. She was only…quiet. But you must have seen her," she said to Gareth, "or Mrs. Brightmore or the girls. She went to Englefield to call on them two days ago. Did…did anything happen there?"

"No," said Gareth. He could only hope his voice sounded normal. "She seemed quite all right to me."

Rosemary Talbot hadn't called at Englefield any time in the last few days.

Two days ago, Fitzpatrick and Waite had opened a door. Olivia had closed it, but had she closed it in time?

———

Gareth had hoped either Olivia or Simon would dismiss his theory: nothing else could possibly have come through when the boys had summoned Balam. Ludicrous idea. Only a layman could have believed him. He would have welcomed mockery.

Instead, Simon swore, and Olivia sighed. "Rosemary had much the same look that the roses did," she said. "Drained. *Used*, I would say."

She'd been silent on the way back to Englefield, and so had Gareth. Not all of it had to do with awkwardness or even thought. Gareth hadn't wanted to speak about the situation until they were within whatever protection the house could provide, and he thought Olivia had felt the same. The windows in the village had looked far too much like eyes.

"Will she recover?" Simon asked.

"I thought so," said Gareth, "but—"

Olivia nodded. "I think what went into the roses was the most destructive and least-thinking part of the demon. Besides, animals are more resilient than plants, by and large. A grown woman certainly has more re-serves than a bunch of cut roses. But whatever happened could have seriously damaged her, I think, if Gareth hadn't been there."

"Ah," said Gareth. The compliment was disconcert-ing. The urge to straighten his shoulders and grin was more so. He cleared his throat. "So there's something out there that's…possessing people?"

"It sounds that way," said Simon, and his hands clenched on the bedclothes. "At the worst time possible, no less, which was doubtless its intent, since it failed to take over *my* mind."

"Why didn't it attempt to control someone in the house, then?" Olivia asked. "There were plenty of people around."

"The wards," said Simon. "They would have expelled it rather forcefully, almost as soon as it entered. If it had possessed me, since I belong to the house, it could have got back in. If it had killed me, the wards would have collapsed, and it would have had access to any number of things I would imagine demons enjoy."

"And now it's…somewhere in the village," said Gareth. "Some*one* in the village."

"Possibly," said Olivia. "We don't know what kind of demon it is or how long it can survive this world without some sort of body. But you're probably right," she admitted with a sigh, "and I don't see any more pleasant alternative." She looked questioningly at Simon, who shook his head. "Then there we are. I wish to God someone knew where Rosemary went this morning. Somewhere close enough to see us coming, I'd think, but that doesn't rule out very much."

"No," said Simon. "Not when we don't know the sort of hosts it can use. I'll read up. Not much else I *can* do right now, is there?"

"No," Gareth said firmly and without letting any sympathy slip into his voice.

"You do have a degree, I suppose. Mrs. Brightmore, your help with research would be valuable, but I'll also need you to reinforce the house's protections. This incident's rather enlightened me on that score. Both of you, keep a close eye on the students. For the next few days, I don't think anyone from the house should go to the village without one of you, or Joan, accompanying them. And all of you should be wary. Don't let anyone touch you, since it seems that's how this thing switches bodies."

"And the people in the village?" Olivia asked.

Simon grimaced. "We can't do anything for them just now. Not until we know more. The demon hasn't made any direct physical threats, so far. We'll have to hope that continues."

Across the room, Olivia nodded once. Her lips were thin, her eyes shadowed, and Gareth suspected he didn't look much better himself.

"We're under siege," he said. "Aren't we?"

Chapter 33

Siege.

Olivia hadn't thought of the word until Gareth said it. There were advantages, of a sort, to being in the company of military men. Precise terms for particular situations, for instance. Comfort was not among those advantages.

She prepared her classes, emphasizing methods of defense: words and symbols, plants and stones, and the warning signs that something was amiss. After consulting with Joan, she also told her students why they couldn't go down to the village and why they should be wary of anyone, stranger or not, who came to the house.

They listened, still and staring and, for almost the first time since Olivia had come to Englefield, silent. The look in Elizabeth's eyes and the schoolboy bravery on Michael's face squeezed her heart.

If it had been safe to send any of them home, the Grenvilles probably would have done it. At the very least, they'd have sent Michael and Elizabeth away. Englefield was warded, while their homes were not, and their coaches and trains certainly wouldn't be. So they stayed, and lessons went on.

Sometimes there was nothing to do. Olivia knew that. In London she'd met women with fading black eyes, who'd asked her silly questions because they hadn't wanted to put the real ones into words. She'd met a ghost far too young for the life she'd led, let alone for her death, and a man who'd been robbed on the way home to his wife and left to bleed in the street. And Tommy had coughed his life away in the rooms she'd never quite been able to get clean.

She'd made peace, of a sort, with having no power over some things.

Having power, she was learning, was no holiday either.

The village loomed up on one side, out of all proportion to its actual size, and the forest on the other. Trapped between them, Englefield—and Olivia—could only wait.

After the first day passed without incident, she started to relax. It probably wasn't wise, but she couldn't help it. The body could take only so much of being on edge. The mind and soul could handle still less. It was either put the demon out of her mind for a few minutes of her time, or go insane and be of no use to anyone if it did show up.

Rosemary Talbot was recovering, Gareth said. Nobody else in the village had been acting too odd when he'd checked. Perhaps the demon had put itself into a tree stump or a rock accidentally, thinking such things were terribly powerful beings in this world.

Olivia didn't have much hope.

All the same, she let the students leave the house on the second day. They weren't to go down the main road to the village, they weren't to talk to any strangers, and they all seemed nervous enough to obey her commands.

Besides, she came with them.

The gardens in November presented a bleak prospect, all hedges and bare dirt, but there was space enough there for the students to take some exercise, and Olivia could see if anyone approached from the road. She'd expected it to be a pleasant interlude where everyone could get some fresh air.

She hadn't expected to see Gareth sitting on one of the benches.

"I hope we're not disturbing you," she said as he rose to greet her.

"No, not at all." The students were wandering off, splitting into their own groups. "If you could use another pair of eyes—"

"Gladly," said Olivia, taking a seat. "The road's clear enough, and I can't imagine anyone coming over the fields without being very obvious, but the fewer chances we take, the better."

"Have you or Simon discovered anything?"

"Not very much. It's surprising how few books actually talk much about demons, or at least about how they act when they're loose in this world. We do have a formula for exorcism"

"Will that be helpful?" Gareth sat down, carefully maintaining a proper distance from her. "It already moves between bodies, doesn't it?"

"Forcing it out is different. The magician has some power over the creature, then. Mr. Grenville says he's done it before."

"Has he? I didn't know that, but there's probably a great deal about him I don't know."

Olivia glanced toward the students. William and Charlotte were talking by the ornamental fountain, while Arthur was telling some story to the younger two children. So far, there was nothing sinister happening.

"I think nobody knows a great deal about anyone," she said absently. "We don't excel at understanding."

"No," said Gareth, and a shadow crossed his face. "Purposeful obfuscation's more our line. As a species, I mean, though I don't know if any others are better."

"Animals, perhaps. I'd have to ask Charlotte. I think they're simpler. Perhaps that helps. Or perhaps they're no better than we are, and they simply have less to understand."

The wind blew Gareth's hair across his forehead. Olivia watched and wished she didn't want to. "Do the dead?" he asked abruptly, "understand people better?"

"Not the ones who are still here, most of the time," said Olivia. "A few, like Brother Jonathan, have a purpose, and they're more…whole. More like living people. Otherwise, the ones who stay are generally more confused than the living. Upset too. It's one of the reasons situations could get violent, though I never was around any attempts at murder before."

"Thank God," Gareth said with heat Olivia hadn't expected to hear. "How violent?" he asked quickly.

"Mostly just flying china. Sometimes the dead weren't even responsible. People who had talents of their own would come to séances, and if those people weren't entirely happy, or sane, things could get out of hand. I learned to cope."

"It sounds like a hard lesson," Gareth said.

"Oh, it was." Another look toward the students showed that Charlotte had joined the group near Arthur, and William was off on his own, studying one of the bushes. Everything seemed innocent enough. "I'm amazed I lived through the first time, really. The spirit was a child, and so…you can understand why it'd be upset. I talked to it, and that worked. Thank God. I didn't realize how lucky I was until later. I didn't realize what *could* have happened."

Gareth gestured toward the students. "Something like what *they* called up?"

"Probably worse," Olivia said. "They had the sense to set up a circle. They made some attempt to protect themselves and the school. I didn't even take it that seriously. I'd just got the book to—" She stopped for a second and cleared her throat. "Because I thought it would be convincing."

Without surprise, she watched Gareth's face close up. "Ah," he said, and then, "You…"

She didn't need this.

Arthur and William were talking now. They were quiet, but William's face was…sulky, perhaps. Olivia couldn't quite identify the expression, and it didn't matter.

"If you'll excuse me," she said and got to her feet, "I'd better make sure everything's going well."

"Of course," Gareth said and let her go.

Olivia didn't look back. She didn't want to see relief on his face.

Chapter 34

THESE DAYS, GARETH'S NIGHTMARES WEREN'T EVEN THAT bad. Everything still went wrong, everyone still died, and Gareth still stood and watched or sometimes tried to help with hands as large and clumsy as bricks. No part of it was pleasant. But he'd grown used to the dreams, familiar enough that a part of his mind recognized them and knew what was going to happen. He couldn't quite keep himself apart from the horror, but there were worse things.

Waking up was one of them.

His dark room was perfectly still, utterly calm. There were no enemy soldiers here or the ravening demons that had started to keep company with them in Gareth's sleeping mind. Nothing had happened.

That was the problem. In his dreams, everything had already gone merrily to hell. Waking to find that nothing had, Gareth inevitably ended up staring into the darkness and thinking about all the ways it *could*. Every time, there seemed to be more. Englefield was quite an education that way.

Not entirely fair. The threats had always been there, though Gareth hadn't always lived a few feet away from impulsive youths with the power to call them up, and the lessons at Englefield were making the world a better-defended place, or they would.

Fine, high-sounding sentiments. None of them

stopped some hateful part of Gareth's mind from exploring all the possibilities he'd never known about before:
crawling things with too many legs, power that could
warp a man's body, hellfire, lightning…

This time was worse than usual. He knew the darkness around him was empty, yet still it seemed to have
grown eyes.

Familiar by now with the treachery of his mind,
Gareth knew he wouldn't be able to stop counting the
possible disasters. Not lying idle, anyhow. He rose,
donned his dressing gown, and slipped quietly out of
his room.

Darkness and stillness held the house firmly. If there
was a light anywhere, Gareth didn't see it, but he was
decent at moving in the darkness, as a general rule, and
quite good at it now, at least on the path from his room
to the kitchens. He didn't walk particularly silently,
but he managed well enough, not bumping into any
tables or knocking over vases. In the kitchen, Nellie,
the cook, had left out the usual late supper, complete
with wine. One of the few favors Gareth had brought
himself to ask of the servants. He'd have to give them
a bit extra for that at Christmas, and that was coming
soon enough. Unnervingly soon. Had he really been at
Englefield four months?

Had it been *only* four months?

Time, Simon had said one evening at university,
went strangely in other worlds and for beings from
those places. At times, Gareth thought it moved quite
strangely enough for mortal men in the normal world.

He poured himself a glass of wine, sliced some bread
then looked down at the knife. The blade shone in the

dying firelight. Steel, not silver. Not cold iron either. Modern steel contained too many other metals, and Olivia had said that iron didn't always work anyway. Kitchen knives weren't much good against creatures in the darkness, unless they were the kind of things any sharp edge could hurt.

The demon roamed beyond the walls of Englefield. Simon had said so. And knives would hurt only whatever poor bastard it was using as a host.

Not that Gareth would have been much use even with Excalibur. Perhaps especially with Excalibur. The Royal Medical Society had never really covered sword fighting.

He broke the bread in half, took a bite, chewed, and swallowed mechanically. Around him, the kitchen kept its quiet. There were faint sounds from the dying fire, quiet creakings from the walls as the house settled, and that was all. He might have been the only person left alive.

Gareth took a large sip of the wine.

Quiet had never bothered him before. He'd also never spent so much time considering potential weapons. Absurd. He'd been to war.

But it had been...he couldn't say an *ordinary* war. He didn't know that there were ordinary wars. But Egypt had been a war of flesh and blood, gunpowder and steel. When the latter met the former, the results had been horrific and all too often on his hands, but Gareth had known what to do and done it. The strangest thing he'd regularly encountered had been his power. His doubts and failures had been, for the most part, those of any man.

Now the walls didn't seem solid enough, and the shadows were too solid. In the daytime, he could tell himself Simon and Olivia had warded the place well. He didn't see Simon's face gone green and half-dead, and he didn't imagine Olivia's in the same condition or an alien soul looking out of her eyes...

He fought back the urge to break something or to shout. Anything to end the silence.

Gareth finished the wine and made himself eat the rest of the bread, though he realized about halfway through he wasn't particularly hungry. It didn't matter. He'd made himself eat often enough in Egypt. The body was a machine: the machine required fuel. Black moods were not a factor.

The food calmed him a little, as he'd known it would, anchored his body a little more solidly to the present time and place. It wasn't quite enough, nor was a single glass of wine, but there were habits Gareth did not want to risk acquiring. He'd seen them enough before, in other men.

Prayer, strong drink, or bad women.

He tried to put the voice out of his head. There had been no decision this time, no moment of failure. He had to adapt. That was all.

Besides, he'd tried praying on other nights. Like the food, it had calmed him only a little, and the other two recommendations weren't available. Rather, there were bottles of drink in the library, which Gareth would almost certainly make noise reaching, and there *might* have been one woman in the village who'd be amenable to coin. There usually was. Her hypothetical existence did him no good at all in his current state.

He thought of Olivia then, remembered her astride him, half-naked, flushed, panting. She'd responded far more thoroughly to his passion than the few other women he'd been with. Natural enough, perhaps, given the choices available to an army surgeon abroad. And he was certain her reactions had been genuine. If nothing else, Gareth didn't think she'd have given him the satisfaction of knowing he'd pleased her if the pleasure hadn't overwhelmed her control.

Not the first few times.

The tension at his groin, admittedly, did distract Gareth from his previous lines of thought. It also left him sitting alone at a kitchen table, hot and hard and unable to do anything about it.

Bed would help. Gareth stood up. He'd go back to bed, bring himself what release he could manage, and hope some physical relaxation and the wine would send him back to sleep, and that afterward, his thoughts wouldn't turn back along either of their previous courses.

Sometimes it actually worked.

He left the fire banked behind him and the kitchen dim, but even so, he had to pause a little way up the staircase and let his eyes get used to the full darkness again. Now, in mid-November, all the drapes were drawn at night. Perhaps an atom of moonlight might have gotten through, had the night not been cloudy. As it was, even waiting helped him only so much.

Upstairs, there were sounds. Not many, not at two in the morning, the time Gareth saw on the clock, but a few. For instance, one of the boys snored loudly enough to be heard through a door. It was something of a surprise the other two hadn't smothered him in his sleep.

Perhaps Englefield was doing fairly well as a moral force.

There was no reason he should have been able to tell Olivia's door from the others. He'd never gone in. He'd never had occasion to go in. With the exception of the early days, when Elizabeth had still been prone to uncontrolled levitation, and Simon's recent crisis, Gareth had never bothered entering anyone's room but his. He would have told a servant if he'd wanted to talk to Olivia.

For the most part, he hadn't.

Her door was two down from his, beyond one of the infernal small tables Simon or Simon's housekeeper had installed as a danger to anyone wandering around at night. Gareth stopped in front of it, put his hands in the pockets of his dressing gown, and told himself to move on.

Olivia would certainly be asleep. Gareth had intended the thought as a reproof to himself, a reason why he shouldn't disturb the woman. She would be tired, and she'd had a long day. Instead, the thought of her sleeping conjured an image as powerful as any she'd produced for her audiences: Olivia curled on her side, white linen in disarray around her body, her dark hair coming out of its braid. Or turned over, perhaps, sprawled on her back or her stomach, unknowing and open to the touch of hands...or lips...

Gareth's experience with women was limited, and that of sleeping women almost more so. Still, he was under the impression they wore little beneath nightgowns.

He flexed his hands inside his pockets, ran his thumb over his curled fingers, and tried to think of all the reasons he shouldn't even imagine exactly what he was about to do.

It was late. They both had positions to maintain. Her character was doubtful, or at least her past was spotted. He'd heard something about forgiveness being divine, but Gareth wasn't sure bedding the woman was the sort of "forgiveness" the Bible prescribed.

As long as he remained at Englefield, some connection with Olivia was unavoidable. He hadn't managed to resist a certain degree of intimacy. There was no real point castigating himself for that. She'd been willing, and he was human. But did he really want to repeat his error?

He took one hand out of his pocket and tapped at the door.

The sound wasn't at all loud. Gareth was sure nobody in the other rooms would hear it, and not at all certain Olivia would. Not until the door opened a crack and he saw her face, sleepy and worried above golden-brown wool.

Clearly, she hadn't been expecting him. She paused, caught between alarm and curiosity. There was no anger on her face, at any rate. And then she said in a whisper, "Gareth. Is something wrong?"

Gareth shook his head and watched as she relaxed, her expression becoming purely curious, and then…less than pure. Her gaze drifted downward from his face, paused at his neck, and showed every sign of progressing farther, but Olivia jerked it back up.

Damn willpower, anyway.

Gareth put a hand on the door frame, just close enough to hers that their fingers brushed together. No very intimate contact, but he heard her catch her breath, and he felt his body tense.

Anything could happen this late at night.

He lowered his voice to a whisper. "Let me in."

Chapter 35

"YES."

Olivia hadn't thought to say it. Not at first. In the moment after Gareth spoke, she thought *that's a dreadfully demanding way to make a request* and *it's the middle of the night* and *are you absolutely sure you should be doing this*? She didn't wonder whether she should be accepting his advances. She knew she shouldn't.

But she was standing very close to him in order to whisper through the crack in the door. Close enough to feel the heat from his body and to be aware of how little they were each wearing. Close enough to pick up the sharp scent of his cologne and a faint musk that was more personal.

In other words, too close for either propriety or good sense.

When she opened her mouth, Olivia said none of the things she'd been thinking. "Yes" hovered in the air between them, faint as moth wings, and then she was moving to the side, letting Gareth into her room.

He closed the door behind him, gently. Discreetly. It made a quiet little click, and then he was reaching for her, a darker shape in the night.

Olivia went to him. There was no conscious thought in it. She simply moved as iron to a magnet, until her body was flush against his and her arms were around his neck and he was kissing her, the taste of wine faint on his lips.

Whatever there had been a moment ago, little gentleness remained in him now. Gareth wound one hand in her hair while he kissed her, and his other cupped her backside, holding her all the more firmly to him. His arousal would have been quite obvious even through proper clothing. With only their nightclothes in the way, it felt like heated stone.

The responding hunger in Olivia's body was instant…and insistent. Had she been tired? Had she been asleep, in fact, five minutes ago? Nothing from her neck to her knees remembered as much, and whatever feeble opinions her brain might have ventured on the subject were quickly outvoted.

Her room was comfortable enough but by no means large. A few half-stumbling steps backward brought Olivia to the edge of her bed. She pulled Gareth down with her, hands on his shoulders. No hard task. Her intent was certainly clear enough, and he was quite willing to comply. His body settled on top of hers, a delicious weight that made her arch upward and whimper.

It was too late, in many senses of the word, for self-control.

———

Gareth had abandoned quite a bit of his reserve the second after he'd knocked at Olivia's door. Most of the rest had gone when he'd spoken. His request was not the sort to leave Olivia in any doubt of his intentions. And that he'd made it at so uncivilized an hour, without any provocation, was an admission in itself.

Therefore, when he finally had her in his arms, he wasted no time in moving them both toward the bed,

and when Olivia drew him down to meet her, he didn't
bother teasing or questioning. She was soft and warm,
there were no corsets or buttons to deal with this time,
and his mind was drowning in sensation. In desire. When
she arched her back to press against him, and when she
made a throaty little sound of arousal in his ear, Gareth
didn't even think about holding back. Rather, he groaned
her name, retaining just enough control to be quiet about
it, lest the damn servants or the blasted students over-
hear, and thrust against her, achingly hard.

Gareth wanted to take her then. He wanted to shove
her nightgown up and plunge inside her, to grab her
hips and lose himself in her body. Ungentlemanly as
that would have been, he didn't think Olivia would have
minded, not given the way she was writhing beneath him
or how damp the fabric between her legs was getting.

But he wanted more.

Biting his lip, Gareth pulled himself back from the
edge and rose from Olivia's body, then rolled to the
side. She made a slight noise of protest, but then he slid
his hands down, pushing her dressing gown off her
shoulders. She laughed quietly, shrugging herself the
rest of the way out as Gareth shed his own clothes.
"You're lucky I hadn't tied the belt," she said.

"I'd have needed a candle."

"There is one," Olivia said thoughtfully and then
caught her breath as Gareth reached for her again, finding the hem of her nightgown and sliding his hands underneath. Her thighs were firm and smooth against his
fingers, the muscles tense with excitement. Her voice
came again, faint now. "If you want."

Tempting thought. Gareth remembered the view he'd

had of her breasts bouncing in a steady rhythm as she'd ridden him on the chair. He thought of how many times he'd imagined her naked and spread out before him, flushed with desire.

But finding a candle would have meant he had to stop touching her.

"No," he said, and then, "Not now."

"Ah."

In the darkness, she moved, though not enough to displace his hands, which were heading steadily upward, tracing over her inner thighs. The fabric over them slid up then disappeared.

Helpful woman. Surely she deserved a reward.

Olivia whimpered again when Gareth brushed his fingers over her sex. When he slid one inside her, she buried her face in her pillow to avoid making louder sounds. Gareth wrapped his free arm around her and pulled her toward him, a difficult task to accomplish while still moving his hand between her legs, but one that proved very worthwhile.

The feeling of her naked body against his was overwhelming. Somewhere, there were disparate sensations: her breath hot on his shoulder, the small, hard points of her nipples pressing against his chest, the warm satin feel of her stomach against his cock. But it all blended together, became white heat and electricity.

If there was a man who could hold off under such temptation, it wasn't Gareth.

Another quick motion brought Olivia beneath him. At the pressure of his body, her thighs opened readily, and then…Ah, then he was inside her, and she was lifting her hips to welcome him farther, her legs wrapping around his waist. Gareth bent his head and kissed her then, muffling the sounds they made at that first moment of connection.

They moved together in the darkness. Gareth became thankful for it, much as he would have liked to watch Olivia. In the absence of sight, his other senses intensified. His world was full of the scent of her arousal, of her rapid breathing and half-caught moans, of the sharp points of her nails digging into his back, bracing counterpoint to the slick heat surrounding him. Of the tension in her frame, building with every thrust...

...and then breaking, in a climax Gareth could swear he felt in every inch of her trembling body. She didn't scream this time. The sound that left her mouth was somewhere between a sigh and a sob, ragged and thankful at the same time.

He heard his name inside it.

The sound went through Gareth like the feel of her had done earlier, a bolt of sensation that took him far past any attempt at self-control. He plunged forward in one final stroke, throwing his head back and spilling himself in a rush that left him gasping and dazed.

Still in the grip of instinct rather than thought, Gareth somehow had the presence of mind to roll onto his side afterward rather than letting Olivia take his weight. It took him a few minutes to realize he'd wrapped his arms around her, rested his chin on top of her head, and brought her with him. Even with recent events, he was a little surprised Olivia didn't protest. She'd been quick enough to disengage herself last time. No servants or students to come across them here, though. Maybe that was it. Also, she was probably tired.

Gareth certainly was. He could feel his thoughts fragmenting, drifting down into darkness that smelled of perfume and sex. Olivia was warm in his arms, her breasts moving more regularly now as she caught her breath. Absently, he stroked her hair, curled a strand around his finger...and let go of both the hair and her, pushing himself away abruptly.

"I should go," he said, speaking and standing while he still had some strength of will left. He felt around for his dressing gown and fumbled it on. "Bad for both of us if I fall asleep here, I'd think."

"Mmmhuh?" The sleepy confusion in her voice almost brought Gareth back to her side, and damn what anyone else thought. Olivia shook it off quickly, and the next words she said were brisk and matter-of-fact. "Yes, rather. Good of you to realize it."

"Er...yes." There must be, he thought, something more to say at this point. He wished he'd ever gotten around to having a proper mistress. Such liaisons as he'd experienced had always been decisive in their conclusion, and without much in the way of parting speeches. "Thank you. Good night."

"Good night," she said and drew her blanket up. "Sleep well."

There was nothing else to say, nothing that would not have seemed even more ludicrous. Gareth opened the door and left.

Chapter 36

A NIGHT'S SLEEP BLURRED THE EDGES OF OLIVIA'S MEMORY. When she woke, she could almost have thought she'd dreamed Gareth's presence in her room and the events that had followed. Lord knew she'd had similar dreams often enough.

He had been careful too. There were no bruises on her neck or thighs, no stubble marks to alarm the maids. Not much at all to give evidence of their...

Sport was perhaps the most tactful term, aside from the words a doctor or a preacher might have used. Certainly Olivia wouldn't have ventured to use *love-making*, not with the way she and Gareth had dealt with each other over the last few months.

He had been surprisingly tender when she thought about it. Not gentle, exactly, but concerned for her pleasure without the edge of competition that had come into their earlier interludes. And there had been that moment afterward, just before he'd left, when lust had been satisfied and something like affection had seemed to take its place.

That had been only because he was tired, Olivia told herself. He *had* left, after all.

She didn't let her thoughts proceed any further along those lines. The man could work with her, the man wanted her, to their mutual satisfaction, but she'd seen his opinion of her quite plainly the first day she'd arrived, and then again when they'd spoken in the gardens. Only a fool would have believed it changed on the strength of a few moments of passion.

Schoolroom days were long behind her. Girlish daydreams belonged in the past with them.

Olivia picked up the lengths of rope, coiling them slowly. The class had gone well, objectively, very well, for her first class in skills other than magic. None of the students had asked where she'd learned how to escape bonds. Some of them had likely guessed, but that didn't matter. They knew her. There'd been no contempt in their eyes, and no suspicion.

It should have been more of a relief.

Mostly, Olivia just felt tired—tired and prickly. She needed to have a cup of tea and a quiet hour by herself. Perhaps a nap before dinner.

She didn't need Gareth's voice behind her, and she certainly didn't need to flush with anticipation when she heard it. Especially when he started off by asking, "Do you really think this is wise?"

"I think it's useful," she said, spinning to look at him. "Or probably will be."

"Ah," said Gareth, clearly not believing her.

Very well, Olivia thought. She'd clearly hallucinated whatever tenderness she'd thought had been between them. She'd behaved like a stupid schoolgirl, and over a man who was looking supercilious and fidgeting with an edge of the chair.

She knew why he was here.

"You don't have to worry," she said, striving for

matter-of-factness in her voice. Really, she wanted to shake him, to demand whether he was concerned she'd weep or try blackmail or both. "I told you before. And I'm hardly going to expect anything *now*."

"No. I didn't think you would." Gareth glanced over his shoulder, clearly making sure the door was closed and they were alone, then looked back at Olivia and sighed. "I'd like to ask you a rather personal question. You may choose not to answer, naturally"

"Thank you," she said, trying not to sound too sarcastic, and motioned for him to continue. She expected some question about their night together. Whether she was *sure* there'd be no adverse consequences, perhaps, or perhaps something to do with her future plans.

Instead, Gareth paused then said, "After your husband died, before you came here, what made you choose to pose as a medium?"

Really, Olivia thought, she *should* have expected that. She looked back at Gareth flatly. "Money," she said and smiled a little. Not pleasantly. "Why else?"

Taken aback for a moment, he recovered quickly. Olivia remembered that from their first days. The clashing steel that had lain below all their conversations, in this room and elsewhere. Now the blades were out again.

"There wasn't anything else you could do?" He sounded somewhere between scornful and horrified.

Oddly, it was the last that drew her into responding, when she hadn't planned to justify herself. "Oh, I'm sure there was," she said with a glance down at her body that made her meaning clear. "But I had a silly girlish aversion to dying at thirty from the pox."

"I didn't mean—"

"I assure you," Olivia said, feeling her eyes narrow and her shoulders draw back, "I would have appreciated any helpful suggestions at the time. Tom had no family living, and his inheritance had gone toward his rank. Then he fell ill, and your colleagues are not cheap, sir, nor do they give refunds when their treatments fail. My dowry and his salary together gave me three months' rent after the funeral, discounting trifles like food and clothing. I was too young and too poorly educated for a governess, and I was far too gently born for a maid. I knew how to dance, how to ride, how to play the piano, and how to be charming. When I saw a way to support myself with the last of those, I took it. Blame me for that if you'd like."

Gareth stepped back a little at the force in her voice, force Olivia hadn't intended. Memory was more powerful than she'd given it credit for. Speaking had brought back gray days and restless nights, when she'd watched her money dwindling little by little and stared alternately at the paper and her hands.

"I…" He halted and cleared his throat. "Your family?"

"Father died before Tom did. Our estate was entailed, and my cousins would have made very sure I knew what my status was." Olivia sighed, some of the anger leaving her. "These days I might have lived with that. Looked for another husband, perhaps. At twenty I could not have supported living as a poor relation. Not then. It would have taken far more willpower than did asking a showman to take me on as an act. Perhaps if Hawkins had refused to teach me…but he didn't."

The walls seemed to swallow her words. They gave

back silence. So did Gareth, and it filled the room for a few moments.

"Then you regret it?" he asked, vicar's son to the end.

Olivia closed her eyes. She could say yes. She wouldn't be lying, precisely. And then Gareth would see her as a victim. He'd switch from suspicion to sympathy, and everything would be so much easier than it had been.

She opened her eyes and met his. "I don't know," Olivia said.

Gareth blinked. "You don't know?"

"I don't. I can't. If Tommy had lived, if there'd been another way, if I'd gone to my family...I'd have been more comfortable and less desperate, and I wouldn't have been lying to people. Yes. But I wouldn't have ended up here either. I wouldn't know anything but the normal world and the surface of things. I wouldn't have met...people whose company I value." She drew a breath and continued, before Gareth could read much into that last statement. "And yes, the lying did bother me somewhat. But, Gareth"—she spread her hands, palms up and open, in a gesture that begged him to see—"*lies were what most of them wanted*."

Gareth shook his head quickly, an instinctive denial. "I can't believe that."

"Can't you?" Olivia asked. "Truly? With everything you've seen of the world?"

He was silent. She pressed the advantage, such as it was. "I never played some of the nastier tricks. I never made anyone think their money was cursed, or they needed to put me up with them to keep evil spirits away. Nothing like that." Olivia watched Gareth's face as carefully as she'd ever examined of any audience member. He was listening. "Most of the time, I gave shows," she said. "People came to me because they had the evening off, or a spare pound, and they wanted a little otherworldly flavor to their entertainment. Most of them didn't *care* whether I was real or not, only that I was a bit of a change from the music hall."

"I suppose some didn't," said Gareth. He frowned, but not at her—not until a few seconds later, when he asked, "What about the others? The ones who were honestly grieving or troubled? I think you must have attracted some, and I cannot think they came only after you learned real magic."

"No," Olivia said quietly, remembering aged faces drawn in lines of grief, and weeping women no older than she'd been. "But they didn't want the truth either. Not really. They wanted to know the ones they loved were at peace. Mostly, they wanted a chance to say good-bye, to say the things they were never able to tell the living."

Gareth nodded once. "And?" he asked.

"And their loved ones *were* at peace," Olivia said. "Most of the dead are. Most of them also know what's in the hearts of the living, particularly anyone they were close to. The people who came to me wanted comfort. I gave them that."

"You gave them an illusion," Gareth said. His voice was flat.

"And you've never told a dying man he'd be all right?" Olivia had to take the shot. She could no more have passed it up than she could have refused Mr. Grenville's offer of employment. All the same, she had no pleasure in seeing it connect.

"A dying man won't be easy prey for the next fraud to come along." Gareth's eyes were dark, cold green. "And I very much doubt your...patrons'...comfort was ever the first thing on your mind."

There it was, and here they were. The afternoon light was gray on the carpet. A soft, heavy weight settled on Olivia's shoulders then quickly spread through her whole body. "No," she said, and it took tangible effort to shape that one word, let alone the ones that followed. "No, I didn't. I made my choices for myself alone. Is that what you wanted to hear?"

Gareth said nothing.

Olivia swallowed past an unexpected tightness in her throat. She'd known this would happen. She'd been prepared. The pain would pass. "I have some work to do, I think," she said. "Please excuse me."

The doorknob was too large in her hand, but she got the door open before Gareth could come to assist her. There was that.

Chapter 37

"I DON'T REALLY REMEMBER ANYTHING," SAID ROSEMARY Talbot.

Like Simon, she'd improved dramatically in health over the past two days. She was sitting by the window now, embroidery in her lap, and she had lost most of the horrible pallor she'd had when Gareth had first come to the house. There was color in her cheeks again and life in her eyes, although at the moment, her gaze was on her hands, and she was chewing uncertainly on her lower lip.

"Are you certain?" Gareth asked. "I give you my word I won't think anything you say is too odd."

"I think having as little memory as I do is quite odd enough," Miss Rosemary said, sighing. "I *had* decided to invite the ladies from Englefield down for tea. I recall that, and I recall putting on my coat and hat to go up to the house." She wrinkled her brow. "I think I remember walking up the road, but that's…blurred. And after that, I've no memory at all, nothing until I woke up yesterday."

Gareth nodded. Given Simon's lack of clear memory, Miss Rosemary's wasn't completely surprising—simply unfortunate. He glanced around the parlor, trying to think of any questions that might lend additional clarity to the situation.

He wished Olivia had come along, but she was

staying close to Englefield at the moment, adding her power to Simon's defenses and discussing how the school might best provide a guardian to take Brother Jonathan's place. Gareth had heard all of that from Simon. He hadn't spoken to Olivia, except in passing, since their argument. He hadn't thought it would do either of them any good.

Thinking certainly hadn't. Gareth's ideas simply wheeled and circled like carrion birds. She had been desperate. She'd had other resources. She had been young. She didn't regret it. She had been scrupulous, after the fashion of her profession. Gareth cared about her. He didn't, couldn't, entirely trust her.

He could see no path forward.

Perhaps it had been better that she hadn't come, logistics or not. Yet now that Gareth had walked through the crisp air to the village, now that he was sitting in the vicar's neat house and sipping tea, he found it harder to resent Olivia's past and easier to remember her way with people and her insights into matters Gareth had to admit he barely grasped.

And he'd thought of her instead of Simon. Perhaps that had just been his recognizing Miss Rosemary might talk more easily to another woman, but he didn't think that was the case.

He picked a small china shepherdess up from a table then put it back down. "Physically," he said, "you're doing quite well, but I'm concerned about how little you remember."

"So am I, Doctor," she said.

"Do you have any memory"—Gareth pressed…very gently, and very careful not to seem as if he was too concerned about this particular detail—"of giving Mr. Grenville some flowers for his wife?"

"No," said Miss Rosemary. "Though I'm glad to hear I did. It's nice to know one behaved well, even when one doesn't remember it."

"Then I'm glad I could oblige you," Gareth said and smiled at her, using his best bedside manner. In case they were wrong about timing, he asked, "Did you have a particular reason for inviting the ladies to tea when you did?"

Miss Rosemary blushed then, and looked down at her hands. "I confess it wasn't entirely the pleasure of their company. I've a friend, you see, very nice girl, but her father's come on hard times. She's quite smart, and I'd been wondering…" She looked up at Gareth, bashful and hopeful at the same time.

"That's nothing to be ashamed of," said Gareth. "I'm sure Mrs. Grenville would be glad to discuss it when you're feeling more yourself."

Simon had mentioned additional teachers. The students would need to learn science and history and French, as well as more esoteric things. And while the three of them and Olivia did a decent job filling in the gaps, it would have been nice to have someone devoted to more normal subjects.

"It's a…rather unusual place," he added. "She'd have to be a fairly open-minded girl."

"Oh, she is, or I wouldn't have thought of asking." Her father's a great admirer of Mr. Ruskin."

No guarantee that the prospective addition wouldn't run screaming when she caught a glimpse of Mrs. Grenville's classes, or Olivia's. All the same it couldn't hurt to discuss it.

"I'm glad to hear it," he said, "and I'll let Mrs. Grenville know. Meanwhile, I want you to take care of yourself."

"I'm very good at that," said Miss Rosemary. "I promise. Oh, hello!"

Her last statement wasn't directed to Gareth, but rather to a small shape that wound its way in through the swinging door. Looking closer, Gareth saw the gray-and-white cat that had run away from the house when he and Olivia had approached before.

"Hello, puss," he said genially. Army life had taught him to like cats, both for the company and because the alternatives were worse.

This particular cat, Gareth saw, was not looking terribly healthy. It moved toward a saucer of milk in the corner, but much more slowly and unsteadily than Gareth would have expected, and he could practically count its ribs through its fur. Something had taken a bite out of its right ear too. "Poor old fellow."

"Yes, isn't he?" Miss Rosemary sighed. "Between me and him, Elizabeth and Papa have had far too much to worry about over the last few days. We'll have to shoulder more of a load in the future to make it up, won't we, Shadow?"

"He's been in a bad way too, hmm?"

"In a fight, we think, or maybe hit by a cart and stunned. Fred Gordon, one of old Mr. Gordon's nephews, brought him back a little while after I woke up. Said he'd found him by the side of the road. Poor thing. Though really, he's been very lucky for a runaway. Papa would say something about the wages of sin, I think."

She laughed, and Gareth laughed with her. He

gave a few last instructions before he left, and gave Shadow a scratch behind the ears, which the cat grudgingly permitted.

He felt *good*, Gareth realized on the way back. He had many things to worry about, yes, but walking through the village, he didn't feel them dragging at him the way they had back at Englefield.

Perspective did amazing things. Perspective, fresh air, and a good walk…and the chance to talk with the Talbots, who reminded him of home. They were generous people too, with Miss Rosemary stepping forward for her friend like that.

Her friend was lucky. Some girls weren't.

Gareth saw Olivia's face in his mind, and the way her eyes had blazed when she'd spoken of the past. Of course he'd known about poverty. His father had seen families in need often enough, and his mother and sister had made up baskets for poor families. But he'd never really thought about the forms it took in the city or for a woman on her own.

Not that it was any excuse. Not when she didn't even regret it.

Stones crunched and clicked beneath Gareth's boots, and something in the sound suggested his own voice, lecturing: *There will be times when you make the wrong decision. There will be times when there's no right decision.*

That was different. It had to be. Going forward with the best information one had, making the best choice possible. No, one shouldn't regret that, however it turned out. However, choosing to base a life on lies…that was another matter.

The world based too much on lies as it was. He'd had quite enough experience to know that.

A sardonic voice in the back of his head spoke up: *You're blaming her for Egypt, then?* The thought went through Gareth with a jar, as if he'd missed a step and landed hard on both feet.

Of course he wasn't blaming Olivia for Egypt. Of course he was just being guided by general principles. It was a matter of honor, of character...

Quite so, said the voice, which Gareth wished he could believe was a demon or a spirit or anything other than his conscience. *And you'd have been just as doubtful of her character if she hadn't been the woman you'd seen before you shipped out. Naturally.*

He had no answer. That didn't mean he was wrong.

But, he might do well to talk with Olivia again when he had a moment, and he thought it might be better to do so outside. It was harder to be angry at her there.

He wasn't sure that was a good thing. But...

Olivia could have told him she *was* sorry. She could have probably made him believe it. And she hadn't.

Chapter 38

MRS. GRENVILLE WROTE AS IF THE PAPER HAD PERSONALLY offended her. Every stroke of the pen was a slash, every dot a thrust. Olivia, sitting across from her in the drawing room, kept her eyes on her own research for as long as she could, but eventually couldn't concentrate anymore.

Not that concentration had been easy to begin with. Olivia's night had been restless, full of dreams about scurrying, shadowy things like cockroaches, and she'd woken just as tired and out of sorts as she'd been the day before. More so, because now she had Gareth's predictable idiocy to remember. Intellectually, she hadn't been surprised. She'd known what to expect.

She still wanted to slap him.

The situation with the demon was affecting her, she knew, just as it was affecting the whole household. Mr. Grenville had been curt and weary, the servants had gone about in poker-faced silence, and her lesson that day had absolutely lacked energy.

And Joan was clearly taking *something* out on the paper.

"Upsetting information, I take it?" Olivia asked, keeping all but a slight edge out of her voice with a significant exercise of will.

Joan looked up, eyes narrow. "Stories I'd heard in London. Names. Places. That kind of thing." She didn't go back to writing. "Figured I might as well do something with myself."

"It could be useful," said Olivia.

"Could be. Right now, it's just cataloguing how *inventive* people can be." Joan nearly spat the word. "You never know what they'll come up with next."

Olivia lifted her eyebrows. "Like teaching magic to children?"

"*Someone's* going to teach them. Some of them don't need teaching to be dangerous. At least we're—" Joan bit off the stream of heated words and took a long breath. "Yeah."

"You shouldn't draw too many conclusions from what you're reading," Olivia said. "You're seeing only one side of people there, remember."

Joan sighed. "Yeah. It's just…I don't *get* it—what they do."

"Meaning no offense," Olivia said, "but you never seemed very sheltered."

"No," Joan said. "It's not what they do. It's that they do it here. And they don't need to. Desperation, sure. Even *fun* I can sort of see. Some people are sick bastards. I understand that. But the people I heard about, just about all of them can keep themselves comfortable in other ways. They've got plenty of food, nobody's attacking them, and they're willing to shed blood for the Outsiders, for demons, in your terms, so they can make a few more pounds. Be a little better looking than the next man. Be in *charge*, as if that was ever anyone's sane idea of a good time. It's goddamn stupid, is what it is."

Rain crawled down the window by Olivia. She watched it for a moment, seeing the misty green expanse of Englefield's lawns stretching away, gray-green under gray skies. Her irritation faded away, but only weariness replaced it.

"I don't know," she said finally. "I think it's easy to be desperate for something you don't need, if everyone around you has it, or if they convince you you need it. Not that it's an excuse. But if you ask ten men what the necessities of life are, you'll probably get eight different answers."

Joan nodded. "We adjust. For good or bad. That makes sense. But"—another gesture to the notebook—"going this far—"

"I don't think it happens all at once." Olivia didn't realize she was interrupting until she'd spoken, and then she froze for a second, prepared for sharp words. They didn't come. Joan simply sat and listened. Olivia went on. "I don't…I've never encountered these people. I can't speak with any sort of certainty. But I would imagine it starts with small compromises. Nothing that requires blood sacrifices or binding promises. Nothing that kills or enslaves, just a spell to make young women find you more attractive, perhaps, or a mild jinx on your enemy."

"You wouldn't see anything wrong with it," Joan agreed, but her upper lip curled in revulsion, as if she was looking at a slug. "Not here."

"Not most places, I'd think," Olivia said. "Even most of our stories don't say there's anything wrong with love potions or with a bit of mischief. And maybe there isn't, always, except…except it's easy to think you *should* have what you *can* get. It's easy to start thinking you're better than normal people, that normal rules don't apply to you. Especially when you're young. Look at Michael.

Before he came here, he didn't see any reason why he *shouldn't* call down rainstorms to suit his convenience. Or, rather, he didn't see any reason why he should think about other people's convenience before doing so."

Joan sighed and leaned back in her chair. "And there's not much difference between thirteen and thirty sometimes. Especially not—" She paused and shook her head. "Not for people who're used to getting their own way."

"Or who aren't and are angry about it. Or who are...tricked. I can't explain the masters entirely, any more than you can, not what makes one man turn to evil and not another. But the men who follow them, some of them...I have to wonder whether some of them started out seeking something greater and realized their mistake only when they thought it was too late to turn back."

Olivia felt the urge to apologize, though she didn't know to whom. She tried to dismiss it. After all, she had never even dabbled in the darker magics or tried to seduce anyone else into doing so. But Gareth had said the men and women who believed her would be more open to other charlatans, less scrupulous ones, and she couldn't discount that possibility. Now she considered, for the first time, the chance that she might have led a few in her audience into something real and quite sinister.

"There's great good in seeking a...deeper meaning in life," she said aloud. "Most people take no harm from it, and it puts many of them on a better path than they might have found otherwise. Maybe a truer one too."

"Sometimes," Joan said. "Sure." Then she went back to her notes, philosophy abandoned now that she'd had her chance to wax wrathful. Olivia doubted if, an hour later, she'd remember much about the conversation.

Olivia's mind, however, remained unsettled, if she ever had been able to call it truly settled over the last week or so. She still couldn't say with certainty that she regretted her choice after Tommy's death. She was certain she could have chosen worse occupations. But she found herself thinking about the faces she'd seen in her audiences. Had any of the curious young men and women who'd come to see her turned to bloody bargains to get their way in later life? Had any of the grief stricken, the elderly, the desperate gone from her to another "medium," one who had drained them of any means of support? And if so, how much of that had been her fault?

Surely she was not completely to blame. The people for whom she'd performed had still possessed their will, and the people who might have lured them into one trap or another were certainly the most accountable. Olivia was too old for extravagant self-reproach, and she couldn't believe her hands were as bloody as all that.

Neither were they so mildly tainted as she had always thought.

And what did Olivia do about that? Lyddie was dead, she had no idea where Hawkins and his show had gone…and neither of them had made her join up. She'd come of her own free will. There was nothing to be found there. Of her clients, she'd known few names and remembered still fewer, and she didn't know what reparations she could make.

Then…

Elizabeth's scream shattered her thoughts.

~~~

Elizabeth was close at hand, and Olivia and Joan were quick. Before the scream had completely died away, Joan was across the hall and opening the door to the room from which it had come. Olivia, though she couldn't claim such speed, was close at her heels.

As she might have expected, Elizabeth was hovering near the ceiling again. Below her, Charlotte was facing what looked, for a second, like a human figure with a dreadful face. It was grayish and hung in loose flaps of flesh. Jagged teeth surrounded a gaping maw. Olivia caught her breath.

"You vile little *pig*," Charlotte said and boxed the figure's ears with quite a bit of strength.

Olivia stepped forward, ready to defend her student even as she realized the scene wasn't quite what it appeared to be, and the monster reached for its face.

"Ow," it said in a muffled boy's voice. "I had that coming, didn't I? Sorry, Lizzie."

"Arthur?" Olivia asked as he drew off the mask. On closer inspection, it appeared to consist of a pillowcase, some broken bits of glass, and a substantial amount of both paint and glue. It was rather well done, in all honesty. That didn't do much for her temper. "What in the name of God is going on here?"

All three students started talking at once.

"Donnell." Joan's voice cut through the clamor. Her glare silenced it. "Get down from there. I know you can."

Elizabeth sniffled and wiped her eyes, but nodded. She looked over briefly to Olivia, who gave her a reassuring smile, and then closed her eyes and started breathing deeply.

Joan turned her attention on the next easiest student

to deal with. "Woodwell, don't hit when you're angry. If you ever stood a chance of talking things out with the guy, it's a lot harder if you hit him. And if you didn't, now he knows how you fight, and you probably need to kill him." She paused, seemed to realize they were staring, and added, "That doesn't apply here. Don't kill Waite."

"I'll try to restrain myself, ma'am," said Charlotte, sounding like it would be a challenge.

"Waite, really, what the hell?"

"Um," said Arthur. He didn't seem shocked. Olivia had overheard Joan teaching the students to fight, and thought all of them were used to worse language by now, but he looked down at his shoes for a moment before meeting Joan's eyes again. "Wanted to find something out, ma'am, so I was hiding in the closet. I didn't think Lizzie'd be coming in." He added, looking upward, "And I am awfully sorry about *that*."

"Oh," said Elizabeth, opening one eye to look at him. "If you didn't *mean* to be horrid, I accept your apology. But still, it was a nasty thing to do."

"It was an idiotic stunt," Mrs. Grenville corrected her, "and this is one of the better ways it could've ended. Trust me on this, Waite. You do *not* want to give me a scare. Or Simon. And we're not made of sheets, by the way."

"Yes, ma'am. Sorry."

Joan looked over at Olivia. "You have this under control? I should make sure Simon's not trying to rush in and save us all."

"Yes, I'll be fine," Olivia said. When Joan had left and Elizabeth was on the ground, she sent them off to get some tea, and turned to Arthur. "Now," she said. "What did you have to *find out* that was so important it merited childish pranks in a house where someone's trying to recover?"

"It's just that…" Arthur looked toward the door and shrugged. "I wanted to see what one of us would do when something jumped out."

Olivia lifted her eyebrows. "So you were trying to get yourself killed?"

"No, ma'am. I'd put up a shield of power, the way you taught us. I thought I'd find out. It probably wouldn't be anything, but we'd know. Given the way things are."

"Arthur," Olivia said with what felt like the last remaining store of her patience. "If I had three wishes, I think I'd spend all of them on making you, for once in your life, *think* before you acted. I realize it's not something you've had to do often, but I strongly suggest you develop the habit."

She knew her voice was harsh. Arthur faced her with tight lips and flaming cheeks, and simply nodded. He looked miserable. Most of the time, that would have moved her. Now she just wondered if it was an act. Surely he'd had worse scoldings.

"Go help in the kitchen," she said. "I'm sure they need something peeled or chopped or sliced. And I'm sure that's a far easier punishment than you deserve. If you have an idle moment for the next three days, it won't be for lack of trying on my part."

She watched Arthur leave, stiff-backed and quick. Then she sank into a chair, wondering why she felt so drained when she hadn't done anything.

Chapter 39

"MRS. BRIGHTMORE?"

Olivia looked up at Charlotte's voice, then immediately straightened. How long had she been slumped in the chair? What had she missed? What had gone wrong?

But Charlotte's face held neither alarm nor reproof, only concern. Concern was bad enough, but Olivia would take it. It had been that sort of day. "How's Elizabeth?" she asked.

"Just fine," said Charlotte. "She's gone up to our room to read a bit before dinner. The boys are doing the same, I think." She rubbed the back of her neck for a second, working up to whatever she had to say, and Olivia braced herself for some unpleasant statement. "I think you should come outside with me."

"What? Why?"

Charlotte shrugged. "I can't explain in here."

Olivia blinked. "It's raining," she said.

"It's stopped."

"The ground—"

Charlotte tossed her head impatiently. "I'll buy you a new pair of boots. We'll stay in sight of the house, if that's what you're worried about, and you can run away if it looks like I'm going to touch you. Though if you think I'm possessed, you should be trying to knock me down about now. Just come with me. This is important. Ma'am."

Clearly it was important enough that Olivia wasn't going to get a minute's peace unless she complied. "Oh, very well," she said and got up, a difficult maneuver, for the chair seemed to have its own gravity.

Fifteen minutes later, in coat and hat and carrying an umbrella just in case, Olivia followed Charlotte out Englefield's front door. The rain *had* stopped, and the wind had blown the clouds away. A field of stars stretched brilliant overhead, and a full moon was rising to the west. Something tight and uncomfortable inside her began to loosen its grip.

Charlotte led her out to the gardens. For a wonder, she didn't talk, and Olivia didn't complain. There was relief in the silence, just as there was in the stars overhead— more than she'd ever been able to see in the city—and in the feeling of cold air against her skin. She took a deep breath, and it felt like her first in days.

They stopped by an ornamental fountain, ghost white in the starlight. "Feeling tired?" Charlotte asked.

"I...no." Olivia shook her head. As exhausted as she'd been inside, she was perfectly energetic now. She felt as though she could've gone on walking all the way to the village. "It must be the fresh air."

"Some of it. Maybe," Charlotte said. "Some of it isn't."

"What do you mean?"

"There's something wrong in there." Charlotte waved a gloved hand toward Englefield. "The animals feel it too. Things are...wound too tight. Today was just part of it. Elizabeth told me she's been having nightmares again. Bad ones."

Olivia nodded. "Everyone's nervous about the demon," she said. "Being shut inside together doesn't particularly help either. Everyone starts noticing everyone else's flaws. Your animals are probably picking up on that." She put a hand against the fountain, bracing herself, and asked, "Or do you think it's something else?"

"I don't know," said Charlotte. "I've been stuck in close quarters before, and it wasn't usually this bad. But then, it wasn't with a houseful of people who could kill me with a thought, and there wasn't a demon lurking around. So maybe it's just that."

"I'll check all the wards again," Olivia said. "Maybe Mr. Grenville's illness left something damaged."

"Do that," said Charlotte, "but take a walk around for a bit first. It's how I've kept from running mad." She grinned. "Assuming I have. Well worth a pair of damp feet."

"Are you coming with me?"

Charlotte shook her head. "Works better on your own, I find. Besides, I've got to make eyes at the cook. Maybe she'll give me some scraps to feed Star."

With a wave, she turned and headed back to the house, becoming a dark shape against the stars. Olivia stood for a few moments and watched her draw near to the lighted windows, then found the nearest path and let it lead her onward.

Charlotte was right. As Olivia walked, she felt weight and constriction lift away, as if she'd just stepped out of an iron cage she'd been wearing for the last day or two. It was wonderful, and would have been better if it hadn't made her worry.

She looked over one shoulder at the house. Mr. Grenville's protections were sound ones, and Olivia had been reinforcing them, but would they hold against something as nebulous as mental influence? None of the students or servants had gone to town for two days without her, Joan, or Gareth accompanying them, and she'd watched visitors carefully. But had someone slipped past?

There was only one way of knowing, and that discovery would take a while. Best to start in the morning, when she'd have a little more time, even if that meant another uneasy night.

The path turned around the house, leading toward the back to the stretch of land overlooking the dormitory and the forest. Olivia followed it, and her thoughts turned as well, to the discussions she and Mr. Grenville had been having about the forest's guardianship. She'd seen enough of city life for a while, and staying in one place sounded quite nice. She wouldn't have minded taking up the responsibility, but she wasn't sure she'd have the skill for it, or the sense of the land and living things. Charlotte might have done better, but she clearly had no desire for the post.

The next time Olivia had an opportunity to enter the forest, she would talk to Brother Jonathan about it, though heaven only knew when that would be. Certainly the current state of affairs—

A figure stood nearby, motionless and leaning against one of the trees.

Olivia's breath caught in her throat. She froze and looked again.

The figure was a man, or at least man-shaped, though the darkness prevented any clearer impression. He stood with his head turned away from her. He hadn't moved, so he probably hadn't seen her yet.

Olivia ducked behind a nearby rowan tree and picked up a fallen branch. Rowan wood was some protection against magic. She could amplify its power a little, and if nothing else, the branch was a stout one. Thus armed, she took a few steps closer, trying to be silent, but she had never learned much stealth. The figure looked up before she got very close, and Olivia caught her breath for another reason entirely: the light of the full moon bathing Gareth's face.

Chapter 40

OLIVIA WAS EXACTLY WHO GARETH HAD BEEN HOPING TO see, and precisely who he'd been dreading would appear. Wrapped in black clothing, with the moon lighting her pale face and the wind tugging at her hair, she looked more aethereal than human for a moment. She might have been an apparition his troubled mind had placed before him.

She also clearly had no real idea how to hold a weapon. Gareth's experience of such things was only secondhand, but even to him her grip on the branch she carried was clumsy and uncertain. Either a spirit or a hallucination would have made a better job of it. Either one would probably have had better weapons—or none.

So he recovered enough to manage speech, though his first words were only: "Good evening."

"Good evening," Olivia said with a rather dubious glance up at the sky. "Finally." She spoke a little too quickly. Nervous. Of him, or of the unknown figure that had prompted her to arm herself, however inexpertly?

He would have had to admit her courage, but he'd stopped trying to deny it some time ago.

"I didn't think anyone would be out here," he said and then realized he'd spoken as if in complaint. "You have every right to be." This had all been much easier when he'd been *trying* to cast barbs in her direction.

"Yes, but I can understand how you'd think

otherwise," Olivia said before Gareth could think of any other way to soften his words. She sounded calm and amiable enough, if a little weary. "Charlotte suggested a walk would do me good."

"Miss Woodwell's a bright girl."

Olivia looked up at him. In the moonlight, her eyes were very dark. "You've felt it too?" she asked with far more hesitation than Gareth was used to hearing in her voice.

"Yes," Gareth said and considered what to say next, while the wind picked up and died down fitfully around them. "Tension. Irritability. Weariness. It happens sometimes. We're not good at facing threats that don't show themselves."

The rest of his feelings had been, in his experience, far less common.

He didn't dream of Olivia. When he did dream, there were mostly nightmares, and sometimes he didn't dream at all, simply woke out of habit. When he did, his first thought was to seek her out.

Gareth's second thought over the last two days had been to reject the notion. Most simply, he'd thought she had her duties the next day, and they would be somewhat more arduous with Simon absent. Waking her would not have been the act of a gentleman, even such a flawed one as he managed to be most times. If not for their conversation and for the train of his thoughts coming back from the Talbots', he might still have done it.

But he still didn't know, concretely, what he felt. He wouldn't have been at all certain how to express it if he had. Midnight was not an hour that lent itself to either.

Still, his good resolutions were frail compared with his memory of Olivia's passion. The longer he stayed outside, he'd reasoned, the more soundly he'd sleep, and the less he'd think of her.

Now she was here.

Gareth looked away from her, out across to the dormitories and the forest beyond them: oak and pine, ash and beech, dark, ancient shapes under the moon and the stars, more ancient still, and all holding secrets whose smallest portion he hadn't comprehended until he'd reached Englefield. Not too long ago, Gareth knew he would have shied from that concept, from the awareness of all he didn't understand. Now it sat more easily on his mind.

The woman beside him, another dark shape, was part of the reason, but that wasn't all. Not all of the reason, or all of her.

She hadn't spoken yet.

Gareth turned toward her. "I can't be around you without wanting you," he said, his voice rough and clipped. "I have tried. God knows. Perhaps with a few dozen years of mental discipline—but I can't."

The air between them seemed to heat, to thicken. Olivia's face was grave when she replied, but there was an edge of irony in her voice. "I would imagine either of us would have stopped if we could," she said. "Quite a while ago, I'd think."

Gareth searched for something to say without insulting her. She knew what his feelings had been on their first meeting. He didn't think she could help thinking of them now, but he didn't want to speak of them, all the same. Perhaps regret *was* futile, perhaps his behavior *had* been justified, but he still wished he hadn't hurt her. "The struggle is a bit distracting."

"Yes," Olivia said quietly. She folded her arms under her breasts and fell silent. Between them, the heat faded a little. In its place came stillness and waiting. Any words now would be weighty things, nothing to be forgotten or discounted the morning after. Lead and steel, not fairy gold.

Off in the distance, an owl cried, seeking its prey.

Olivia took a long breath and squared her shoulders. She started to step toward Gareth, and then, clearly thinking better of it, stopped.

"I can leave," she said.

Lead and steel indeed. Gareth felt like he'd been hit in the side of the head with a bludgeon. Numb and almost dizzy, he stood and watched as Olivia continued.

"Not right away. Not completely. I—" She stopped whatever she was going to say, swallowed. "I care about your happiness, but not, I'm afraid, enough to forsake everything I've found here. Before, when I was tricking people…it was never the right thing to do, even if it worked out well in the end. This, with the Grenvilles, is. But I don't have to do it here."

Gareth stared at her. "The *school* is here," he pointed out, because of all the objections he wanted to make, it was the simplest.

"I'm sure there are other duties I could perform. Finding students, perhaps, or teaching those whose parents won't let them stay here. Research. And there are other teachers. Miss Grenville will be coming home, eventually. When she does, or when Mr. Grenville finds another likely candidate, I can ask him for more remote tasks."

"My God, Olivia—"

She lifted her chin. "Let us be practical, please," she said, but there was a softness in her eyes that looked anything but pragmatic. "We…desire each other. Immoderately. In other situations, perhaps there would be other solutions. But my life was as it was, and I made what choices I did, and you cannot approve of them, or of me. I will not ask you to."

Gareth never thought for a moment of doubting her sincerity.

The determination in Olivia's voice, the angle of her head as she looked at him, the quiet patience in her dark eyes. Gareth couldn't have named one single thing that affected him. All of them hit him with the same force, and the thoughts that had been diffuse and chaotic suddenly lined up.

He stepped forward and reached out. Olivia's shoulders were rigid under his hands, her body stiff with surprise, and the branch she still held in one hand made their position more awkward than Gareth would have liked. He thought of asking her to put it down then realized he had more important things to say. She hadn't stepped away from him and she hadn't tried to twist out of his grasp and these were encouraging signs.

"You're half-right," he said, looking down into her eyes, watching her conviction turn to confusion. "But only half. I can't rejoice in your past or think it was good, even if…even *though* you and I and Englefield might have profited from the results. You wouldn't believe me if I pretended otherwise. But…" Gareth brought his hand up to cup the side of her face, stroking his gloved thumb down her cheek. "What you did to survive wasn't what you were. And it's certainly not what you are now."

Her eyes widened, filling his gaze. "And," she said, struggling to keep her voice light and not quite succeeding, "what am I, then?"

"Brave. Dedicated. Brilliant. Lovely." Gareth bent his head and brushed his lips against hers, a caress briefer and gentler than anything that had passed between them before. "Loved."

Olivia stopped breathing at that point. Only for a few seconds, but Gareth thought shocking her back into normal respiration was clearly his medical duty. He pulled her to him and kissed her again, lingering this time, until she dropped the stupid branch and her arms came up around his neck.

As Gareth was beginning to entertain serious thoughts of taking her on the ground, despite the hour and the cold, she slid her hands down against his shoulders and pushed away, gasping. "Are you sure?" she asked. "The things I'll be teaching—"

"Are useful. If I think they're not, I'll object *then*."

"You might not be the only one who recognizes…who I was, you know. It could be embarrassing for you to be seen too publicly with me."

"God save me from ever becoming that sort of man," Gareth said. He tilted her face up with one hand. "If this is your way of rejecting me, you're doing a damned poor job of it."

"No," she said and shook her head. "No, I love you. I just want you to know what could happen."

"And nothing that happens will be the end of the world." Gareth laughed. "Hopefully." He felt free, almost weightless, as he hadn't felt since he'd left England years ago. He felt as intoxicated as he had in the grip of magical power. "All we can do is go forward."

Olivia relaxed into his arms again. "Or back, in this case," she said.

"Hmm?"

"If we want to sleep indoors tonight," she said and glanced over his shoulder toward the house.

Her body stiffened even as Gareth heard the footsteps. In an instant, he'd released her and turned, putting himself between Olivia and the dark figure moving toward them. "Who's there?" he demanded and hoped to be neither shot nor dismembered for his pains.

The figure froze, becoming, as Gareth's eyes focused, tall and lanky and unsure. It was still under a tree, the shadows obscuring its face, but the voice was unmistakable. "Sir?" Waite asked.

Some of the tension left Gareth. Not all of it. There were still many questions to be asked.

Olivia stepped up beside him, the tree branch in her hands again. She wasn't holding it threateningly, not now, but nothing in her posture suggested a joyous welcome either. "Really, Arthur," she said, "this is *outside* of enough."

Chapter 41

ALMOST AS SOON AS SHE'D SPOKEN, OLIVIA REGRETTED HER exasperation. True, Arthur had picked a bad moment, but when she got a clearer look at his face, she knew he wasn't out on some boyishly stupid errand. His eyes were wide and desperate. His face was pale.

And as she watched, a drop of blood ran down from his hairline.

"Arthur, what happened?" she asked, seizing one of his shoulders and dragging him out of the shadows. "Gareth, he's hurt…have a look."

Arthur tried to shake off her grip. "I'm all right, ma'am. It doesn't matter about me. Someone has to go after him."

"Who?"

"William. We were in our room, and he hit me. Tied me up afterward, but I remembered what you taught us. He was gone when I got out. I think he's gone mad. Or something."

"Or something," Olivia repeated, knowing only too well what *something* was. She remembered the way William had been keeping to himself and how he'd wandered off when all of the students were outside. He'd looked strange when he'd returned too. "But he wasn't gone that long," she said aloud, "and there was nobody there. I was watching for people."

"We all were," said Gareth, refocusing on her. "We

were watching for *people*. Not animals. I should've known when I saw the vicar's cat." His face showed the same realization and horror Olivia knew must have been apparent on hers, but he turned back to Arthur and spoke calmly. "You're surprisingly well off for taking a blow to the head. Where is Fitzpatrick going, do you know?"

"He didn't say," said Arthur. "He didn't talk at all. But he took a pair of candles, a flask of water…and a knife."

The implements didn't mean much to Olivia, save that the thing in Fitzpatrick was going to attempt some kind of magic, a sort it couldn't do on its own. If she'd been trying a spell and either needed as much power as possible or were inhuman enough not to care if the magic slipped her control, she knew where she would go.

"The forest," she said. "We probably don't have much time. What's in there?"

Arthur was carrying a small bag over one shoulder. At Olivia's question, he took it off and handed it to her. "What I could find, ma'am," he said.

Inside were a candle and matches, a shaker of salt, a small bottle of water, a pair of silver cuff links, and three twigs of holly, probably cut from one of the bushes near the front door.

"Holly protects the home, mostly," she said through numb lips. "I'm not sure it will do much good in banishing anything, though I suppose one never knows."

"The school's our home. And I suppose this world is too, if we're dealing with things from outside of it. I thought that might count enough."

"It might." Olivia said. Arthur's voice and her own sounded far away and quiet. Her mind spun then centered and stopped. She was aware of Gareth at her side,

reassuring even though he didn't speak. "Go inside," she
said. "Get Mrs. Grenville. Tell her what's happened and
that I've gone to the forest."

"Miss Woodwell too," Gareth said suddenly. "First.
Have her send us a guide. She can ask one of the birds
to find a young man in the forest then lead us there."

"Yes, sir. Ma'am." Arthur looked between them for
only a second, waiting for more instructions. When none
came, he dashed off for the house, moving with the
speed only youth and fear could provide in combination.

She and Gareth, Olivia thought, would have only the
first on their side. She turned and headed toward the
forest, walking as swiftly as she could, but didn't run.
There would be a great deal of ground to cover, and
much of it would be uneven. Breaking her ankle again
would be the last thing she, or anyone, needed.

Quite possibly, it would be the last thing she did.

Gareth's presence was no surprise, no more than his
use of *us* had been. The practical side of Olivia thought
of course he would come. This was as likely as not to
end with William badly injured. But she didn't think
William's welfare was Gareth's only reason for joining
her, or even his primary one, and the knowledge gave a
little warmth back to a heart that had gone cold with fear.

He still limped a little, she saw, though not nearly
as badly as he had when he'd arrived at Englefield.
Noticing that made her remember the rowan branch, still
in her hand, and she passed it to him. He took it with
a quick smile but didn't speak any more than she did.
They would need their breath.

Just past the dormitory, Olivia glanced back toward
the house and saw that lights had gone on all along the

top row of windows. A few moments later there was another scream overhead. Olivia froze for a moment, until Gareth put a warm hand on her arm and pointed upward. "Owl," he said. It flew onward, toward the house. A little later, as they approached the edge of the forest, the owl passed over them again, flying ahead into the night. Olivia thought of Charlotte with thanks, and with hope.

Even in winter, the forest blocked a great deal of the moonlight. Haste would be even more foolish now than it had been earlier. Olivia gritted her teeth but slowed down. The respite let her catch her breath.

"What do you think the demon's trying to do?" Gareth asked.

"I'm not sure," said Olivia. "It probably doesn't want to go home, or it wouldn't have come in the first place." She hated to say what came next, but she owed Gareth honesty. Especially now. "There's an outside chance it hates this world enough to destroy it, but it came from Balam's…home…and from what I've read, most of the creatures there find this place amusing."

"That's some relief, I suppose."

Olivia sighed. "It doesn't *intend* to destroy us, exactly. I don't think it cares very much if it happens, any more than a child would care about breaking a toy, and I'm not at all sure it understands this place enough to avoid it. Especially if its aim is what I think it might be."

"What's that?" Gareth was barely limping now. Olivia hadn't expected that, even with the stick, but she thanked God for small favors.

Certainly they'd need them. "Sending out invitations," she said, "and opening a door."

They didn't stop walking. She couldn't see Gareth's face. She didn't need to.

"To its home?"

"That's probably what it intends. Out in the forest, it might knock down a wall instead. Metaphorically speaking."

"Good Lord."

"You see what I mean."

Olivia ducked under an overhanging branch. The path wound ahead of them, shadowed and narrow. At least there *was* a path, so far, and William had probably stayed on it. Probably. Hopefully.

"Do you have any idea," Gareth asked slowly, "what's likely to be on the other side?"

"No. That's where the metaphor fails a little. You see there isn't really an 'other side.' Bear in mind that both Mr. Grenville and I have started researching this comparatively recently. There are many places outside our world. A hole in our walls might open to any, or all, or a different place under a new moon and a full one."

"Ah," said Gareth, which seemed to Olivia like the only sensible response to what she'd just said.

"Of all the...not-here places I've ever heard of," she added, "there are *some* that are comparatively harmless. Even pleasant, in their way."

"Some?"

"Not very many. From everything I've read, most of the others aren't hostile, exactly, simply...inimical, like a desert or the peak of a very tall mountain."

Or the bottom of the ocean. Olivia didn't say it. She also didn't mention the places that *were* hostile. She'd heard only a little about any of this, but that little had already been enough to haunt her dreams at times. Gareth had seen Balam. He could draw his own conclusions.

Shrieking, a shape dropped out of the sky toward them.

Olivia froze and ducked, throwing up an arm to shield her face, but the great white-faced owl stopped its dive a foot or so above her head, a few inches above Gareth's. As Olivia rose again, it flew one quick circle around their heads then took off to the North, sailing just a little bit below the tree line.

They went after it, putting on as much speed as either of them dared, given the darkness and the ground. The darkness was of no help in following the owl either. Olivia looked ahead several times, fearing she'd lost it, only to see the motion of its wings after squinting for what felt like an age. She thought of the white birds people had mentioned seeing in the forest but didn't let herself wish for one. Having any kind of guide was blessing enough, and if any god was listening to her prayers, she didn't want to anger it with ingratitude.

A few yards onward, they came to the fork in the path they'd encountered with Charlotte. To Olivia's surprise, the owl paused above it and waited until she and Gareth had caught up, then flew off in the direction they'd taken before.

Memory flickered through Olivia's mind. "I think William talked with Charlotte," she said, stepping around a fallen branch. "Asked her where we'd gone and so forth."

"Would she have told him where we were?"

"Of course. Perhaps nothing specific. I think she'd have got suspicious if he'd asked for precise directions. He might not even have known he wanted them then.

I don't know how immediately or how thoroughly this thing took control. All the same, he could easily have asked how far we'd come. She wouldn't have thought to keep it secret."

Gareth sighed. "Neither did we."

"Reasonably enough, I'd think," said Olivia, letting her voice go hard to match the vague impression of guilt she heard from Gareth, and felt herself, in all honesty. "Telling someone a place makes magic harder to control should *not* be an advertisement to try some magic there, and we had no idea a demon would be sifting through his mind."

The path they were on was snaking now, winding its way around trees and large rocks. It *was* still a path and not a game trail, but they'd come farther in than they had when Olivia had been testing the place. She couldn't tell how much farther. Squinting ahead for a minute or so, she saw the owl was still in front of them…and then she started to see something else. A different texture to the dark, as if it rippled like water. Olivia shook her head and closed her eyes for a second, trying to clear her vision, but the distortion was still there when she opened them.

"We're getting close," she said.

"I thought so," said Gareth, and his voice was strained. Olivia glanced over at him, but there wasn't enough light to see the expression on his face. And she could have done nothing, anyhow.

Almost nothing. "Will you be all right?" she asked. "You can stop here, I can try to bring William to you, if he's injured."

"If you can," Gareth said. "No. I can keep going. I'll stay with you. This…whatever it is, shouldn't do me any permanent harm, I think."

"You think?"

Gareth's laughter had an edge to it, but it was still welcome. "I *am* the doctor here," he said.

There was no real way to argue with that. "Just turn back if you start thinking you're in any danger," she said. She wouldn't beg him to go back now. He hadn't told her to stay behind. Each of them had their duty here. "And, Gareth—"

She stopped, half because she suspected he knew what she was going to say, half because of the way her voice sounded, slow and fast by turns. Olivia put a hand to her throat but knew the problem wasn't there.

Above them, the owl had stopped in its flight. She looked up at it and nodded acknowledgment and thanks. It had been a good guide, and she wouldn't ask anything to go farther into whatever lay ahead. Besides, their path was obvious now.

When they turned another corner, they started to see light up ahead, pale green light that danced and wavered in the sky. There was a rhythm to it, but Olivia couldn't quite find it. She didn't know that she wanted to.

She stopped walking and reached out a hand. "The branch, please? Just for a moment."

Gareth passed it over.

Olivia had no knife, but the cut she needed to make was a small one. The back of one of the cuff links served well enough, and while Gareth went rigid beside her, he made no move to intervene. Pressing her bleeding finger against the rowan wood, she called out three words in Enochian and felt the branch go hot and cold at the same time.

"Careful," she said, handing it back to Gareth. She

put her finger in her mouth. Undignified, she knew, but dignity was the least of her concerns now.

He took the branch gingerly, closing his hand slowly around one end. "I should have brought gloves," he said as he started to walk.

"We should have brought many things," Olivia said.

They fell silent. There was nothing to say, really, only the knowledge of what lay ahead, or rather, the knowledge that they didn't know what that would be. Couldn't know. Darkness closed around them, light danced in front of them, and fear moved slow and icy through Olivia's blood.

But she wasn't alone. Whatever happened, she wouldn't be on her own.

She looked at Gareth. She couldn't see his face clearly, she couldn't touch him without slowing down, and talking would only have emphasized how wrong everything around them was becoming. Nonetheless, the simple fact of his presence was enough to stave off the worst of her fear. He was there. He was solid. He would not break or change. Not essentially, anyway.

For his sake, she wished he wasn't there. For hers, she was glad he was.

They went a few yards onward, across ground that now shook, though Olivia would have wagered nobody had ever heard of an earthquake near Englefield. A rock grew and shrank in her sight even as she followed the path around it.

Then up ahead, there was a hole in the world.

Chapter 42

AFTER HAVING WOUND THROUGH A MILE OR MORE IN THE close darkness of the trees, the path opened abruptly into a clearing. The green light came from the center of it, rising from the ground and then spreading into the sky, moving in patterns that resembled no flame Gareth had ever seen. Moonlight could reach the clearing too. In a circle perhaps twenty feet across, a man could see as well as if dawn had come early.

Gareth didn't really want to.

The trees were bending. Not as they might have done in a wind, which would have been strange enough for sturdy oaks and pines on that calm night, but rather twisting back and forth as if they were made of rubber. Coming in and out of focus, not only to Gareth's vision, but to the world itself.

Nor were the trees the only distorted things simply the most obvious. The earth was unsteady, and the very air seemed off, summer-hot one moment and cold the next, damp and dry at once.

The twisting, pulling sensation that had accompanied Balam's entrance was back in Gareth's mind, but now it felt multiplied tenfold. Closing his eyes brought no real relief, though it meant he didn't have to see the trees against the light. He would have reached out for support, but the only thing to lean against would have been one of the trees.

There was the rowan staff. That seemed to keep its

shape, and the earth below it seemed more solid than that beneath his feet. And there was warmth at his side too. A voice, low and urgent, talking to him.

Olivia.

He couldn't abandon her. He had his duty, but more than that, he couldn't leave her to face this horror alone. Gareth bit down on his lip and tasted blood. The external pain returned him to his senses a little, enough so he could open his eyes and look again.

Now he saw the light rose out of water, a small, shallow pool. A brass pitcher sat beside it, and other, smaller shapes Gareth couldn't recognize straightaway.

Fitzpatrick stood near the pool his head thrown back—so far as to defy everything Gareth knew about human anatomy. His arms moved in gestures Gareth didn't know.

At Gareth's side, Olivia flung a hand out, pointing at Fitzpatrick with all the innate grace that had served her in front of crowds in London, and shouted three words in that language Gareth didn't understand. The words split the air, louder than a human voice should have been, and the night shuddered around them.

Fitzpatrick froze.

Briefly, Gareth let out his breath in relief. Then he saw the light hadn't vanished, hadn't even diminished. In its glow, Olivia's face was tense, her breathing quick. "I can't hold him for very long," she said.

She withdrew the salt and silver cuff links from Waite's bag, stepped forward and put her free hand on Fitzpatrick's face. Gareth stumbled forward, then stopped himself. Olivia knew what she was doing. His interference wouldn't help anything. Not right now.

The best he could do was to learn more. He took a breath, steadied himself against the onslaught he knew would come, and focused inward and then out.

There was more pain. He had expected that, and still it took him hard. In the first moment of sight, Gareth fought the urge to double over or simply to be sick. His whole body seemed to become a flare, a trumpet of alarm, screaming *wrong wrong wrong wrong wrong* at the shifting world.

He clamped his white-knuckled hand on the rowan staff and slowly floundered his way toward solid ground.

Fitzpatrick and Olivia were glowing shapes in his view, and Fitzpatrick was, physically, not too badly off. The silver-gray threads that made up the boy's shape grew brighter and darker in time with the rhythm of the dancing light, but neither the scrying nor the twisting of the world had affected him very much. There were no wounds, no breaks in his body.

However, there was another color just under the silver, a color Gareth had never seen before and he could not have named. It bore some resemblance to the gray sludge that had infested Simon, but that had been only a small part of the demon. It was fully present in Fitzpatrick now, immaterial as it was. The malicious half sentience Gareth had sensed in Simon was ancient and hateful cunning now. The light writhed and twisted under Olivia's touch, reaching toward her, but it could not touch her. A green-gold radiance surrounded her hands, and the nameless color recoiled from it.

Olivia chanted, and the green-gold color pushed itself forward, surging from her hands into Fitzpatrick. The demon struck, fruitlessly, then retreated, farther into Fitzpatrick's soul. Olivia's light pursued it, and it ran again.

Gareth began to hear names in what she was chanting. He recognized a few of them—Michael, Tyr, Athena—but others were unfamiliar. Nevertheless, they seemed to be working. The demon kept retreating. He saw bits of it leaving Fitzpatrick's body. It didn't go toward the light, though.

He looked away to see where it *was* heading…

…and, for the first time, looked at the gash in the world with magical eyes.

In Olivia's metaphor of walls and doors, the demon had managed to knock out a load-bearing beam. It probably wouldn't be the end of the world, from what little Gareth could tell about such things, but at this rate, the situation certainly didn't look good for Englefield or anywhere nearby. The dislocation around them would intensify…and it would spread.

As if that wasn't bad enough, something was pressing against the other side. Shapes. Some of them were immaterial, like the demon, and he saw them only as vague impressions of color. Some of them looked like Balam or similar creatures. At least one was bigger. Much bigger.

They would all come through soon. Even fleeing Fitzpatrick's body, the demon was opening the gate. Soon, there'd be no need. It would open itself, or the beings on the other side would force the issue. Gareth felt the knowledge like a blow to the chest.

Then, and only then, did he think to wonder how he knew.

He'd never read magical theory. He'd certainly never

been around anything like this disruption. And his idea of what was happening was fairly rough, but Gareth was certain he was right…as certain, he realized now, as he had been when he'd been fourteen and known how to make a cut hand stop bleeding.

Even as Gareth understood that, he heard Fitzpatrick crumple to the ground. Olivia stepped back, sweat running down her face despite the cold night air. "I…" she panted. "The gate…"

"It's a wound," Gareth said. "The—nature of the world is injured."

Understanding came into Olivia's face quickly. "Can you—?" She gestured. Vaguely, but Gareth knew what she meant.

Could he heal this wound?

Looking at the light now, he could half-see the strands of power he'd worked with in people. These were far finer and constantly moving. Many of them were snapped in half, with so many loose ends dangling into…what? Gareth wasn't sure he wanted to know. He wasn't sure he was *able* to know.

"I can try!" he yelled back.

Olivia was at his side again. "I'm with you," she said. "Wait a moment."

Then she was in motion, opening Waite's bag, drawing out the candle, and placing it on the ground. A sweep of a stick she'd picked up created a circle. A few more gestures wrote symbols Gareth couldn't have read even on a chalkboard at bright noon, even if his head weren't pounding. He struggled to breathe. Struggled to wait.

Flame caught, first on the match in Olivia's hand and then on the wick of the candle. It was a small spot, barely visible against the witch-light, but it was one point to hold onto.

Olivia's face was another. It was set, determined and steady as she picked up the candle. Pale, perhaps, though the light made that hard to tell for certain. But it didn't matter. Whatever she felt, Garth knew there was no danger of her backing down. Not now, not ever.

She turned to the North and raised her voice, gesturing with her free hand and shouting a series of quick words that might almost have been Latin. As Gareth watched, she spun quickly and went through similar motions to the east, then the south, then the west before returning to the north and calling out a final phrase.

The candle flame looked larger now, and it seemed to be spreading down over Olivia's hands. Nevertheless, she didn't look worried or pained, and so, when she reached out, Gareth instantly took her hand in his. He reached out at the same time, magically rather than physically, sending his talent and energy toward the first of the fine, broken strands of the world.

Making the first connection was like trying to find the proverbial needle in the haystack, if the needle had squirmed away from his fingers and the haystack had been in constant motion. The broken threads writhed. The gulf between them yawned and pitched. The world shuddered. After his first failed attempts, Gareth drew back and watched, until the movements fell into a pattern. Then he lunged.

Grabbed.

Spliced.

His task became easier and harder at the same time. Easier because he was working with the broken end of the strand now. Each end *wanted* to find the other, just as the flesh of a mortal body *wanted*, in its own mindless way, to be whole. Now that Gareth had made a connection to one end, he could see more clearly how the other moved, and the connection was simpler.

Harder because his power and the force Olivia was passing to him were flowing out to bridge the gap between strands. Harder because Gareth had, without realizing it, opened himself to more than just the threads of the world.

The hole had its own power. As mindless as the threads, it pulled at him nonetheless, and pulled with considerable force. If he slipped forward a little, he would go through, and emerge—where? Gareth didn't think anyone on Earth knew that. The power Olivia was sending him gave him a handhold, though. Otherwise, he would have succumbed almost immediately.

The power might very well have killed Gareth had he not connected to the strands when he did, and it still might. If what Olivia had given him to help Simon had been a cold drenching on a hot day, this was standing under a waterfall. Magic coursed through him, beating at every fiber of his consciousness. There was far too much for a mortal body to contain. All Gareth could do was direct it.

So he did, stretching energy across the gap between one end of the strand and another, grabbing the loose end and tying it into the new string. The new length was amber gold and bronze. The weave it attached to was radiant, but colorless. A man could have spent quite a while marveling at that. Gareth didn't have time.

He reached for the next strand and the next, conscious as he did so of Olivia's presence. Her hand was still in his. More importantly, her power moved within him, linked to him, sustaining him in the midst of chaos. She was no rock, Gareth became aware as he worked, or a chain to keep him in place. Neither of those would have given him much aid in this present nightmare. Neither of them might have survived long.

Instead, Olivia shifted with the world like a rider on a trotting horse. She moved as it did, reacting and responding but never quite letting it get out of control. The power coursing into Gareth ebbed and flowed regularly. It never sputtered, never quite died, never overwhelmed him any more than it *always* overwhelmed him.

He was certain Olivia never doubted herself. He thanked God for it, or whatever gods there might be.

As Gareth completed the third strand and the fourth, he saw the edges of the hole growing closer together. The movement was only slight at first. He didn't have time to observe it at length, nor did he have the nerve to tempt fate and draw any conclusions. Instead, he went back to his work.

And with the sixth strand, the hole was definitely smaller. With the eighth, the rest of the broken strands met. With the twelfth, their ends started twining together, each finding its mate and joining again.

He poured more power into the weave, giving it strength to heal itself both quickly and thoroughly. Now his body was realizing it was late at night and he'd walked very fast over a great distance to reach the clearing. Now he was feeling the drain on his own energy. Despite the power Olivia had given him some strength, apparently, had to come from his personal stores. Cold would come soon, and hunger.

At first, Gareth thought the rejoining strands had made a sound—a creaking kind of sound, like a door swinging shut.

Then Olivia screamed.

Chapter 43

DURING HER TIME WITH DR. GILLESPIE, OLIVIA HAD COME across a battered volume of Milton and had read the words *they also serve who only stand and wait*. At the time, her inclination to *serve* anyone was rather small. The line had been just a pretty phrase. In the midnight forest with Gareth, she found it echoing in her head.

She wasn't even waiting. Not really. Mending the rift took far longer than healing Mr. Grenville had, she was working with far less stable energy than she'd been using then, and, oh, yes, the world around her was trying to pull itself apart while she did so. Olivia kept alert, shifted her stance, grasped and released power as it became necessary. She watched Gareth and William and the rift. There was plenty to occupy her, yet she found space enough in her mind to wonder how Gareth was faring. The eerie light showed the tension in his body, his set jaw and thin lips as he stared into the wound in reality. His hand was tight on hers, almost painful.

She wanted to scream with impatience. She wanted to sob with fear. She did neither, and when she saw the rift begin to close, ever so slowly, she didn't jump into the air and yell with joy, as strong as that impulse was.

There were things to do. Closing down the conduit of energy was one of them, and that fully occupied her consciousness for a little while, because it required the most delicate balance Olivia had ever managed. If she shut off the flow of power too rapidly, Gareth would have nothing but his own energy to work with. If she took too much time about the process, he'd have nowhere to shunt the extra power.

Admittedly, Olivia had never seen what would happen when the mortal frame had to deal with too much magical energy. The results could be wonderful. Conversely, she somehow doubted the likelihood of that, and so she went to work, shutting down the connection a little bit at a time. She didn't even let herself look up when she heard a strange creaking sound. It was probably the wind in the branches.

Then something grabbed her around her waist.

Her first impressions were jumbled and senseless: the smell of rot and dead leaves, darkness, and something that held her far harder than anything human could have. Screaming, she shoved at it and felt slime under her hands. It didn't give. Olivia shrieked again, kicked backward. Her foot sank into something squashy. She tried to remember the one offensive spell she'd learned to cast without preparation.

Fire ripped its way out of Olivia's body and into whatever was holding her. The magic took much of her strength with it, and when her unknown assailant dropped her hard to the ground, the blow knocked the wind out of her for a moment.

She stared upward at a dark mass of—she didn't know exactly what. There were branches in it and dirt and leaves. This was the form the demon had made for itself when she'd cast it out of Fitzpatrick in this place where the world was thin. This was its last attempt at achieving its goals. Banishing it would not work, not here, not when the gate was still a little ways open and she had no protective circle.

Olivia didn't know what would.

A mouth opened below the eyes, a mouth as large as she was. The beast lunged forward.

When it reared back abruptly, roaring with the wooden noise Olivia had heard before, her mind didn't recognize what had happened at first. Instinct propelled her body more quickly, and she rolled out of the demon's path before she saw Gareth drawing back the rowan staff for another blow.

She couldn't find the rowan branch, but she grabbed another stick at hand and fumbled for her book of matches. Her mind was racing all the while, the aether still clouding her vision. There was still a line of power between the demon and the gate. Now that Gareth was distracted, the demon's will was opening it again, faster than the world could fix itself.

Connection could go both ways. If the demon could influence the gate, then the gate could affect the demon. At least, Olivia hoped that was the case.

As the demon lunged for Gareth, Olivia struck a match and used what remained of her power. The stick she held burst into flame. She jabbed it toward the demon and danced backward as the beast turned toward her again. The stick was burning faster than she would have liked. She wished she hadn't noticed that.

"Close the gate!" she yelled to Gareth. "Finish it!"

He hesitated just a moment. Then he turned back to the gate, knelt…and tossed his staff toward Olivia. She caught it in one hand and held it to the remains of her stick. It seemed to take forever for the wood to catch.

The demon hissed like wind through the trees and bounded toward Gareth, reaching out with tentacles of wood and dirt. Olivia lunged desperately forward. She heard her skirt tear. She also heard bark crackling as some part of the foremost tentacle caught fire. There was another roar.

She stumbled forward, pressing her advantage, thinking she should have taken lessons from Mrs. Grenville. Her dress caught around her ankles. The staff weighed down her arm. She ducked but not fast enough. A lashing tendril slammed into her side.

It hurt, no question about that, and Olivia rocked backward on her feet. She was still *on* her feet, though. She'd expected to be across the clearing, against a tree or dead. Waving the staff, she stared at the demon through the jumping firelight. Was the creature smaller? It looked smaller.

This time, its roar was more of a shriek. In the aether, something was pulling it away. It was draining through the gate, shedding bits of its assumed form as it went. More and more of it dropped away, faster the further it diminished, like an avalanche in reverse.

In desperation, it charged toward Olivia once more. She hadn't been expecting that, and she was tired. The sharp sticks that served as its teeth closed on her sleeve. She felt them against her arm for one second. Then she jerked backward, and her sleeve tore away.

The demon fell. When it hit the ground, its body shattered into a jumble of leaves and soil and rocks and twigs. The gate sucked the rest of it back inside and sealed itself together. Olivia stood, staring at a spot that looked like anywhere else in the forest.

"Are you all right? Did it hurt you?"

Gareth's hands were on her shoulders. His voice was breathless.

"Yes. No. Shouldn't you know that already?" Olivia asked with a laugh she knew bordered on hysterical.

She switched her gaze out of the aether and looked up. Moonlight and candlelight were all that illuminated Gareth's face, but they were enough to see his weariness…and his smile.

Chapter 44

THE DEMON WAS GONE, THE GATE WAS CLOSED, AND everyone was alive. Gareth would feel drained soon, and cold. Already his leg was beginning to hurt, but none of that mattered at the moment. He pulled Olivia into his arms and kissed her, holding her to him for a moment that didn't last nearly long enough.

Consciousness of their situation and of his duty intruded far too soon, and Gareth pulled away enough to speak. "I should try to wake Fitzpatrick," he said, sighing, "and then we should leave."

Olivia nodded and stepped away. "They're probably panicking up at the house." She moved about the circle quickly, picking up Fitzpatrick's implements and her own, while Gareth unearthed a handkerchief. "Do you know," she added thoughtfully and with a little uncertainty, "I think we just did something like what Brother Anthony spoke of. Being the guardians of this place, I mean."

"I...suppose it is. Repairing, at least." Gareth eyed the remaining water in the pool doubtfully. Since Fitzpatrick had likely poured it out of the pitcher, he'd probably used it to open the gate. He didn't know if some enchantment still lingered. He would rather not test the theory, but he wanted some water to wake Fitzpatrick up.

Olivia stopped in front of him and passed over the

flask Waite had been carrying. "I think we've made ourselves part of this place tonight," she said, "or made it part of us. We'd probably learn to make the place stronger too, in time." She coughed and looked away. "If it would be something you wanted, that is. Learning more magic, staying here as much as you'd have to, for as long as you'd have to...I don't know if you'd want that."

Gareth didn't even have to think before he answered. "With you? Yes."

Her answering smile banished all the chill from the night air.

Gareth made himself turn away and kneel by Fitzpatrick. He bathed the boy's face and neck until Fitzpatrick woke gasping, squirming—and then freezing in place when he saw where he was and who was there. "Sir?"

"Fitzpatrick." Gareth kept his voice quiet, kind but not too gentle. Too much gentleness would make the boy suspect something was badly wrong. "How are you feeling?"

"I...all right, sir. Ma'am," he added, half a question as he saw Olivia. "Confused."

"I'm not surprised," Olivia said. "What was the last thing you remember?"

"Sitting in my room. I'd been in...oh, some kind of funk," Fitzpatrick admitted, looking away from Gareth and Olivia, "and I didn't want to be around anyone. I was an absolute beast to Waite about it too. Strange, but I don't feel any of that anymore."

"When did that start?" Olivia asked.

"I'd been in a mood for a while, ever since...ever since Waite and I tried the summoning, you know. But it got really bad only the day we all went outside. I tried to pet some stray cat, make myself feel better. It scratched me, and…" Fitzpatrick looked around. "Ever since then, I felt rotten. Only it wasn't just a bad mood, was it?"

Olivia drew a breath, looked at Gareth, and then shook her head. "No. It was the demon. I think you managed to fight it off for a day or two, which is longer than most, but it took you over completely in the end."

"Oh," said Fitzpatrick, and his eyes were wide and scared. He looked very young. "Did I hurt anyone?"

"Not badly," said Gareth. "You hit Waite, but you didn't do any real damage."

"I'm lucky, then. And lucky you came after me."

Gareth nodded. "Luckier still you'd learned something about magic," he said, remembering Olivia's classes before he'd stopped going. "Mrs. Brightmore gave you the chance to resist as long as you did, I'd say."

"Thank you, then, ma'am," said Fitzpatrick, who still looked dazed.

In that moment, so did Olivia. "Catch your breath for a few minutes," she said. "Then we'll start back."

There wasn't much either of them could do about the pool, but there were still circles to wipe away. If Olivia had ever been careless about wild places, she certainly wasn't going to be so here, not even to the extent of waiting until morning. She cleaned while William recovered, leaning against a rock, since he seemed inclined to avoid the trees as much as possible.

Despite his obvious exhaustion, Gareth insisted on helping once Olivia admitted the process took no particular magical skill. "It's hardly pulling stumps," he said brusquely, handing her the brass pitcher. As she took it, he caught her hand and lowered his voice. "Besides, there are some advantages to your company."

After a brief glance to make sure William had his eyes closed, Olivia gladly allowed Gareth to pull her into his arms—arm, rather, as he was leaning on the rowan staff, but that one arm held her tightly, and his chest was solid and warm. She rested her head against him and closed her eyes.

Gareth bent and brushed his lips across the top of her head. Knowledge followed the tender gesture, sinking into Olivia's mind. Now she thought of everything that had happened, how close their escape had been, how blindly she'd gone into the situation, and how thoroughly Gareth had trusted her at the last. She drew a breath, ragged now, and stepped away from him a little. "I can't," she said quietly, "not now. I'll start shaking or weeping or…I don't know."

"It'll probably do you good," said Gareth, his arm still around her waist.

"Not bad for you either," Olivia said dryly, tilting her head back to look up at him and regaining a little of her composure through pride. "Just not now, for either of us." She leaned forward, pressed a kiss to his jawline, and then slipped back to her tasks.

—⁓—

When they left the clearing, the owl had disappeared. Apparently not even Charlotte's persuasions could keep a hunting bird in place for almost an hour, which was how long Olivia thought it had taken to close the rift and recover afterward, though she couldn't be sure. Gareth's pocket watch said the time was a little past two in the morning, but it wasn't as if either he or she had checked it before entering the clearing.

It wasn't as if it mattered, anyway.

They walked back slowly and carefully, William between them. He *could* walk on his own, to Olivia's relief, and his steps became steadier as he kept going, but he was still pale and silent. She and Gareth felt it better to keep him surrounded as much as they could. He seemed to appreciate the company as well, glancing back every so often as if to make sure Gareth was still bringing up the rear. Olivia also looked back frequently, to be sure the men were still all right. They must have looked like a regular troop of owls.

Even Gareth cast a glance or two behind him. At first Olivia wasn't sure why, since nobody was supposed to be following him…

And then she realized: nobody was *supposed* to be following him.

She gulped. As far as she could make out from Gareth's expression, he didn't look alarmed after any of his quick inspections, and Olivia couldn't make out either shape or movement on the dark path, so there was nothing to be alarmed about. It was important to remember that.

It was also difficult. The immediate situation was much less intimidating now, but the forest was only slightly less so. Even without a rift, reality was thinner here. Even though Olivia was part of it, in some manner she didn't really understand, she *didn't really understand*, which was unsettling in itself. And the forest was still the place where men had seen colored lightning and odd animals.

It was still the place where children had disappeared.

She and Gareth would come back. They would talk to Brother Jonathan and learn the art of guarding the forest. One day, they might even bring their children here. Olivia thought they'd do all of those things in daytime, though. She couldn't imagine entering the forest at night. Not willingly.

Shadows pressed around them. Some of them waved in the wind, and when it picked up, making the tree branches above them caper in the broken moonlight, Olivia had to look away. Behind her, William made an inarticulate sound in his throat.

"Nothing to worry about," she said, her voice full of brisk energy she didn't feel at all. It would be a long time before any of them could look unflinchingly at something as ordinary as trees in the wind. Longer, probably, for William. He'd seen more of the world beyond the gate, but he'd had no part in the final triumph. Poor boy. Even if he had nearly gotten them all killed. "We'll be home before long. Hot tea all around, I think."

"Good luck finding anything to make it at this hour," Gareth said. "I've never managed."

"You haven't looked hard enough." Olivia didn't mention the household would probably be up. No point alarming William further. When she looked over her shoulder, she thought he seemed a little more at ease.

So she spoke of inconsequential things, of how good it was to have fresh cream these days. How she'd bought a set of teacups once only to find—in the midst of a visit—the handles were prone to falling off at the slightest provocation. Of mishaps in the kitchen and the scullery when she'd been young. She let her words become a thread that rolled before them, leading them out of the forest. Gareth's voice joined hers occasionally, telling his own stories. His sister's early attempts at cooking, and rushed and comical moments of domesticity during wartime.

The forest was still dark around them, but the darkness stayed a little farther away now.

Then suddenly, they were out. The trees retreated from them, and they were standing at the base of the hill below Englefield. The dormitory rose above them, an empty shell, but the house in the distance was solid and strong, and light poured out of the windows.

A figure rushed toward them, silhouetted against the light. For a moment, Olivia couldn't make out who it was, and her throat tightened. But then she got a better view, and she recognized Mrs. Grenville. A very *odd*-looking Mrs. Grenville, granted. She wore men's clothing in some tight black fabric, her hair was braided back, and there was a long knife stuck into her belt. That knife didn't look like it had come from the scullery.

Olivia wasn't inclined to ask questions. She suspected she'd have plenty to answer before long.

For now, Mrs. Grenville asked only one. She looked over the three of them, then out toward the forest. "Everything all right?"

"Yes," Olivia said and couldn't help turning toward Gareth as she did. Despite everything, a smile touched her lips. "And I believe it's going to be."

"Right, then," said Mrs. Grenville. "You all look dead. Let's get back inside." She turned and started walking. To Olivia's considerable surprise, William was the first to follow her. He went quickly, caught up, and said something to Joan in a low voice. Joan stopped for a second. Then she nodded, and the two drew ahead, speaking quietly.

Without the necessity of being bright and cheerful for William, Olivia felt a great weariness descend on her, turning her feet to lead. There was satisfaction in it, though. She'd done a hard and a dangerous day's work, bed waited up ahead, and she suspected she wouldn't be alone when she got there.

Drawing closer to Gareth, she reached out one of her hands. There was nothing dramatic about the gesture this time: no anchor, no power, no task. Simply the desire to touch—the desire for connection. Nonetheless, Gareth linked his fingers through hers as eagerly as he'd done out in the forest.

Hand in hand, with darkness behind them and light ahead, they went back to the house.

Acknowledgments

I'd like to thank Professor Robert Mathiesen for information about occult weirdness, in general, and Victorian occultism, in particular, and for much support and encouragement. As always, many thanks to my family and friends, to the editorial and marketing geniuses at Sourcebooks who make my writing presentable, and to my readers, past and future.

The Lord of Illusion

by Kathryne Kennedy

—᷾—

He'll do anything to save her…

Rebel Lord Drystan Hawkes dreams of fighting for England's freedom. He gets his chance when he finds a clue to opening the magical portal to Elfhame, and he must race to find the slave girl who holds the key to the mystery. But even as Drystan rescues Camille Ashton from the palace of Lord Roden, it becomes unclear exactly who is saving whom…

For the fate of humankind lies with Camille…

Enslaved for years in a realm where illusion and glamour reign, Camille has learned to trust nothing and no one. But she's truly spellbound when she meets Drystan, a man different from any she's ever known, and the force of their passion may yet be strong enough to banish the elven lords from this world forever…

—᷾—

Praise for Kathryne Kennedy:

"Enthralling…a passionate love story."
—*RT Book Reviews*, 4½ stars

For more Kathryne Kennedy, visit:

www.sourcebooks.com

Deliver Me from Darkness

by Tes Hilaire

Angel to vampire is a long way to fall.

A stranger in the night…

He had once been a warrior of the Light, one of the revered Paladin. A protector. But now he lives in darkness, and the shadows are his sanctuary. Every day is a struggle to overcome the bloodlust. Especially the day Karissa shows up on his doorstep.

Comes knocking on the door

She is light and bright and everything beautiful—despite her scratches and torn clothes. Every creature of the night is after her. So is every male Paladin. Because Karissa is the last female of their kind. But she is *his*. Roland may not have a soul, but he can't deny his heart.

"Dark, sexy, and intense! Hilaire blazes a
new path in paranormal romance."
—Sophie Jordan, *New York Times* bestselling author

For more Tes Hilaire, visit:

www.sourcebooks.com

Untouched

by Sara Humphreys

———

She may appear to have it all, but inside she harbors a crippling secret...

Kerry Smithson's modeling career ensures that she will be admired from afar—which is what she wants, for human touch sparks blinding pain and mind-numbing visions.

Dante is a dream-walking shapeshifter—an Amoveo, who must find his destined mate or lose his power forever. Now that he has found Kerry, nothing could have prepared him for the challenge of keeping her safe. And it may be altogether impossible for Dante to protect his own heart when Kerry touches his soul...

———

Praise for the Amoveo Legend series:

"Sizzling sexual chemistry that is sure to please."—*Yankee Romance Reviewers*

"A moving tale that captures both the sweetness and passion of romance."—*Romance Junkies*, 5 blue ribbons

"A well-written, action-packed love story featuring two very strong characters."—*Romance Book Scene*, 5 hearts

For more of the Amoveo Legend series, visit:

www.sourcebooks.com

The Wolf Who Loved Me

by Lydia Dare

--- ❧ ---

Lady Madeline Hayburn has money problems...

Specifically, she has so much of it that she's dogged by fortune hunters, including her bewilderingly attractive, penniless neighbor, with his wild nature and uncouth manners...

Weston Hadley has an identity crisis...

He's just turned into a wolf while Madeline was watching. Now it's up to the regal lady to tame the wild beast...if she can...

--- ❧ ---

Praise for Lydia Dare's Regency Werewolves:

"Ms. Dare has been added to my must-read authors!"
—Night Owls *top pick*

"Sexy, witty, and wildly passionate!"
—Star-Crossed Romance

*"Deliciously witty and sensationally sensuous...
delightful historical romance."* —Fresh Fiction

For more Lydia Dare, visit:

www.sourcebooks.com

Enraptured

by Elisabeth Naughton

ORPHEUS—*To most he's an enigma, a devil-may-care rogue who does whatever he pleases whenever he wants. Now this loose cannon is part of the Eternal Guardians—elite warriors assigned to protect the human realm—whether he likes it or not.*

Orpheus has just one goal: to rescue his brother from the Underworld. He's not expecting a woman to get in the way. Especially not a Siren as gorgeous as Skyla. He has no idea she's an assassin sent by Zeus to seduce, entrap, and ultimately destroy him.

Yet Skyla herself might have the most to lose. There's a reason Orpheus feels so familiar to her, a reason her body seems to crave him. Perhaps he's not the man everyone thinks…The truth could reveal a deadly secret as old as the Eternal Guardians themselves.

"Filled with sizzling romance, heartbreaking drama, and a cast of multifaceted characters, this powerful and unusual retelling of the Orpheus and Eurydice story is Naughton's best book yet."—*Publishers Weekly*

For more of the Eternal Guardians series, visit:

www.sourcebooks.com

Kiss of the Goblin Prince

by Shona Husk

The Man of Her Dreams

He is like a prince in a fairy tale: tall, outrageously handsome, and way too dark for her own good. Amanda has been hurt before, though. And with her daughter's illness, the last thing she needs right now is a man. But the power of Dai King is hard to resist. And when he threads his hands through her hair and pulls her in for a kiss, there is no denying it feels achingly right.

In a Land of Nightmare

After being trapped in the Shadowlands for centuries with the goblin horde a constant threat, Dai revels in his newfound freedom back in the human realm. But even with the centuries of magic he's accumulated, he still doesn't know how to heal Amanda's daughter—and it breaks his heart. Yet for the woman he loves, he'd risk anything…including a return to the dreaded Shadowlands.

Praise for The Goblin King:

"A wonderfully dark and sensual fairy tale."
—Jessa Slade, author of *Seduced by Shadows*

For more of the Shadowlands series, visit:

www.sourcebooks.com

About the Author

Isabel Cooper lives in Boston with her boyfriend and a houseplant she's kept alive for over a year now. During the day, she maintains her guise as a mild-mannered project manager working in legal publishing. By night, she writes romance and indulges in very geeky hobbies. Despite spending most of her life in bizarre academic environments, she has yet to develop strange powers: perhaps she should have gone to graduate school? For more, visit *isabelcooper.wordpress.com*.